WINSTOI

THE CANN

Barking dog wishes
It Darlan; with
ways in memory of
Ted, Jenny, Sean
and ; your Roxy
and BonBo!! 23/

i

By the same author

Published
Barking at Winston: Book One: The Winston Tails
The Event of the Nose (short story)

Stage Plays
The Silence
Taking the Wrap
Big Hec
Moses Brown Is Waiting
Star Quality

BBC Radio Four
Pamela Myers Show (drama)

BBC Television
Nicola's Bullet (documentary)

Selected Community Publications
(as compiler/editor/co-publisher)
Pie in the Sky
Dancing in Mid-Air
Fabulous Just
Closer Links
Eyes Open
… from the Car Crazy project …
Igloos in the Sun

WINSTON AND
THE CANNY LASS

BOOK TWO

THE WINSTON TAILS

Barry Stone

Berry Press • London

First published 2014 by Berry Press
Reprinted 2014
Reprinted 2015
Reprinted 2016 (twice)
Reprinted 2017
Berry Press
PO Box 71267
London
SW11 9GQ

ISBN 9780956693211

Typeset by Mike Davis

Printed and bound in the UK by
Martins the Printers,
Sea View Works,
Spittal, Berwick Upon Tweed,
TD15 1RS

Front cover illustration, *Times* cartoonist David Haldane
Cover design Mike Davis

With love for the kids that were

1

It was the legendary summer of 1976 when I, Brucie-Dog, was rescued from the kennels by a red-headed fifty-five-year-old artist and her two sets of twins: Rachael and Craig, fifteen; Vanessa and Jack, sixteen.

I fell in love with the family at first sight. Ginger was surrounded by a red mist that any canine would see meant she was passionate about life. As for the kids, well, their joyful colours made me dizzy, though I also associated a worrying white with Craig. I soon discovered that this was largely because of his alcoholic dad, Raymond: in the months before his recent suicide he had increasingly attacked his son for being queer. Queerness was also despised at the kid's school so Craig had known tough times.

Still, he was a survivor and it was clear from the outset that the family needed a dog to help them after Raymond's death. That lucky mutt was me: a mange-ridden collie-cross. Other visitors to the kennels had looked away from me.

By the early 1980s I was what humans call middle-aged, though my black and tan coat was thick, wavy and shiny, and I considered myself a fine-looking animal. Other dog-walkers on the beach where Craig took me every day frequently remarked on how handsome I was.

Those good looks had only come about because of the love Ginger and the kids lavished on me: it made me gleam for joy. I admit to a little vanity, but most of my delight in my appearance was down to Craig: every time a fellow dog-walker complimented me, the kid's pride put a beautiful redness all around him. Those were the moments when I truly believed that his warm heart would survive until he was ready to share it with a companion, such as the one and only Marcus Wright. He was the flirtatious young human who – aside from being at school with Craig – had been the kennel lad on duty when the family rescued me. It had been obvious then that he was seriously keen on the kid.

But at twenty-one Craig showed no sign that he would ever accept his queerness or depart the home to which his big brother, Jack, and his two sisters were now only summertime visitors. I feared that in staying on with his mum he would miss out on love. Marcus Wright had long since moved hundreds of miles away to London. I had often prayed to my old saviour, Her Hoityness, the stuck-up but kindly Alsatian that had stopped me losing hope when I was taken in by the

RSPCA. Perhaps she could have saved Craig from a loveless life.

Now, you may feel I was being disloyal towards Ginger. Without Craig at home, there would have been nobody to look after her. A couple of years after my recovery from the distemper that had nearly offed me when I joined the family, the kids' mum had suffered a mini-stroke. It had left her, weirdly, with an on-off French accent. I feared that, on top of all the bad feelings about himself that Raymond and school had caused, Craig would slip into the role of her companion-cum-carer. I redoubled my prayers to Her Hoityness to help him create his own life, as his brother and sisters were doing. Ginger had always encouraged them to be independent.

There's a danger now that I'm giving the wrong impression of the kid. With his queerness pushed down deep where he didn't have to worry about it, he was far from miserable.

Leastways, that was how things stood until September 1982, when Vanessa married an unusual lanky human with the Polish name of Zenon. That was the day when a bang that shattered all twelve panes on Ginger's double-storey bay window shook everything up.

Bang was the word the family always used when they were looking back on Vanessa's wedding day, but there was an explosion on the road outside Ginger's house. It was the culmination of changes that had started a year earlier: Rachael, Craig's twin, had completed her first year at sports college, and the older twins, Vanessa and Jack, had been predicted to get first-class degrees in fashion (Vanessa) and fine art (Jack).

Ginger was thrilled by their impending success and, to the alarm of all the kids, insisted that, until the summer ended, they were to be at the breakfast table for eight o'clock every Saturday morning. She wanted to spend 'quality time' with them. They were worried about their mum's dodgy health and didn't want to upset her so Rachael, Craig, Jack and Vanessa did their best to comply without winding each other up. To be fair on all, the household had become much less argumentative than it had been in the past. Still, I dare say things were always bound to take the stroppy turn they did.

One Saturday morning Jack grumpily declared that he was tired of Ginger serving bacon so undercooked it could still have been hunting for truffles.

Vanessa snapped that his jokes were funnier when he didn't bother telling them, while the younger twins rolled their big green eyes in disdain at their elder brother's wit.

This was a bit hard on Jack. He had been the last to arrive at the table, too sleepy to notice Rachael smirk knowingly at Vanessa, who was scowling at her. They were at loggerheads, and I was intrigued from the moment Rachael entered the kitchen, a minute or two after her sister. That, on top of the bacon contretemps, drove the ever-watchful Craig to ask, 'Just what the hell is it with these two ladies this morning, our Jack?'

Jack yawned and ran a hand through his unruly black hair. His nice square shoulders lifted in the quick shrug that meant, 'Who cares?' The indifference was a cover for the smart he still felt after the ridicule of his truffles quip.

Craig continued, 'I mean, our Rachael's obviously up to no good! And this one …' he jerked his head at Vanessa, seated to his right '… she's been like Vesuvius ready to blow ever since she got up.'

Rachael sniggered because he'd opened for discussion the mysterious situation between her and Vanessa, but Jack gave his twin sister a long, questioning stare.

He might have been studying her newly tweaked look: her spiked-up hair – which was a different colour every week – was a vivid blue she'd never used before, while her left furry-caterpillar eyebrow was a deep green, its companion an exceptionally bright purple.

Jack, though, was intent upon assessing her mood, and while his seemingly endless scrutiny caused her cheeks to turn crimson, the green of her eyes became so very dark that bullets might have zipped from their glossy black pupils. That meant anger, which was no big surprise to me: the more Rachael had smirked at Vanessa, the more blackness had filled the air in the kitchen. It suggested that anything might happen.

I was worried that Ginger – who'd been making five mugs of tea – was about to be disturbed by a truly nasty scene so I reared up on my hindquarters and plonked my front paws on the cluttered table. A big yap escaped my barking box just as Craig slung his arm about my neck. 'Hey up, everybody!' he cried. 'It's the one and only Brucie-Wucie-Lucie-Darling!' He'd always called me that and I loved him all the more for it.

Jack and Vanessa burst out laughing, and young Rachael niftily took her chance to feed me the half-raw bacon on her plate. The all-round joy that was driving away the blackness reassured me that, after my years with the family, I really was doing what Ginger had asked in the beginning: helping her with the kids.

Then she proved that, irrespective of my observations, she had an all-seeing eye in the back of her head: 'Oh, you crafty, crafty thing, our Rachael! Feeding bacon to Brucie when you think I'm not looking!'

Rachael was hardly ever scolded by her mum – I couldn't resist doing a stand-up version of my seal wiggle. Ginger stamped her foot upon the lino, which had been specially laid when the family moved to the house twenty years before. Its unusual seahorse pattern had been chosen because of their move to the seaside. Now it was well worn.

'Dog! Stop wobbling the table!' she cried.

That set reds, greens, yellows and blues swirling all around her, and amused the kids, me and even the family parrot, Picasso. He was a baldy old thing who'd been bought from a market stall by Ginger's parents to mark her birth in 1921.

'Dog! Get down!' continued Ginger.

I raised my head and began a series of howls that first Craig, then the others crooned along to.

When the crazy fun came to an end, the atmosphere in the kitchen was as soft as a puppy. I wanted to plant my paws on Ginger's shoulders and lick the big nose that Raymond had, long before, battered out of shape when he was drunk.

3

Before I could get near her, she'd put the mugs on the table, stood back, and said to the kids, 'Oh, come on, you rotten lot! I'm not so far gone that I don't know when something's in the air. So, whatever the trouble is between our Vanessa and Rachael, let's thrash it out as a family.'

The girls appeared equally uncomfortable. Instead of piling the pressure directly on them, though, Ginger moved her gaze to Craig, who raised his chunky eyebrows until they almost met the severe fringe of the pudding-basin haircut his sisters were always complaining about. 'Don't blame me!' he protested.

Jack held both hands flat in the air and pressed downwards for calm. 'He's right, Mum. It wouldn't be fair.'

Vanessa cleared her throat. 'Well, actually, Mum …'

Rachael was biting her lower lip and screwing up her eyes as if someone had pulled the pin on a grenade that had been dropped beneath the table.

Craig and Jack eyeballed each other: what could be so daunting to say that Vanessa, of all people, couldn't complete her sentence?

'Well actually what?' enquired Craig, directing his eyes at his big sister and speaking with an exaggerated curiosity that I feared would get him a tongue-lashing from Ginger – until I moved to a position near the hall doorway that gave me a clear view of his mum's face. Most of the time it still showed the smiley energy that I'd loved at first sight; in times of stress such as this, though, it looked sadly ancient. Her natural redness had become a murky brown.

'Please tell me what's wrong,' she begged, with a hint of French that made the kids start. 'Please, please, please!' she continued, now kneading her eyes with her fists and stamping her feet with such force that I feared the ceiling – which had big cracks where the bath was always overflowing – would crash down upon them all.

Rachael was out of her seat and cuddling her mum, who broke free, stamped her foot once more and demanded to be told what on earth was going on.

'Mum,' Jack responded, as he glowered across the table at Vanessa, who was now inspecting her purple-varnished fingernails, 'ask the bloody girls. Me and our Craig don't have a bloody clue!'

4

Vanessa gave her brothers and Ginger a resigned smile, then looked at Rachael. 'Go on, then, little sis, tell them the news you've been dying to break.'

Rachael went very red. She'd only been teasing, she stuttered, and it was for Vanessa to reveal her own personal business, not her.

'Oh, for God's sake!' Jack exploded. Craig quipped that there hadn't been so much democracy in the family since the choosing of my name at the kennels, though that was immediately surpassed when Ginger interrupted: as democracy was obviously somewhat ponderous, would the person in the know please pipe up before there was a flaming great row. It was the kind of conflict, she said, with a flourish that thrilled me because it brought her redness back, that only her mad brood could create.

'Brilliantly put, Mum!' said Jack, who, with Craig and Rachael, was creased up with the laughter that made Vanessa's face and neck turn crimson. She was still checking her elaborate fingernails.

'Oh, come on now, our Vee,' chided her twin, who, I knew, wanted the mystery resolved before Ginger became distressed.

Vanessa understood: she was normally the one to steer them out of trouble. Now she was being so obstinate that Craig was urging, 'Yeah! Come on, Vanessa! It's not fair! You're making poor Mum suffer!'

Vanessa gave a loud sigh. 'Go on, please, our Rachael. You tell them. I'll fill in the details.'

You would've laughed if you'd seen the puzzlement that flickered across Rachael's face at that particular promise, and maybe even more so if you'd seen how eagerly Ginger, Craig and Jack were waiting to hear whatever was on its way.

Vanessa smiled, which encouraged Rachael to splurge: 'Well, if youse must know, our Vanessa's pregnant!'

5

My front legs gave way and I clobbered the seahorse lino. My collapse was mainly due to the loss of muscle control I occasionally suffered. It had been put down to nerve damage caused when my cruel first human had touched my spine with the live electric cable he kept to torture me.

If I'd wanted sympathy for old wounds that morning, though, I would have been disappointed: Ginger and the kids were so absorbed in Vanessa's news that, despite the clatter of my fall and the yelp that escaped me, nobody even glanced in my direction. In fact I, too, was eagerly awaiting the next development. If anything, my sudden collapse had made me extra attentive.

Vanessa cried, 'Me? Pregnant? Oh, no, I bloody well am not, little madam!'

Her younger sister looked as if she'd been hit on the head with Ginger's heavy preserving pan. Vanessa had once given her twin brother concussion doing precisely that. Jackie and Craig wisely stopped the laughter to which Vanessa's alleged pregnancy had reduced them. The long silence that followed was ear-splitting.

What I remember even more clearly is that, upon repositioning myself by the window, I could see Ginger's eyes, which told me she was doing her best to understand what was going on. There was a touching sing-song note in her voice as she reminded them that, at twenty-two, her elder daughter had no reason to justify being pregnant to any of them.

An even angrier Vanessa insisted she was not having a flipping baby, while Rachael – who everyone could see was fighting back out of pride rather than reason – retorted that, oh, yes, she bloody was.

Craig inserted his right forefinger into a circle made by the thumb and first finger of his left hand, and told his brother that if she was up the stick, then this was what their Vanessa had been getting. It was behaviour that made my tail droop between my legs and my heart thump so hard it hurt.

As I had dreaded, in the next instant Craig was the target of anger that had Jack snarling at him to grow up and Vanessa snapping that he was thoroughly disgusting. Rachael's rebuke trounced the lot: her red-faced twin had just proved beyond doubt, she said, that he was the retard their dad Raymond had always claimed him to be.

'Ouch.' Jack winced as the glass door to the yard and the workshop where Craig fixed cars for a living slammed behind him.

'Be careful you don't break anything, our Craig,' Ginger shouted.

There was yet another tricky silence before a guilty-looking Rachael reminded the older twins that it hadn't been only her who'd scolded their brother, and that what he'd been doing with his finger had indeed been vile. Vanessa was quick to agree, then pressed her sister, who was obviously trying to evade the subject she herself had raised, to explain why she believed she was pregnant. Rachael replied hotly that Vanessa knew full well that people apart from herself were whispering things about her. That heralded a reawakening of their argument.

'I've had enough, Mum,' Jack told Ginger. 'I'll be off to buy some oils when the art shop opens at nine.' He got up and strode through the open door and along the shadowy hallway. The glass inner door was silvery and turned my eyes to slits.

'Good luck with those two witches, Mum,' he called, as he left the house. Briefly his body was a dark outline with a large, shaggy head that reminded me of poor old Raymond.

6

But then all thought of Jack was gone from my
mind, and his sisters became so slippery-eyed
with embarrassment at their behaviour that
good old Ginger made it clear she was taking charge.
She rolled up the sleeves of her orange blouse, craned
forward on the breakfast chair where she'd now parked
her bum and, gripping her knees with her knobbly old
artist's hands, let out a sigh that meant the silly quarrel
between her daughters was going to be settled.

The wide smile she adopted became as fixed as the
grin of an empty-bellied eastern dignitary contemplat-
ing the Queen's corgis, and while the sunlight poured
through the glass door at her back, her brow and cheeks
turned a spooky white that made her hair seem extra
red, and her eyes bigger and greener than before.

It was a truly weird presentation, to which she unwittingly added by giving several slow nods that, while
intended to encourage talking, made her seem so heart-
breakingly lost that Rachael busied herself with stack-
ing the breakfast plates. That drew a questioning frown
from Vanessa. When she realised that her sister was

hiding tears from Ginger, she clicked her fingers and looked at the old aluminium saucepans on the shelves beside the ancient cream-enamelled gas cooker.

'I know what we need!' she announced, and darted across to fetch the heavy preserving pan with which she'd once concussed Jack.

Rachael clashed the last plate onto the stack and cowered in her seat, her arms crossed protectively over her head as she cried, 'Our Vanessa! Don't you bloody dare hit me with that thing!'

Her fear was matched by a flare of anger from her mum, who shrilled for the pan to be put back where it belonged before somebody got hurt. That made me bark with relief: it confirmed that for all her coming-and-going oddness, my beloved old Ginger was not becoming completely lost to the kids or to myself. Added proof came with the blast, 'Shut up with your damn barking, dog!'

Rachael removed her arms from her head, and retorted, 'Ha-bloody-ha,' when Vanessa told her sister that she wasn't at risk because she herself wasn't in a homicidal mood. However, as the heavy old pan was placed upon the table, with a thump that made the stacked plates clatter, I wondered if she was preparing to knock Rachael out cold after all.

Things moved so fast that my new worry was gone by the time Rachael had assumed a bolt-uprightness which amounted to a complete denial that she had been scared. It was a mix of toughness and fun that put green and yellow around her, and made Ginger place the tips of her fingers to her nose as if she was praying, when in fact she was chuckling. Out of all the kids, it was Rachael, she often claimed, who had inherited her own wilfulness.

She was equally amused by Vanessa now: she had whizzed to the drawer below the sink and was just as quickly returning with the wooden spoon that Ginger used for stirring jam. It was a mission of such giddying determination that I couldn't stop my seal wiggle, and Rachael – who'd finally realised what her sister was doing – was laughing as she clamped the pan between her hands, ready for Vanessa to stir an imaginary brew.

"'Double, double toil and trouble; Fire burn and cauldron bubble,'" they chanted, as Ginger clapped, a joyous red surrounding them all. They were three witches together, not two, as Jack had teased when he was leaving the house. Now they repeated the spell and my ears pricked. Ginger was flushed and happy as she announced that she really was batty enough to travel by broomstick.

'You're a funny old thing, Mum,' declared Rachael.

Vanessa plonked a kiss plumb on the middle of my head. 'Artful old bugger,' she said to me, with a sideways glance at her mum.

Ginger, in response, sat bolt upright and cooed, 'Oh, I say, our Vanessa! I do agree! He is! He is! He most certainly is a most dreadfully artful bugger!'

Runaway delight flooded me with the familiar warmth of liquid gold. Rachael looped her arms about Ginger's shoulders, and mouthed, 'Thank you,' to Vanessa, who smiled and carried the stacked plates to the sink.

There she wiped the tears her mum's fleeting absence had brought to her eyes on the same blue towel that earlier Ginger had used to dry the mugs for the tea. 'Mum, I really am sorry,' she began, casting an apologetic look at Rachael. 'Maybe I should've said months ago. I'm not pregnant but I am engaged.'

'Are you really, darling?' My beloved Ginger had sounded so puzzled that Rachael dropped a kiss of reassurance on the top of her head.

The betrothal had come out of the blue. Soon Ginger and Rachael would be told the details. So firmly did these enter my already cluttered doggie-brain that, in retelling the tale, my canine second sight takes a shortcut into Vanessa's mind. Be ready, then, for her story in her voice . . .

7

Mother went to bed one night as her normal self and woke up speaking in a French accent. We thought she was putting it on for fun. She had our Jack calling her Joan of Arc and our Craig asking for croissants, until our Rachael noticed that she couldn't lift her mug properly and slopped her tea on the table. That left us in no doubt that things were out of her control. Quite a shock for us all on an ordinary Saturday.

As for the Frenchness, a doctor at the hospital raised our spirits with funny tales about the effects of mini-strokes, especially the one about the patient who spent three months believing she was the Queen of Hearts from *Alice's Adventures in Wonderland* (which our Rachael said would have suited Mother best because she could have shouted, 'Off with his head!' about our Craig, whom she argues with most). And yet the same doctor, who was only trying to understand what was going on inside Mother's head, then asked – while our guard was down, mark you – if she had ever played games that perhaps disguised a forgetfulness problem?

I was mystified until my twin brother, Jack, recalled how she'd make us kids scour the house for her mislaid handbag, and our Craig's eyes told me he'd thought of more such examples. Mercifully, the hospital came up with a diagnosis before the boys supplied a full inventory of forgetfulness going back years. The doctor told us she'd had a rare condition from birth called arteriovenous malformation, which means a tangle of excess blood vessels in the head. Our comedian doctor described it as 'spaghetti on the brain'. Or maybe I should say our would-be-comedian doctor: no sooner had he given his diagnosis than he was trounced by our Jack, who declared that at last we had proof that Mother was 'past-a her best'. It wasn't that funny but at the time it made me laugh until I nearly got the hernia I would gladly have accepted in exchange for Mother's Frenchness to be gone.

In the event, it took three long weeks. It was lucky that it happened in the middle of summer when we were all home from college: otherwise our Craig would've had to deal with it alone.

I'm not making excuses when I say that I would happily have told the family all about my fiancé, Zenon, but the doctors were asking more questions: when and how had our mother's nose been so badly broken? Were we aware that she talked so loudly because an injury to her jaw had impacted on her inner ear? Did we know this and did we know that? I thought their all-seeing X-rays would be best dumped in the nearest bin. Think how you would feel if you were falling in love with a man whose Polish parents had come to England to escape the Nazis while the history of your own parents' relationship – which had been damaged by the war – was being picked over by doctors, who were implying that your mother had had earlier haemorrhages, caused by your father's drunken blows to her head.

For once I was grateful for our Rachael's pragmatism. She'd been the least sympathetic of us about Daddy's alcoholism when he was alive, but now concluded that if he heard about Mother's haemorrhages, he would turn in his grave. Who would want him to suffer that? 'Certainly not Mother,' Rachael said.

I wanted to kiss her because, no matter what any doctor says or thinks, our mother and father did love each other – the wartime photograph of them in our front room proved it. But what was their love worth when you remember what they ended up doing to each other? That was why I kept my Zenon a secret. With my warring parents as the only example, how could I be certain that we could share love without physically or mentally damaging each other?

Yet it was only when I was with Zenon that I felt complete. And Zenon felt complete only when he was with me. The paradox behind this was that, although

I'd kept Zenon a secret from her, the unexpected joining of our lives had actually come about through Mother's brilliance as an art tutor.

8

The wine merchant's where I met Zenon was owned by a short, round, middle-aged bachelor called Mr Garrity, who'd been the subject of laughter in our family after he'd joined one of Mother's evening classes. Impressed by her lively teaching style, he'd soon proposed they should go as a twosome on a painting tour in the South of France, where his wine came from.

To be fair to Mr Garrity – who was a really nice man – this episode was disproportionately funny: a month earlier, our old friend Bill the copper, who'd been divorced for ever, had made himself the butt of endless truncheon jokes by asking Mother to marry him. We got away with sheer filth partly because, after she'd turned him down, Bill went into a huff that kept him away from our house. Our Jack pointed out that if he'd called round for his usual skive-from-duty cuppas, and overheard what we were saying, we would have got life sentences for gross obscenity. Yet my twin brother had always respected Bill: he'd first met us when a seaward-facing statue of Sir Winston Churchill was unveiled on a promontory at the bottom of our road in 1975.

What a day that was. Bill wisely stood back from the chaos when Daddy was drunk and naked in our small front garden. If the police had been officially involved, the story would have made the *Gazette* and caused hideous bother for us all. In fact, when Bill came to check on us a few days later, he was kind to Daddy, who said later that Mother had an admirer waiting to fill his shoes.

That remark made me feel uneasy because, although I didn't realise it at the time, it signalled that Daddy knew things couldn't go on as they were. Also, of course, a part of Bill must have been weighing up his chances – though if, later on, he'd asked any of us kids about marriage, we would have advised him that Mother's ways would drive him insane before their first anniversary.

Bill the copper and Mr Garrity weren't the only men who were attracted to her. She always claimed that being 'saddled with four ill-behaved and otherwise in-solent bloody teenagers' meant she was hardly a great catch, but until she started to become more erratic, Mother had no shortage of offers from lonely men, all of whom she rejected in a way that gave us glimpses of the mischievous teenager she must once have been.

While Bill continued his epic huff, the irrepressible Mr Garrity went on his painting tour with a different widow. He was so pleased when one of his Carcassonne watercolours was accepted for display in the public library that he repaid Mother's teaching, which he actually described as brilliant, by giving me my first ever summer job. I served beside a blonde art student called Lisa-Jane on the trade counter at Mr Garrity's Liquor Emporium.

There, a tall, slender man of twenty-seven, with appalling clothes and a thick black beard, took the order cards from the counter staff, then delivered the wine to cars and vans at the rear of the building. He performed his duties without fuss, while saying as few words as possible. I still marvel at that: until my arrival at Mr Garrity's I'd always been thrown by quiet men (or boys, if I think back to school where the silent ones set my teeth on edge – I was used to my brothers' noise).

I guess I was seduced by Zenon's calm. I practised his surname – Kalaknowski – during slack moments at the counter. The notion that I must at all costs say it correctly was accompanied by a sensation I can only compare to warm honey. It consumed me so rapidly that I fled to the loo to scold myself in the mirror for resembling a lovelorn character in a teen magazine.

I couldn't wait for day two at work when I'd confirm what my apparently no longer reliable mind had been unable properly to register, which was that Zenon – who had a very still way of facing you as he accepted the order cards – had one eye the blue of zircon while the other was the green of jade. The disparity was somehow so harmonious that it had only struck me hours later.

Kal-a-know-ski … Kal-a-know-ski … Kal-a-know-ski …

I practised like my life depended on it.

9

Lisa-Jane had a lovely smile that made her mouth lift at the corners, like the tips of a crescent moon. I noticed it particularly on my second morning at Mr Garrity's because she smiled at me so much that, in the end, I couldn't prevent a scowl, which drove her to the opposite end of the counter.

We both knew, without anything being said, that the cause of my tension was a man I'd met only the day before. Our interest in him surged when an amused customer popped in to tell Mr Garrity that he'd seen Zenon squirt ketchup onto an ice cream he'd bought from Tony the Italian Number Two (who drove around in a red and yellow van, with a big plastic hot dog on its roof and chimes that could be heard half a mile away).

Mr Garrity winked one of his mocha-coloured eyes at me and said, in a voice like Marlon Brando's in *The Godfather*, 'Ah! You see how it is, Vanessa. He is in love, this man who cannot tell raspberry sauce from tomato ketchup. In love,' he stressed, wrapping his left hand over the right and pressing it to his heart. His chubby face contorted with exaggerated emotion, making me and Lisa-Jane laugh. I wasn't irritated by her now: it wasn't her fault that everyone could read my haywire emotions. Including, of course, the flipping customer, who gave a departing smirk, which left me in no doubt that he had seen a link between my arrival at Mr Garrity's and Zenon's conversion into a bumbler who'd topped his ninety-nine with the wrong red stuff. A minor error by any standards but in terms of what it signified it had Mr Garrity raising his hands and declaiming, 'It's amore! Amore!' he repeated, so insistently that, to my bewilderment, my mind flipped back to when Daddy had played the same kind of barmy games. This gave rise to such a rush of happy-sadness that I had to distract myself by shifting my gaze to Lisa-Jane. She gave me an extremely curious look and announced that she was off to the loo before she wet herself.

Mr Garrity lowered his arms and nodded towards the rubber swing doors that led to where Zenon was. 'Take it from an old fool who never seized the chance of love when he was young,' he advised, in his normal voice, yet with a sadness that touched me. 'Your Zenon is an exceptionally fine young man.'

Although he had referred to Zenon as my young man, sending a wave of pride through me, I suddenly saw how I appeared in Mr Garrity's eyes: all at a loss with my unnecessary-seeming hands, my ankles crossed as if I wanted to corkscrew an escape through the grey-painted concrete beneath my feet. It would have been a relief to do just that because, after all my years of self-control, I wanted to confess the hideous emptiness I'd felt when Daddy had drowned himself just as I'd believed he was at last going to stop drinking and do right by Mother and us kids. It was a horrid betrayal that, nonetheless, had the effect of making me love him more than ever and determined not to let my family down by being sad, especially with Mother, who was trying so hard to keep a lid on her own feelings.

With the benefit of good old Mr Hindsight, I can see how naïve I'd been in thinking I could endlessly contain my grief at Daddy's suicide, which now became a maelstrom that confused me until it wasn't Zenon I wanted but Mr Garrity. His eyes were so dreamy and lonely that I ached to make him happy.

Thank God, then, for the chimes of Tony the Italian Number Two, which were distant but still loud enough to make Mr Garrity shake himself out of his trance, his jowls wobbling as he came alert. 'Go to your Zenon, young lady!' he barked, slapping the counter and turning his back on me.

'Yes, madam, how may I help?' I heard him ask a customer, who had arrived as I pushed through the rubber swing doors. My mad, dangerous craving for Mr Garrity evaporated.

'Zenon?' I called warily, into the chilled cavern where the white wine was stacked twenty feet high to the left, the red to the right. A red-painted central aisle led to the bay into which the customers reversed their cars and vans for loading.

'Zenon?'

Go on, Vanessa darling . . . I heard Daddy whisper, as if he was with me, not just inside my head.

I began the walk down the red aisle, the wine racks towering to either side, my heart thumping so fast and hard it could have burst.

'Help me, Daddy,' I whispered, looking left and right for Zenon in the first of the six lanes of racks that crossed the path I was now treading.

'Help me, Daddy.' I crossed the second lane with no sign of my Zenon.

10

When I was younger and the everyday bickering of us kids sometimes became nasty, I was usually the one who smoothed things over. Before you get the idea that I reckon I was better-behaved than the others, I must point out that on rare occasions – such as when I knocked our Jack out cold with the jam pan – I excelled in a fight. But, that said, I'd be untrue to myself if I didn't claim to have a bit of calm within my nature that had set me slightly apart, and often proved beneficial. As it was when I eventually found Zenon in the white section of the last lane of racks. He looked at me from where he was sitting, like a broken Action Man, on some tall aluminium steps with rubber wheels, and my heart steadied.

'I can't think!' he said. His eyes had lost the previous day's harmony: the green one seemed to go one way and the blue the other (like somebody I'd seen on TV who'd had a lobotomy). 'I – I can't work!' He tugged at his hair with his left fingers while holding his right hand as it twisted forward and back beside his ear.

It was hard for me not to step forward and draw his

troubled head to me so that I could kiss his crown a thousand times. I decided against that because his agitation was so extreme he might have drowned.

'We should meet up to talk away from work,' I proposed, marvelling at how I was feeling the honey glow I'd first experienced twenty-four hours earlier.

'Where? When? What time?' Zenon rose from the steps with an urgency that made me hope he was going to take hold of me and kiss me.

'The bench below Winston Churchill's statue, eight o'clock tonight,' I replied, without thinking. I was struck by how unfazed I sounded.

As I look back now, that calm still seems amazing. Right from the off I was desperate for the intervening hours to pass, yet wondering how on earth I'd make the rendezvous without piquing the interest of my brothers and sister.

'Eight o'clock it is, then,' confirmed Zenon. He moved off the steps and backwards beyond them. He swept his hair off his brow and asked if I could credit that he'd squirted tomato ketchup onto his ice-cream.

His unworldliness reminded me of our Jack and Craig, whom I'd always worried over in respect of their dopey-boy ways. This caused me to smile. Zenon's odd-matched eyes narrowed. 'Are you teasing me?'

'Oh, no, Zenon, darling! Please! I'd never do that because I love you!'

Even though I'd fallen for him partly because he communicated with long pauses as much as with words, I was too taken aback by myself to stay with him: his eyebrows soared up as if little bombs had gone off beneath them. The grin that broke right across his bearded face made me feel as if I was walking on air, not the long red-painted aisle that led to the rubber swing doors, beyond which Mr Garrity discreetly remained in his office.

When I got back, Lisa-Jane demanded to know all, her pale blue eyes wide with excitement. She suggested I could keep my nosy family at bay by saying I needed to walk the dog to clear my head after being so long in the warehouse, a plan I thought brilliant. I wondered briefly if Zenon was as nutty about animals as Mother and the rest of us.

'Zenon Kalaknowski,' I said perfectly, many, many times in my head. As if that would fill the agonising gap that yawned until eight o'clock. If I hadn't seen him then on Churchill's Promontory, I might have thrown myself where Daddy had ended it all, so compelling was my honeyed sense of love.

'Thank you, Daddy,' I whispered. Just once: I didn't want to be disloyal to Mother, whom, for the time being, I intended to keep in the dark.

11

Sometimes our Brucie-Dog's eyes were amber. Not unusually they were brown, with a blue centre, and if he was really watching you, they became so incredibly blue that, if you were in an off mood, you felt comforted. Even though I was wary of setting any dog beside people in terms of importance, when I returned from Mr Garrity's it was the bluest eyes our Brucie could muster that soothed me during the two long hours before my meeting with Zenon.

Far from noticing anything different about me, our Rachael was busy limbering up to help at an over-sixties exercise group, and my twin brother was upstairs completing a self-portrait in oil that had already got us calling him Narcissus. Craig was willing to forgo his usual evening dog walk as it meant he could get some MOT-test welding finished.

That left me – the only one who'd fallen in love in the past twenty-four hours – with a curious feeling of neglect that might have been something of a downer, except that Mother was watching me, like an owl, and had even smiled at me once or twice, behind the others' backs, as if we were somehow in cahoots.

'Well,' she eventually said, finding me alone as she prepared to make the first of many trips to water her irises at the front of the house, 'if you don't mind me saying so, you seem not quite yourself this evening, our Vanessa. There's nothing wrong, is there?' she went on, smiling oh-so-broadly. I felt myself turn as red as the large plastic watering-can she'd got balanced on the back of one of the breakfast chairs. A puddle was forming on the seahorse lino because the can's seam leaked if upward pressure was applied to its base.

'Mother dearest,' I pointed to the wet floor and did my utmost to sound bored when really I was flattered and concerned by her interest, 'if you'd only stick to your own business, you'd see you were drowning the bloody seahorses!'

That was an old family joke, like the one about us kids being able to swim the length of the hall after she'd slopped water along it all the way to the garden. Usually it annoyed and amused her in equal measure, but that evening her response matched the tone I'd been aiming for. 'Do seahorses actually drown, then?' she enquired, picking up the heavy watering-can with both hands, and leaving me with an unnerving sense that my palm had been read without my consent. That, most infuriatingly of all, was precisely how our otherwise inexact mother sometimes was.

'Enjoy your stroll with our Brucie,' she called from the porch.

I replied tartly that I would, even though I'd realised there was more dignity to be had in saying nothing.

'Roll on eight o'clock,' I told Picasso, who merely tucked his head beneath his threadbare wing. It was a gesture our Rachael had once described as the parrot equivalent of 'Do Not Disturb'.

12

L ooking back, I could understand the contradictory game I was playing. I needed my family to intuit that something amazing was happening to me, but I didn't want them to stick their big noses into my business. Especially since my powerful feelings for Zenon were unlike those I'd had for any previous boyfriend.

Which confronted me with a sartorial dilemma: I wanted to look special, but not so special that my walk with Brucie would arouse interest. I decided against the gold velvet two-piece I'd made out of one of Mum's curtains on the day when our beloved mutt had joined the family (and which I'd recently remade with neat stitching: I'd long considered it a lucky outfit).

The solution to my problem was a compromise: a red tracksuit top borrowed from our Rachael, ordinary blue jeans and – my pièce de résistance – the shiny yellow shoes on which I'd long ago painted ladybirds.

There was no danger of me forgetting that exercising our Brucie was the supposed focus of my walk: he had been at my side all the time I was downstairs, then fol-

lowed me to my attic room and sprawled across my bed
with his tail hanging over one side, his chin resting between his outstretched paws on the other, his blue, blue
eyes upon my every move. Just like he truly was my
guardian angel. It was not an unusual position: Brucie
thought all the beds in the house were his.

'What are you looking at, big daft dog?' I asked, getting down low and tickling behind his gorgeous silky
ears. 'Brucie-Wucie-Lucie-Darling,' I added, in a par-
ody of our Craig. It sent a quiver from his little black
eyebrows to his tail.

'Brucie-Wucie-Lucie-Darling,' I repeated, struck by
terror now: it was crazy to believe Zenon would ever
wait for me on Churchill's Promontory. Surely no fully
grown man could fancy my stumpy legs and plump
belly.

Have faith, Vee darling. You're my beautiful girl,
whispered Daddy, as Brucie lifted his chin and looked
right into my eyes, his ears pricked as if he, too, had
heard the words that encouraged me to take him downstairs, attach his chain and leave to meet Zenon via our
Craig's workshop.

'See you later, Vanessa babe!' cried my ever-playful
brother. He had panda rings around his eyes where the
dense green welding goggles, now pushed up into his
hair, had been hard against his skin.

'See you later, Brucie-Bruce!' he added, as our dog
pulled me down the lane and towards the seafront.

13

But as we rounded the corner at the bottom of the lane and stepped onto the pavement, our Brucie locked his legs, pulled back on his lead and faced me. The left and right sides of his brow were concertinaed, like they'd been knotted between his eyes. His sudden refusal to cross the seafront road – especially given his urgent pace so far – might have been a puzzle.

Yet Brucie-Dog was nothing if not a remarkably intuitive beast and, sure enough, I really needed an extra minute to prepare myself before we continued to where Zenon was sitting against the right armrest of the seaward-facing bench beneath Sir Winston Churchill's feet. It was an oddly isolated position that left the bigger part of the light blue slats with a sweeping bareness that set my mind turning until it connected with an episode of several hours before. Lisa-Jane had left work sharpish for a dental appointment, and Mr Garrity had come out of his office to log the day's sales on the equally sweeping bare trade counter.

'What you have to understand about your young

man Zenon,' he had begun, his voice full of apology that he was yet again trespassing in my space, 'is the gap.'

'What gap?' I asked. It hit me then that his feelings towards Zenon, who'd worked at Mr Garrity's every summer for years, were fatherly.

'Well,' he went on, briefly tap-tapping a biro against his lower lip, 'he's known much pain, Vanessa. His parents escaped the Nazis and were killed in a car crash when their boy was ten. His grandfather, from his father's side, he too was alone, and came to England to be Zenon's parent until his own death. But could Zenon tell me, "Oh, he was a loving man, thank you for asking, Mr Garrity"? Could he say to me, "Oh, he was a good man"? Or that his grandfather had saved his childhood as best he could? No, Vanessa, none of these things. But your Zenon takes his time. He thinks. The next day he answered me thus. "Mr Garrity, Grandfather Kala-knowski was from a town in central Poland where everybody drank a locally made fruit juice. Very sweet. Very thick. Syrupy, in fact. Similar to that in our tinned fruit cocktail. In England he was the Pole who drank the juice and threw away the fruit. That was my grand-father Kalaknowski for you. The fruit-juice drinker."'

Mr Garrity had placed the biro, with which he'd continued to fiddle, upon the counter top, and at last looked squarely at me, his dark brown eyes filling with pity as he saw that my fingers were clenched against the loneliness that Zenon must have been through: losing his parents, who'd earlier fled the murderers who had caused the flipping war, and then the grandfather, who had been his only family.

'I don't tell you this to cause distress,' he explained. 'I tell you this so that you will understand. The gap is the difference between what is greatly felt by the heart and what is expressed by the tongue!' He gathered up his papers and, en route back to his office, paused to look at me once more. This time his eyes were so full of compassion that I burned to thank him for caring so much about my – our – Zenon.

Somehow, though, it was right that only he should talk and, pressing this advantage, he was pretty damn quick to conclude, 'Your Zenon, Vanessa, needs to be loved. But remember that while he could tell me about the fruit juice, he could not, in the plain language to which you may be accustomed, say how much he truly loved his grandfather.'

And then, as if he was now in cahoots with Mr Cupid-dart Garrity, cunning old Daddy whispered in my ear, Love, Vanessa darling, reach out to love.

Advice that he repeated as, with my minute of reflection over, I led big, happy Brucie-Dog off the high granite kerb, over the blood-red surface of the seafront road, and towards the promontory.

The sun was setting over the town behind me, casting a ruddy glow that brought a welcoming pinkness to the shiny white marble figure of Sir Winston and the vast flat silvery-blue sea.

14

Zenon had been so far away in his thoughts that, as I sat on the bench and shuffled against his side, he turned to me in incomprehension. 'You came!' he cried, upon quickly gathering his wits. His adorable green and blue eyes had widened as far as they could. 'I was convinced, I mean totally convinced, Vanessa, that you'd change your mind!'

Even before he'd finished speaking, I'd released our Brucie's chain and was moving in to kiss Zenon, with something akin to an exploding star going off inside my head as our lips met. There was passion that, for all the dizzying emotions of the two days past, I truly had not anticipated. When we eventually stopped, it spurred me to exclaim, 'I really, really meant it when I said I loved you, Zenon. Really I did.'

He declared that he'd fallen so deeply in love with me that he couldn't imagine a future without us being married. Far from seeming premature, as you may just be thinking it was, this statement had the exquisitely odd effect of making me feel that at last I was coming home. Or that I was being nudged in the direction of a loving place where I'd always been meant to go.

Trust this man! Trust him with your soul, whispered Daddy, as Zenon gently kissed the top of my head. Our now slouched position on the bench meant we were more like long-familiar lovers, cuddling on a sofa.

Oh, I will, Daddy, I most certainly will. I was peering dreamily beyond the sea rail to the horizon from where millions of ladybirds had once flown. That was the day when we were on the beach and Daddy had been stitching a moccasin from a kit that Mother had given him for his birthday. 'And we'll always be soul-mates,' I heard myself add, just as Zenon's right hand came to rest on the head of our Brucie, who, while we'd been kissing and talking, had stayed close by.

'I know,' agreed Zenon, making me love him even more. 'Soul-mates for ever.'

I couldn't help but marvel at the directness of expression that Mr Garrity had led me not to expect. Next Zenon explained that he knew about the long struggle between my parents, and how it had ended with Daddy jumping from the very spot where we were sitting on the promontory. His openness so astonished me that, pushing him aside, I stood up. 'I see what this is! You've been primed for our meeting!' I cried, the words spilling from my mouth. I'd made the link between Zenon knowing all about my family and Mr Garrity.

'Exactly! Mr Garrity!' he confirmed, with a chuckle

that left me in no doubt that he knew our employer had told me about his parents' flight from the Nazis and Grandfather Kalaknowski's recent death. 'That gossipy matchmaking devil!' he exclaimed, leaping from the bench with a grin that, in a trice, blasted my vexation across the sea and beyond Norway. 'He shouldn't be a wine wholesaler! He should be a dating agent, bringing lonely hearts like yours and mine together, Vanessa!'

At this point our Brucie added to the fun by barking and rearing upwards. Zenon grabbed his paws and craned forward to accept the big wet licks that were aimed at his slightly pointy nose. 'He's mad, this animal of yours!'

Then Daddy thrilled me: You see now how it is, Vanessa darling? Trust in love. Always, always trust in love.

Zenon lowered Brucie-Dog to the ground, picked up the leather handle of his chain and extended his free hand to me. 'This way,' he said, as we began the walk along the seafront towards the far end of the beach, where every thirty seconds the lighthouse cast an arc of yellow into the darkening yet still quite pink evening air.

'Where are we going?' I wondered, not really wanting an answer, as the mystery was a pleasant accompaniment to the glow that was warming my insides.

'You'll soon see,' he replied confidently, placing his

left arm across my shoulders so that we walked as one.

My thoughts drifted to Mr Garrity. His description of Zenon's home life had been so quirkily done that I could not resist alluding to its strangeness. 'According to our match-making employer, your grandfather drank positively gallons of fruit juice.'

Zenon laughed and held me tighter to his side. He knew I was embellishing what Mr Garrity had actually said about Grandfather Kalaknowski and his fruit juice. To have been so easily read by him made me tingle. We really were made for each other.

'You'll know all about Grandfather soon enough,' he promised.

I was blissfully content to leave it at that.

Forty minutes later we'd reached the end of the long promenade, where a strip of small hotels ended to our left, and to our far right the beach gave way to jet black rocks and little pools that were fleetingly illuminated by the lighthouse. It was as if the brand new night was readying itself to give up old secrets.

'The dead never die, do they, Zenon?' I said, amazed at myself, yet curiously proud that this thought had popped into my awareness as a conclusion, not really as a question.

'No, Vanessa darling,' he agreed, without looking at me, yet with a note which somehow conveyed that in time I would learn all there was to know about his long-deceased parents and Grandfather Kalaknowski. 'The dead never die while those who loved them remember . . . This way,' he said. We increased our pace a little as he steered us towards some detached 1920s houses that were just along the seafront from the hotels. True to their Bauhaus styling, they had flat roofs and wide, rectangular windows that gave them a look of decks on ocean liners. Each of these unusual properties was brick-built, with a ghostly-white finish. They faced across the road towards some golf links and the sea.

To the right of the sixth and final house was the entrance to the crematorium where I recalled our brave fifteen-year-old Jack halting Daddy's coffin to kiss the lid and say goodbye from us all.

'You know what?' I said to Zenon, carried along by a great rush of love for my dopey brothers, my obstinate baby sister and our batty mother. 'You'll like my crazy family, Zenon! You will! You'll really like them all!'

'But of course I will,' he replied, his smiley eyes in perfect harmony as he led me and our Brucie onto the crunchy gravel drive of the fifth house.

15

Instead of branching off the drive to where the front door stood beside a rectangular bay window, whose panes were dark and dimly shiny, Zenon led us straight ahead to where the garage, which adjoined the side of the house, had extra-high black-painted wooden doors.

'Zenon, have you got a lorry or something?' I asked, my curiosity growing as he opened the first door with a Yale key, then swung it to slip a retaining hook into an eye on a post at the edge of the small front garden. 'Or just a tall van, like Tony the Italian's hot-dog thingy?' I persisted, amused by his air of mystery as he opened the second tall door and secured it to the fence shared by the neighbouring house.

He stepped over the threshold and positioned his right hand so that, with a couple of quick karate-like chops, he'd flicked two rows of wall-mounted switches.

'Blimey! Are you sure you've got enough lights?' I cried. Each of the fifteen or so joists that spanned the width of the roof had two long and dazzlingly bright strip lights attached to it.

'Ah,' he replied, shielding his eyes against the glare with his hand, 'as he got older, my grandfather had bad eyesight, Vanessa.'

If that was a cue for me to ask about Grandfather Kalaknowski, it was wasted: all I could do was gawp at the intense blaze of gold that covered the long side walls from top to bottom. Sheer brilliance, which was almost too much for my eyes, but they soon adjusted to the glare, and I saw that each wall also bore a continuous pattern of evenly spaced red, white and yellow dots.

'Bits of cherry!' I said. Zenon wore a touchingly imp- ish smile, and Brucie was observing my every move with a curiosity that made his ears as sharp as darts. 'Plus cubed melon! And bloody peach!' I was becoming ever more excited as I ran from one side of the garage to the other. Zenon's floor-to-ceiling shelves of Del Monte fruit-cocktail empties were Andy Warhol's latest art. 'You kept them! All the cans your grandfather drank the syrup from! You flipping well kept them!'

'Not me exactly,' he said, folding his arms across his chest and turning in a slow circle upon the middle of the red-painted floor, his gaze tracking the many, many colourfully labelled tins. 'My grandfather. Though we both had a bit of a thing about orderliness.' He was fac- ing me without blinking the green eye or the blue, yet with trepidation, which made it nothing like the scary eyeballing our Jack went in for. I became certain that, for the first time ever, he was preparing to bare his soul.

'You don't need to justify yourself to me, Zenon,' I said, noting that a consecutive number had been neatly written in black felt-tip ink on every label of the display. 'Not one bit,' I added. I was taken aback at the sheer fastidiousness, yet also mindful that in all likelihood he feared I would see the need to collect old cans and keep them in perfect order as, well, freakish.

'You mean that for all this fruit-can madness,' he threw his arms wide, 'this collecting mania, you still want me, Vanessa?'

Self-doubt had narrowed his eyes again and, shocked that I was becoming the cause of new suffering, I retorted that if he wanted to claim the copyright on family madness he'd long been beaten to it by my crazy family.

I swear I heard Daddy chuckle, but paid him no attention. Instead I splayed my fingers before Zenon's face and itemised the following:

1. Our family was excommunicated by a dentist who wore a rug on his head.

2. We narrowly escaped the police after Daddy made an approach to the Salvation Army when drunk and naked.

3. My twin brother Jack was in the habit of claiming to be a latter-day Casanova, when everybody knew he was a virgin.

4. In the absence of five hundred press-ups a day, my baby sister would probably turn into the female equivalent of Mr Hyde.

And:

5. My kid brother, with his pudding-basin haircut, once fell seriously in love with a Mark 2 Ford Cortina 1600E.

I was on such a roll that I couldn't resist adding that, of all colours, the car in question had been metallic pink, a detail Zenon grasped as if I'd unexpectedly thrown him a gold nugget the size of a cricket ball …

16

'Eighty-A-Eight!' he declared, with joyous authority, which thoroughly bamboozled me, though by way of part-explanation he just as quickly conceded, 'Ye gods, Vanessa! But it's a small, small world we live in!'

'Is it?' I responded, mystified but reassured by the swift return of his confidence and happiness.

'It most certainly is,' he answered, gently bringing the front of his body against mine and joining his hands upon my lower back. With the side of my head now resting against his chest, he explained that the Cortina 1600E, which our Craig had fallen in love with, was Light Orchid in colour, not pink.

It was a long-familiar distinction that set my mind whirling back to our Craig's pride at rejuvenating the shine on the stylish car. Daddy had thought it a duffer and let Craig smarten it up in readiness for sale. Big Eddie, our family friend from across the lane, had encouraged him. He and his wife Vivienne ran an Elvis-themed hotel called the Heartbreak. When the car was ready, Big Eddie had fixed it so that one of his mates bought it from Daddy. Everybody was proud of our Craig for what he'd done.

To be hearing about the same car from Zenon six years on was somehow disturbing. I was caught un-awares and, before I could think to do otherwise, I'd placed my hands flat upon his torso, then – for the second time that evening – forcefully pushed myself free of his embrace. 'Look! I don't get this! What on earth are you telling me?' I demanded, as his blue eye went once more the opposite way to his green one.

My still-whirling brain filed away that the thickly painted concrete floor I was standing upon was the same dark red as the long centre aisle at Mr Garrity's warehouse. That got me wondering whether Zenon had pinched the paint from poor old Mr Garrity, which, I have to say, was unfair: I was already realising that my Zenon abhorred dishonesty.

'Please – please – don't be upset,' he begged. I opened my mouth to apologise for so roughly pushing him away. 'Ssh, Vanessa!' He placed a finger to his lips. 'It's all so easy to explain. Cortina 1600Es came in many colours, the most popular being Aquatic Jade, Aubergine, Amber Gold, Silver Fox, Saluki Bronze and Blue Mink. But, like Aubergine and Amber Gold, Light Orchid was most common to the E model, not found on the full Cortina range. Yet where Aubergine and Amber Gold were numerous on the 1600E, Light Orchid was rare as hen's teeth . . . well, almost.

'So, if anybody admired a pink 1600E in this town, it had to be the car that was bought new by one of the hoteliers near here because that was the only Light Orchid example I ever knew of. And as for Eighty-A-Eight,' he concluded, with a triumphant grin, 'that's easy too. It's nothing more mystical than the Ford paint code for Light Orchid in 1970, the year of the car we're discussing.'

'But flipping heck, Zenon, how – and, more to the point, why – do you know the code for a shade of paint that the Ford Motor Company stopped making three hundred years ago?'

'Ah,' he replied, all the while scrubbing where his beard grew up the side of his face to become a bushy sideburn that I fully intended to trim. 'That's where you jumped the gun big-style, Vanessa! I wasn't trying to steal your treasured copyright on family madness! I was trying to explain what makes me me!'

So, right when he'd been doing his very best to open up to me, I'd gone and done what everybody in my bigmouth family always did: I'd spoken straight over him. Or, to put it another way, smashed him about the head with words as surely as I'd once concussed our Jack with Mother's pan. Before I had time to begin hating myself, though, Zenon was ready to pick up on the theme of Eighty-A-Eight.

17

'**M**y grandfather,' he resumed, pointing to one of the ghostly white pillars that marked the entrance to the short drive, 'also had a Mark 2 Cortina. Nothing special like a GT or a 1600E. Just an ordinary 1300 deluxe, which he scratched quite badly on that concrete post.'

The information came so assertively that I placed my hands over my ears for less volume. His playful response was to ham up the whisper in which he explained that the Lagoon Blue of his grandfather's car was a far easier shade to match than the metallic pink or – 'Oops! Sorry, Vanessa!' – Light Orchid of the 1600E with which my baby brother had been infatuated.

Because it was gentle teasing and came when I least expected it, it made me stand on tiptoe and offer my lips to his. Unlike our passionate kissing on Churchill's Promontory, the softness of his mouth relaxed me to the point at which I didn't care if he spoke loudly enough for a dog walker, whose cigarette I could see glowing on the golf links, to hear.

In fact it was in his usual voice that he described how

Grandfather Kalaknowski had bought a litre of Lagoon Blue paint from a man who'd mixed it in a clanking old machine behind the shop counter. Zenon had had ten minutes or so to observe a chart that displayed the many Mark 2 Cortina colours for the model's production run, 1966 to 1970.

I was more confused now than I had been at any time in the previous forty-eight hours, as you would've been if you were with someone who was driving you stir-crazy with love yet you couldn't get your head around the significant thing he was disclosing about his life.

And while Zenon's eyes had become even more focused, I was still finding it hard to stop mine sliding away from him. The result was that, wary of my inattention causing yet another bumpy patch between us, I ditched my resolution to keep quiet. 'But, Zenon!' I protested. 'Please! Why on earth do you keep blathering on about a flipping paint chart?'

He paced the garage, rattling off the codes for Aubergine, Silver Fox, Blue Mink, Aquatic Jade, Amber Gold and several other Cortina colours in a soliloquy of sorts. In a bid to avoid his now alarmingly wild stare, I looked to where the dog walker was coming onto a paved area lit by one of the tall lampposts that stood at fifty-yard intervals along the roadside.

'Buster!' the man called to his dog – a large Alsatian. 'Here now.' He had a stoop that made me want to protect him. I was distracting myself from my utter failure to understand Zenon. The man didn't need my protection: on seeing a taxi pass far too fast, he snapped himself upright, flicked away his fag-end and commanded Buster to sit right where he was.

Zenon had gone deadly quiet, and Daddy – I'd forgotten about him – gave me quite a start when he whispered, Never mind Buster, Vanessa darling. Look to your Zenon.

The tender insistence of those words made me turn back to my Zenon as instructed – to see that, in the wake of his crazy-seeming outburst, his eyes had stilled with fear. Now I realised with clanging certainty that he'd been testing me with the barmy paint-code rant to see if I'd dump him for being freakish after all. I felt guilty for ignoring him in favour of Buster and his owner, and thought so hard and fast that, even as I was getting the words straight in my head, I found myself asking, 'Do you really mean to say that after one scan of that colour chart you remember the name of every colour and its code fifteen years later? Is that what you need me to understand? That you have a mind which remembers every tiny little thing?'

It was an interrogation of sorts that now made him eyeball me in a way that more than equalled one of our Jack's scariest glares.

'Yes,' he replied. 'Once I've read something, I remember and see every syllable for life.'

'You mean all the letters, numbers, full stops and commas?' I was doing my best not to reveal that I was utterly in awe of his offbeat mental powers, yet at the same time I saw a hilarious image of his mind as a dustbin so full of gas bills and shopping lists that the lid was about to fall off.

He was backing away from me, mumbling that he'd understand if I'd made a mistake and wanted to marry somebody with a 'normal mind'.

It was pessimism, outright defeatism. I told him not to be so bloody stupid, and, with his wildly unbelieving eyes darting this way and that, strode forward to kiss him with a passion that made my already pounding heart feel so inconveniently large it could have burst my ribs wide open.

Never had anything been as clear to me. My Zenon might have been gifted with a mighty memory and inclined to speak in metaphors but, as Mr Garrity had mentioned, he must have known loneliness second to none.

'My bloody special genius!' I crowed, delighted and honoured that he had trusted me enough to bare his soul.

18

'Test me!' he cried, the second we'd stopped kissing. 'Go on, Vanessa!' He was trailing the tip of his finger along the numbers on some of the Del Monte cans.

'Four hundred and fifty!'

'Ah! Now that, Vanessa, will contain seventeen one-inch stainless-steel slot-headed self-tapping screws!'

His accuracy was confirmed when he led me across the garage to Can 450 and gleefully displayed its shiny metal contents. The fun built as I rattled off number after number, and followed in his wake as he zigzagged between the walls.

The game went on and on until the exhilarating proof of his ability to recall the contents of every single one gave me a stitch. It was matched by his attack of breathlessness, which caused him to bend forward, with his hands upon his knees, and gasp for air.

'Vanessa, we're playing happily enough now,' he began, when he'd recovered enough to straighten his back, 'but the discovery that my mind was different from anybody else's when I was a boy wasn't funny.'

'That I can imagine,' I replied. I kept it brief because I recognised that in opening up his childhood Zenon was placing even more trust in me. Now I was finding it both easy and wonderful to keep my eyes fixed on his as he recalled that, when he was eight, he was sent by his teacher to a school on the far side of a shared playing field: he was to bring her a box of pencils that had been delivered there by mistake. It was a simple enough mission, which went well until he was told to wait at the rear of a class of fifteen-year-olds while their maths teacher wiped a mass of sums from the blackboard. 'A move,' he continued, 'that brought a hail of protest, proving most of the pupils had not completed them.'

Now he twisted his upper body to reposition a can whose label was facing the wrong way. For once, impatience did not get the better of me: I waited for him to go on with the story.

When he looked back at me, it was as if I'd passed another test: he launched into an explanation of how, with 'all the guileless enthusiasm' of an eight-year-old boy-genius, he'd called out the erased sums from where he was standing at the back of the classroom.

The silence that followed had made him fear he was in double trouble: in his helpfulness towards the much older pupils, he'd also inadvertently given the answers. The maths teacher and her class were not so much taken aback as knocked for six. There was no trouble.

'And that,' concluded Zenon, 'led to several meetings with a very pink-faced man who had immaculate silver hair.'

He whirled away from me, his long thin fingers frantically working to turn Del Monte cans on either side of the garage so that they faced the walls. When he reached the end of the shelving, he clenched his hair with both hands, groaned, then righted the cans again.

'Okay!' I cried, aware that I sounded dangerously like Mother, yet unable to hold my tongue. 'Enough of this flipping mad hoo-hah, Zenon! What did the silver-topped man say to you?'

A look of revulsion slithered into his eyes – and barely a second passed before I, too, got wind of the stench that had evidently reached him first.

'Phaaaw!' he exclaimed.

I turned to where Brucie-Dog had done his business on the garage floor. My poor old family mutt had had an accident, which made me feel as guilty as sin. As well as leaving his front legs with a tendency to collapse, the near-fatal distemper he'd fought off when he was young had also left his bowel inclined to open without warning. It happened rarely and only at times of stress. I realised that while Zenon had been turning cans to face the walls I'd been dimly aware of our Brucie-Dog whimpering.

Zenon spotted poor old Brucie's down-turned tail,

flattened ears and immensely sad eyes. Straight away he grabbed a shovel, which was beside a stiff-bristled broom that was resting by the door, and scooped the poo into the garden. 'It's only a bit of crap, Vanessa. I'll get it in the morning. C'mon, let's take him to the links before he dies of embarrassment.'

On the one hand I welcomed his care, but on the other it made me shudder: he had come so close to explaining his difficult childhood to me but had seized on Brucie's accident as a means to procrastinate.

'Two minutes for the dog to get his spirits up, and then you tell me what old Silver Top said,' I insisted, leading our Brucie out of the bright garage, slightly ahead of Zenon.

19

For all my determination to be firm with Zenon, I couldn't manage it. When we'd cleared the road and I'd freed our Brucie from his chain, I was amused that, instead of running about, he became very still, and gave us an incredibly intense stare.

Zenon placed his hands on his hips. 'I'm convinced that animal of yours, Vanessa, is following every single thing we say and do!'

'Of course he is!' Our Brucie-Dog was so very poised that his long, bushy tail was horizontal. But he'd always been the canniest of mutts. Having got our attention with his ultra-stillness, he flicked himself to the side, then barked and barked while running big, crazy circles around us.

'Bloody hellfire! He can make some noise!' cried Zenon, who made a show of clamping his hands over his ears and glancing to where two or three curtains at the houses that neighboured his own were twitching. Rather than trying to silence our Brucie, though, he closed the couple of yards that had separated me from him. If you'd been watching, you might just have agreed that the barking had been intended to encourage such a move: from the moment Zenon took me into his embrace, the barking and running stopped.

The calm did not apply to me. All of a sudden I was crying so flipping hard that it's a wonder Zenon, Brucie-Dog and I weren't drowned in a mini-lake of tears. 'I'm sorry, sorry, sorry for being such a bossy bitch,' I blubbered, gathering just enough wit to add, 'Our Jack once said I was so bossy in the womb that I pushed him into the world first!'

A clogged-sounding chuckle alerted me to the fact that Zenon, too, was crying. He cleared his throat and stated that it was 'vital' for me to hear 'precisely' what the silver-haired man had said about him.

His insistence made me wonder if he'd been the kind of boy who'd torched his school or perhaps even tortured little animals. Immediately I felt so wretchedly guilty for thinking such a thing that, upon easing free of his grasp, I met his eyes and lied: 'Look, Zenon, despite what I said before, I don't really don't give a fig what bloody Silver Top thought about you!'

Clever old Zenon rolled his eyes. Whatever I was thinking, he said, it was okay. He had not been the sort of child who'd chopped up furry creatures with a Swiss Army knife. His black humour made me shiver. I retorted that since we were now speaking of little animals, the torture thereof, his tear-drenched moustache resembled a drowned rat. He accepted a paper hanky from the pocket of the tracksuit top I'd borrowed off our Rachael. Determined not to let my habitual bossiness get in the way again, I crossed my fingers behind my back and asked Daddy to blow a raspberry if I came on too demandingly.

'Just give me a moment to think,' said Zenon, as he returned the hanky and signalled that I should wipe my own tear-stained face. He turned his attention from me to where the lighthouse cast its gleam on the flat sea.

'Brucie-Bruce,' I whispered, as my eyes rested on our adorable wonder-dog, lying on the grass with his chin between his front paws, his eyes glinting in the dark, his brow wrinkling and relaxing as an affectionate grumble came from deep within his throat. 'Take your time,' I told Zenon. 'There's no hurry, no more bossiness, I promise.'

20

While I waited for him to begin I looked at the sky. Some years before, my twin brother Jack, who was doing a series of paintings of the stars, had said that the Seven Sisters were hazy because there were no brothers to keep them at their brightest. That had piqued our Rachael. If Jack was a star, she'd said, his feeble light would have made astronomers dismiss him as a mere speck of dust.

Unwilling to hear his big brother so easily trounced, Craig declared that his lah-di-dah twin obviously thought she was a supernova. Hardly was he done than I chipped in that the only bright star in the family was me. In sum, it was the kind of sparring that, now we were older, I often yearned for.

Yet I was wary. In an unguarded moment, before I'd begun working at Mr Garrity's, I'd revealed my nostalgia for our childhood to Jack.

He'd mentioned a Henry James character who had missed her pain when it was no longer there. I saw that, in being my twin, he was also the voice of my conscience.

So, having shifted my gaze from the Seven Sisters to

the Plough to the Bear and on to Orion's Belt, I further recalled that, upon becoming weary of Jack's star paintings, I'd told him to belt up before I died of boredom hearing about them.

One of the canvases subsequently won a regional oil-painting competition. When I apologised for how I'd behaved, he remarked that my rattiness hadn't mattered. Everybody knew I was becoming an impossibly bossy cow anyway.

He'd taught me something worthwhile. Determined not to risk alienating Zenon, I resisted a growing urge to chivvy him about what Mr Silver Top had said when he was little.

Waiting was not easy for me. Soon done with stargazing, I turned to the moon, which was low over the blue-black horizon. Its beauty threatened to ignite my already incendiary feelings. For all my desire to be quiet until Zenon was ready, I became scared that I'd provoke him into spilling the beans.

Instead of risking an outburst I knew I'd regret, I looked at the uninspiring strip of seafront hotels, beyond which was a neon-lit mock-Tudor pub. The Gay Hussar: Daddy's all-time favourite. After the harm the booze he'd drunk there had done to our family, I could quite reasonably have prayed for it to be demolished. Yet because of Daddy's many quirky friends, who would still be at the bar, I was fond of the old place.

A mile further along the promenade, Sir Winston Churchill was up-lit with the magenta that a writer to the *Gazette* had grumbled made him seem to be in drag. It was only right to accentuate the feminine side of the manliest prime minister in history, suggested a second correspondent.

The debate in the paper had lasted a month, with bad consequences in our house. During a sudden return of her French accent, Mother wailed that our glee at the portrayal of Sir Winston Churchill as a drag artist made a mockery of what Daddy had gone through in the war.

We hadn't intended such disrespect. Jack went up to his bedroom and, angry with himself for stressing Mother, stomped about so hard he could have brought the dodgy kitchen ceiling down.

Forget all that unhappy stuff, Vanessa, whispered Daddy. You and your young man have love. The most precious gift in life. Look to the future, darling.

Zenon at last turned his odd-coloured eyes upon me. He was ready to reveal all about Mr Silver Top.

21

'What you have to keep in mind, Vanessa,' he began, 'is that this was the early 1960s. Things were a lot less . . . I don't know . . . professional. For example, could you imagine today an education shrink who isn't a psychologist, just a retired GP assessing the occasional bright upstart from across the county? I don't think so.

'Anyway, I endured five weekly sessions with him in a little room near the headmaster's study, with the best bit – apart from some of the interesting patterns on the Rorschach splotch cards – being the lingering death of the electric fire. Week by week it made soft popping sounds as its five bars burned out. By the time Grandfather came to hear the results of the so-called tests I'd done, the shrink kept his coat on while I had my hands inside my blazer sleeves.

'And probably because it was the middle of January and very cold, our silver-haired pseudo-shrink, called Dr Hope of all things, ploughed straight in, confirming that, no doubt about it, little Zenon Kalaknowski, yours truly, was a boy-genius. The only pupil in the northern-schools region able to become the proverbial rocket scientist. He was oblivious that Grandfather hadn't properly mastered English and disdained all talk of high IQ as being Fascist. All of which, genius or not, I was far too young to understand.

'But what I most certainly did get, Vanessa,' he said, pushing on with a harder edge, 'was dear old Dr Hope's blithe diagnosis. "Of course, the flip side of his extraordinary intelligence is that the area of Zenon's brain that normally has the capacity for love, Mr Kalaknowski, will never develop. Put simply, that part of the boy will be stunted. As he gets older, not only can you can expect him to become more distant generally, he'll almost certainly be indifferent to, and possibly scared of, the opposite sex. In other words, he will have a brilliant mind but he will be a loner of inadequate emotional expression, incapable of love as less intellectually gifted souls the world over experience it."'

22

He'd stepped aside to where the moon cast a bright haze around his head. Unknown to him, it shone upon my bewildering disappointment that his eight-year-old self had not been diagnosed as having the makings of a serial killer. I rebuked myself for being a mean sensationalist who didn't merit anybody's love, but in the next instant, to my great surprise, I was brimming with sympathy for our Craig.

Until we'd crashed into love at Mr Garrity's Liquor Emporium, twenty-seven-year-old Zenon had been living Dr Hope's prediction that he was a genius-loner. I hadn't understood that Craig had never escaped the cruel things that Daddy had shouted at him when he was young, the frequent savage onslaughts about his emerging sexuality that, as Zenon now awaited my response to his story about Dr Hope – Dr Hopeless – had me silently posing a question that didn't involve him.

Oh, Daddy? Why did you? Why did you do that to Craig who loved you so?

But then, as quickly as Craig had entered my mind,

my thoughts were pulled back to Zenon.

In moving slightly to his left, he'd lost his dazzling corona and I felt able to speak up. 'And you're quite certain Dr Hope actually said that about you, Zenon?' I asked.

'Oh, I'm sure, all right,' he answered, so emphatically that if I'd snapped his words, like a stick of seaside rock, his wounding at the hands of Dr Hope would have been inscribed therein.

Incapable of love.

Scored onto his soul.

Whirling from me to face the vast black sea and the silvered horizon, he suddenly bellowed that Dr Hope had been useless. His fury had been awaiting release for years. When he looked at me again, his eyes were hard and shiny. But not scary as Daddy's had been when he was agitated.

Still, no doubt aware that he might have unnerved me, Zenon shrugged and held up the flats of his hands. The outburst was over. Anger spent.

Go to him, Vee! ordered Daddy, who, I noted, put in his ha'pennyworth only when it suited him. Now! he snapped.

'But Dr Hope doesn't matter any more, Zenon,' I protested. Closing the two-yard gap between us, I didn't care if I was being pushy now. We had a future to share and I didn't want him drowning in the past. 'You're in love!' I cried. 'And I'll always love you with all my heart!'

As he took me into his arms, my eyes filled with tears at the plight of the eight-year-old Zenon, whose future, I yearned to reassure him, would hold love. Dr Hopeless was wrong, I wanted to tell that child. I gripped Zenon tighter.

23

His grasp on me was suddenly limp and I stepped back. Something was clearly amiss – but what? He was looking across the darkened links to where the open garage doors revealed the red and gold space in which we'd played the Del Monte game. 'I'm getting this all wrong, Vanessa,' he said.

I felt as if the coarsest sandpaper had been rubbed against my heart. I saw myself tumbling from the cliff where we'd been standing to where the sea would take my life. That was what Daddy had done when things had become too horrible for him to go on. If Zenon was about to tell me that our love was a big mistake, there was no doubting what I would do next.

Stop that, Vee! Stop it now! Stop before you ruin every damn thing worth having! ordered Daddy. That was a relief. It seemed that, without his help, I was no longer in control of my emotions. They went from one extreme to another. It was both beautiful and terrifying.

Seizing Zenon's arms, I yanked him round to face me. I'd never been one to muck about. Our Jack had learned that when I'd concussed him with Mother's pan.

'What the flipping heck d'you mean?' I exploded. 'The whole evening's been proof that we're madly in love!'

His bright green eye went so far from his equally vivid blue eye, I imagined two shiny metal balls going down distant holes on a pinball table. To my right, our Brucie-Dog gave one of his loudest yaps. Zenon grinned. 'Oh, bloody heck, Vanessa! How can you possibly think I doubt us?'

I felt pretty silly. I'd never been topsy-turvy like this before. Zenon's eyes were back together and firmly focused upon me. I wondered if tumbling into love was a form of insanity. If so, we were at least becoming unstable together.

He set his hands on my shoulders and gently turned me until we were again looking towards his house. It struck me that the garage was like a furnace in the night.

'I was speaking about that!' he explained. 'The flaming garage! Look deep inside, Vanessa,' he instructed, 'to the end wall.'

The unusual height of the doorway meant that my line of vision was unimpeded. Even though we were at least a hundred and fifty yards away, I could see what he meant. 'More doors,' I said. Earlier, when I was testing him on the Del Monte cans, I'd only half registered that the white-painted end wall was actually a second set of extra-high wooden doors. It was now glaringly obvious that whatever was housed beyond them explained why Zenon's garage was much taller than those of his neighbours.

His grip tightened on my shoulders. If excitement could be felt as electricity, I would have got a double shock from his hands. At the same time he brought his face down to beside my left ear. Glancing at him, I saw that his gaze was set directly ahead. Sharing the secret of the garage with me was of immense importance to him. In the moments before he spoke I hated myself for the suicidal thought that had flitted though my mind. Never had somebody opened their heart to me like this before. We were somewhere warm and I wanted us to stay there for ever.

'Guess,' he whispered. 'Go on. Guess what's kept in the inner garage, Vanessa.' Brucie came closer and sat directly before us. His ears were pricked and his big blue eyes were shining. I had to smile. It was like he, too, was anticipating the revelation of the secret. Part of me wanted to say something funny but I knew that if I came across as flippant, it would be wrong. Zenon was trusting me to take him seriously. I tried to speak but couldn't. Seconds dragged by and I felt his impatience for an answer. Daddy came to my rescue again: Go on, Vee, darling. Guess what's so important to your Zenon.

That was the prompt I'd needed. Aiming to be zany but plausible, I dived in. 'I don't know, Zenon!' I protested. Then I sped on: 'Yes, I do! Grandfather Kalaknowski brought a clanky old lorry over from Poland!'

Brucie stood up, barked and wagged his tail at us. Perhaps he thought my idea was good. Amused by my dog, Zenon stood a little clear of me and threw his arms wide. 'Nope!' he said triumphantly.

I'd answered wrongly and he'd enjoyed it. We could now happily play the guessing game. Our hearts were getting closer by the millisecond.

I decided that, if not a lorry, it had to be something like a vintage double-decker bus with an open back. That, too, was incorrect.

'Again, Vanessa!' Zenon insisted. 'Again!' By now he'd moved in front of me to where his eyes reflected the dark gleam of the sea behind me. 'Think harder!' he teased.

Moments passed before another likely answer came to me. Confident of what I was about to say, I clicked my fingers. 'It's an old fire engine, isn't it?

Zipping a thumb and finger across his mouth, he theatrically shook his head.

That was galling. I was used to winning against my brothers. Zenon had me hooked and wriggling, like a fish on a line.

A sailing boat. He shook his head once more. I loved

his impish smile, but I wanted to guess correctly and make us equals again. Brucie-Dog was whimpering and fidgeting. That wasn't unusual. He'd always let us know one way or another when he'd had enough of being outside. Still, I needed to try some more guesses. A Second World War tank, I suggested. Zenon was further amused. He knew he'd really got to me. My last-ditch attempt seemed inspired. It just had to be right.

The thing that was housed in the inner garage, I confidently asserted, was the life-sized mechanical elephant that Bill the copper had once told our family was stored in an arch on the lower promenade, near Churchill's Promontory.

Zenon's brow shot up and his eyes widened to their limit. I was certain that I'd nailed the answer. 'Well?' I allowed myself to smile in anticipation of winning the game.

'Wrong!' he declared.

I was piqued and he knew it. He'd already worked out that I was easy to tease. Our Jack had known the same thing and that was partly why I'd clobbered him with Mother's heaviest pan. He hadn't pulled my leg so readily after that. Our Rachael said it was because he'd lost so many brain cells. Craig, on the other hand, reckoned that my twin had become a little scared of me.

Before I could speak – and maybe say something antagonistic I would have regretted – Brucie was running crazy circles around us and barking. In trying to stamp on his trailing lead, Zenon slipped upon the dewy grass and landed on his side. I burst out laughing. Now it was his turn to be piqued, though he was also laughing. He wasn't precious, I decided. We were going to get along like a house on fire. It didn't matter that I hadn't won the guessing game. We'd had fun and I knew we would always make each other happy.

By the time Zenon had got up, Brucie had pelted halfway back to the house. Seeing him getting near the seafront road, I looked in each direction for traffic. It was late but the taxis, which were usually out and about, tended to go fast. I smiled in relief as he made it to the far pavement unharmed.

Zenon had been watching me. 'C'mon, Vanessa!' he cried, putting out his hand to take mine. 'Even ya dog's crazy to know what's beyond the inner doors!'

We returned to his house. My intention was to scold Brucie for running off. As I got near to him, he rolled onto his back. Those big cheeky eyes would have got the better of Barbara Woodhouse.

'You crafty old mutt!' I laughed.

Wildly kicking the air with all four legs, he wriggled his spine on the ground, at his most adorable.

'He's laughing!' exclaimed Zenon. 'He's laughing at us, Vanessa!'

We stood together, looking down at Brucie. I knew

exactly what Zenon meant. Brucie was laughing. Only somebody who loved dogs would have believed it. 'Boy, is he some canny mongrel!' concluded Zenon.

Daddy chuckled in my ear. It was almost like he and Brucie were working in cahoots.

24

Zenon asked me to cover my eyes while he opened the inner doors and hooked them to the Del Monte shelves. Several rows of switches clicked, and new light shone between the gaps in my fingers. My heart thudded in anticipation and I resisted a powerful urge to tilt my head back and peep. Something told me that the surprise he wanted to give me was one of the most important things he'd ever done.

'Okay, Vanessa! Hands away!'

I trembled. Perhaps the reality wouldn't match the anticipation that Zenon had built up in me. If that was the case, my disappointment would have been a knife to his heart. To my amazement, I feared I was going to faint. Had it not been for Daddy's intervention, I believe I would have done so.

Lower your hands now! he barked.

That shook me. I instantly obeyed – and was slack-jawed with amazement at what I was seeing.

A gleaming royal blue steamroller filled the middle of the crimson-painted floor. Thickly embossed upon the front of its immense round boiler was a cherry-red prancing horse. I'd seen steamrollers many times before but they were rowing boats compared to this liner. For scale and beauty she was truly astonishing.

I tingled at my core. Zenon and the steamroller were now synonymous to me. I could've kissed the shiny red ground in front of the colossal iron roller. Instead, I found my voice.

'Zenon!' I cried, stepping forward to gawp at the metal chimney, which towered fifteen feet above my head. 'It's awesome! Beautiful, amazing, incredible!' I babbled, totally enraptured.

Grinning like the Cheshire Cat, he followed my every move as I circled the glorious machine, which, to its rear, had spoked cast-iron wheels taller than I was.

Zenon proudly rattled off some vital statistics: 'Twenty-two feet long. Eight feet six and three-eighths of an inch wide. Twelve and a half tons in weight!'

His eyes sparkled and I laughed. Then he revealed that, at eighty-four years old, the steamroller was the biggest of its type to have been built by an apparently world-famous firm: Aveling and Porter of Rochester, Kent. The prancing horse, he disclosed, was now the logo of a firm long descended from Aveling and Porter. Its continued use had recently upset the Italian carmaker Ferrari, whose own prancing horse was almost identical.

So happy was he to share his steamroller obsession

that I longed to kiss him again. Yet he clearly needed to reveal all about the steamroller. I did my best to remain patient while he talked.

'So when did you and Grandfather Kalaknowski get it in the first place?' I broke in.

'It, Vanessa? It is a she!'

I cursed myself for being a complete fool. His eyes showed I'd stabbed him clean in the heart and I hated myself again. First I'd had a perverse notion about him killing furry animals and now I was destroying his joy in sharing the steamroller with me. I shouldn't have been wearing my yellow and red ladybird shoes: hob-nailed boots would have been appropriate to the way in which I walked upon the feelings of others.

Suddenly the smile was back in his eyes. He grinned. 'Don't look so alarmed. Even Grandfather Kalaknowski sometimes called her "it".'

If I'd had a second longer to think, I would have stopped my eyebrows going up. Barely a moment after I'd felt them do so, his eyes widened. He'd told a fib about his grandfather and he knew that I'd spotted it. In the event it didn't matter. We were laughing now and I had the comfort of knowing that I would never again refer to the steamroller as it.

I didn't need to be a genius like he was to conclude that the mauling he'd received at the hands of Dr Hopeless had prompted the acquisition of the steamroller.

The long restoration project, I rightly surmised, had been a kind old man's way of guiding his gifted grandson.

25

Clicking his fingers, Zenon strode to where three tightly packed bookshelves were mounted on one of the inner garage's spotless white-painted walls. 'Something extra to show you,' he announced, as his right hand went to a volume whose spine projected several inches from the shelf.

Intrigued, I went to him. He opened it and jabbed his finger at a black-and-white photograph. 'Here!' he exclaimed. 'Get a look at this!' The heavy book began to slide from where he'd balanced it on his left palm. He splayed the right over the centre crease.

'Zenon,' I objected, 'I can't see a thing for your hand!'

His retort was swift: 'You soon will!'

He set the open book flat on a shiny steel bench beside a lathe with well-oiled workings and dinky metal knobs. Everything was impeccable. Stepping aside, he rapped his fingers on the image. 'There you go, Vanessa. It's all yours!'

His eyes were shining and his smile was even more impish than before. He intended to astound me. My apparently lacklustre response came from the wilfulness over which I had no control. 'What is it?'

'Go on and look,' he urged. 'I guarantee you'll be impressed.'

Stepping up to the bench I lowered my eyes to the dully gleaming pages, and was fascinated to see an immense steamroller, which clearly bore the Aveling and Porter prancing horse on the front of its boiler. The clothes of the workers who were laying steaming tarmac in her path told me that the photograph was from the early twentieth century. Eighty years ago.

Just to be doubly sure that I was also getting the identity of the steamroller right, I left the bench to compare the number of spokes on the rear wheels in the photograph with those on Zenon's steamroller.

'Twelve spokes,' he confirmed. The steamroller in the book was undoubtedly the same impressive machine as the one I was standing beside.

'The workers in the photograph called those rear wheels her two big clocks,' he revealed. One spoke per wheel for each hour of the standard clock face.

'But look at the road she's rolling,' he suggested, referring to the photograph. 'Look at the road, Vanessa,' he insisted.

It was with amazement that I realised the slope being surfaced was that of Sea View Road where my family had lived for twenty years.

'Our flipping road!' I cried.

Zenon was in his element. Grinning broadly, he stuck his finger on the terrace of houses that was being constructed to the left of where the steamroller was working. 'Look closer,' he encouraged me.

My family's future home was fronted by scaffolding with men working on two levels. 'Our house being built!' I squeaked. It was undeniably moving to see it unfinished. The house might have been only bricks and mortar but it was at the heart of all Mother had done for us since we were little. Zenon was connecting with the soul of my family. Staying close, he remained silent while I peered harder at what the men were doing. It didn't take long to work it out. 'They're installing the sash windows to the bay.'

Dr Hopeless had diagnosed that Zenon would be incapable of effective communication, but he knew exactly when to hold off. Grateful for his silence, I eventually lifted my head and smiled. I looked back at the book and saw that our decorative wrought-iron gate was resting against the garden wall. A brand new item, awaiting fitment. Something about it made me want to cry. Before I could, Zenon said quietly, 'Look closer for me, please, Vanessa. Not at your house. At the canopy frame.'

I had to laugh, but I hope not unkindly. We were back to the steamroller that meant so much to him.

He pointed to where the shiny blue machine beside

us was missing its canvas cover, leaving exposed the framework of the canopy, which kept out the rain. The tingling at my core returned.

I eagerly returned to the photograph. To do so was an act of love. He came so close that we could have been joined at the hip. Despite the chill that was coming off the sea, across the links and into the garages, I was warm.

He pointed at some italicised lettering, which was too small for easy reading.

'Her name, Vanessa,' he confided, 'is the Canny Lass.'

We bent nearer to the book and I placed my right hand on his lower back. Discovering her name was the equivalent of learning that she had a beating heart and needed to be loved.

That's the way, Vee, darling, Daddy whispered, as a most exquisite tingle came to where the tips of my fingers found the slightly raised ridge of Zenon's spine.

Love him for the character he is and be happy.

'The Canny Lass,' I repeated, thrilled by the roll of the words on my tongue.

And after that there really would have been no dilly-dallying over my next loving moves with Zenon, I'm certain, except that in our eagerness to get upstairs to his bedroom, he failed to push the cumbersome book as far as it would go onto the shelf. Barely had we turned our backs before it fell to the floor. Rudely awakened by the racket this made, our Brucie-Dog yelped and scampered beneath the Canny Lass's boiler.

Whatever was going on in his funny old doggy brain, I, too, had been startled. It was like a bucket of water had been thrown over me, bringing me out of a dream in which I'd been taking advice on love from Daddy. That was scary.

Since long before our family move to the seaside in the early 1960s, he'd been the destroyer of love. This was not deliberate. His mind had been damaged by the horribleness of the war. With moods that swung forward and back, he was doomed to be a wrecker. Accepting words of wisdom on my relationship with Zenon from him suddenly felt about as right as giving the Nobel Peace Prize to Herr Hitler.

26

Our first home was one of several council houses in a street of otherwise privately owned properties. Daddy was a small-time car trader. Money for comforts, or even the basics, was scarce.

When Mother decorated the downstairs oblong bedroom where we kids had two sets of metal-framed bunks, she cut pictures from magazines and pasted them onto every inch of the walls and ceiling. This took a while to do:

1. Aside from *Woman's Own*, her 'one weekly luxury', she had to rely on magazines given in dribs and drabs by other mums at the school where the younger twins were in Reception, our Jack and I in Infants.

2. When Mr Mounsey, the newsagent, who'd recently moved into a 'rooming house' up the street heard what she was doing, he supplied two piles of magazines, but Daddy went into a huff

about this and refused to help with the work.

And:

3. Our then incredibly sweet little Rachael wanted to help with the pasting so some parts were badly mucked up. Because Mother never criticised us when we were being creative, days went by before she could scrape away Rachael's latest disaster area; she told my little sister that cuttings pasted onto the lower walls often went crinkly.

Still, the 'collage on a grand scale', as Daddy grumpily called it, was finally complete, and our bunk beds – which for weeks had been moved around according to which part of the room was being done – were at last back to their familiar places, one set to each side wall.

It was a triumph over adversity for Mother: she was yet to return to the art teaching she'd done before we were born so had no money of her own and was chuffed to bits when she happened upon a tin of Dulux gloss at a jumble sale. Instead of the old white paint that she'd cleaned down, the door, the window frame and the skirting boards in our bedroom became apple green.

While the younger twins were ecstatic at this finishing touch, our Jack and I sensed that we shouldn't be too enthusiastic if Daddy was within earshot. That was how it was becoming in our late infancy: we were instinctively walking on eggs to avoid upsetting Daddy, who, I knew, didn't mean to be horrid.

27

Had it not been for the recent acquisition of a pay-as-you-go grainy black-and-white telly from Radio Rentals, Daddy might have turned on us the meanness he'd obstinately kept up towards Mother about our room.

When the teatime news featured the world boxing champion Muhammad Ali, he allowed our Jack to grip the sleeve of his woolly top and tug him to where they confirmed the identity of the grinning face Mother had pasted next to the overhead light. Daddy's number-one hero, mighty Muhammad himself. In a complete reversal of his apparently scathing opinion of Mother's collage, he threw his arms wide and declared that she had worked a miracle in our room. With the bickering finally over, a pall was lifted from each of us. Not least from Daddy. But the one who really hit the nail on the head as regards the change of mood in the house was our five-year-old Rachael.

28

The morning after Muhammad Ali had been identified upon our bedroom ceiling was sunny, reflecting Daddy's upbeat mood. Happily sandwiched between Jack and Craig at the breakfast table, our Rachael was directly opposite me. Daddy's seat was to my right, Mother's to my left. In sum, each person was in their usual place. I'd say we were sitting upon benches, but really they were old church pews that Daddy had accepted in part-exchange for an Austin A30. It was the sort of deal he did all the time; Mother claimed it had accounted for half our furniture.

Daddy seemed to be getting happier by the minute. He declared that from then on he would get up first and cook the breakfast. Mother good-naturedly protested that she would believe that when she saw it in action.

More than true to his word, the following morning not only did Daddy do all the cooking, he also assumed the character of a heavily accented French waiter, whose courtesy towards us kids was entertaining. Especially for my crazy brothers: while Daddy served up

our bacon, egg and fried bread, they went into parox-
ysms of laughter, which made Mother tick them off.

Years later I would understand that, while she'd been
secretly worried that Daddy's latest down period had
lasted longer than usual, she now feared that his resur-
gent happiness – which, naturally, she'd welcomed –
was not quite right.

Daddy would have argued that she was spoiling the
party, getting unnecessarily irked with our Jack and
Craig and scoffing at his French-waiter act. Rachael was
directly in my eye line as she peered over the breakfast
things to where, chastened by Mother's attitude, Daddy
had sat down beside me.

'Daddy,' she began, 'duh sun is shining in duh house
again.' Her green eyes were deep as rock pools. The rest
of us were quiet. Letting out a long sigh, Daddy sagged
on the pew as if he'd been punctured. Mother, though,
was becoming tense.

'Eat up, our Rachael,' she instructed. Her tone unnerved my brothers who looked across the table to her.
'You too, boys,' she added, with an attempt at breezi-
ness.

Daddy cleared his throat, sat up straight and looked
to where the sun was streaming into our galley kitchen.
'Yes, little darling, the house is sunny again.'

Rachael fluttered her eyelashes and gave him a smile
of such tenderness that now, more than twenty years

later, I want to protect her as I would a six-week-old puppy.

Daddy set his knife and fork on his plate. Disregarding Mother's call for him not to start any of his 'barmy games', he got to his feet. We knew from experience that our Rachael was about to receive one serious attack of rib-tickling; and because this was always hilarious, I laughed with my brothers.

Using the tips of his fingers and thumbs to riddle his thick black hair into a wild mess, Daddy briefly looked down at me. His steel-coloured eyes bulged like Marty Feldman's and I shivered. Setting a clawed hand to each side of his heavily bearded face, he roared at my baby sister: 'I am duh Big Monster!'

Our Rachael's eyes widened as he began moving around the table towards her. Clenching her hands between her thighs, she rocked back and forth. His steps were in the style of the Frankenstein monster that we'd recently seen on telly.

Mother had been pretending to concentrate on her breakfast. As Daddy assumed his place behind Rachael and began to lower his horribly clawed hands, she could bear it no longer. 'Oh, do stop now, Raymond! Please! Stop it before it's out of control. The children have school today.'

Her pleas fell upon deaf ears. Once the game reached this stage it was unstoppable. Jack and Craig scrambled to their feet to either side of our Rachael, who was now curling up, hedgehog-style.

'Don't be so damnably uptight, Missus Wife!' snapped Daddy.

'Well, don't say you weren't warned! You'll make her pee her knickers!' She lowered her face to her breakfast, but quickly looked up again.

'Dad!' our Jack was urging. 'Tickle her till she pees herself, Dad!'

'Yeah, Dad!' added Craig, who, like his big brother, was literally jumping up and down on the pew. 'Make her wet her knickers like last time!' he added.

Daddy gave Mother an exaggerated shrug of resignation that marked the onset of his deepest Big Monster roar. 'I am duh Big Monster!'

Lifting her flushed face from where it had been tucked into her chest, our Rachael pinned me with eyes that were determined not to be cowed. 'Go away, duh Big Silly Monster!' she protested.

It was still funny but also disturbing. I now feared I might be the one to pee her knickers. 'Shut up, you two,' I snapped at my brothers, who only laughed more.

'Duh Big Monster's a big soft teddy!' exclaimed Rachael, whose eyes had not left mine. Daddy peered over her head at me and I did my best to smile. I didn't want him to know that the Big Monster, who'd always made us laugh, was becoming truly horrible.

'Oh, Rachael,' Mother said wearily. 'You silly, silly child. You've asked for it now.'

A shiver went through me. I wanted to tell her that she should have ordered Daddy to stop, but for once her eye was slippery as an eel.

As I looked back to Daddy he frowned. I felt like he no longer loved me. Sometimes when he was arguing with Mother, he would yell that he hated her, then afterwards, he would cry. Scared that he would now hate me, I looked right at him and said the only thing I could think of.

'Tickle her, Daddy! Tickle her your hardest ever!'

Jumping up and down even more excitedly upon the pew, my brothers renewed their calls for the tickling to commence. I joined in with their laughter, but it sort of echoed inside me. When Mother laughed, the sound wasn't right either. Still, at least Daddy had stopped frowning. Slowly lowering his hands, he kept his madly enlarged eyes upon me. Years later, I'd wonder what would've happened if he'd seen that I no longer trusted him with our Rachael. He scared me. 'Tickle her, Daddy,' I urged again.

Suddenly he was his proper self once more. He pulled his hands away from Rachael and shook them back into their normal shape. Now I really did want him to do the tickling: his fingers were no longer ugly. Mother must have sensed the same thing. Her tone was resigned but affectionate: 'Do stop drawing it out, Raymond, for Heaven's sake.'

Craig and Jack had gone quiet again and Rachael was once more balled up like a hedgehog. A feeling for Daddy that I couldn't identify filled me. Later I realised it was pity. He swiftly lowered his hands and tickled my sister until she was squealing like a piglet.

When he'd finished, I felt guilty. I'd been terrified for our Rachael. But I loved Daddy, who'd never hurt us. Mother was deathly quiet. Even my brothers were obediently sitting down. Daddy was thrown. 'What's the matter?' he demanded of them. Nonplussed, they faced him with the big green eyes that we'd all got from Mother. 'Can't we have fun in this house any more?' They'd somehow got smaller on the pew.

'Look now!' cried our Rachael. She pointed to where Picasso was doing something very strange against his plastic water butt.

Daddy laughed in a brutal way and sat down. 'Don't worry,' he said to her. 'The Big Monster's dead.'

Rachael now appeared totally lost. As if he'd cast her adrift.

'Oh, Raymond.' Mother sighed. I thought she was going to cry but she didn't. Ignoring her, Daddy stuffed food into his mouth. When he glanced up at Rachael, whose face was normally full of trust, she scowled. The sun streamed in but the air was as heavy as a shroud.

'Big Monster,' squawked our Picasso, who was beadily eyeing us all. 'Big Monster,' he repeated, shuffling to the far side of his rusty cage.

29

Four hours later I was doing skippies in the yard at St Cuthbert's School. One of the several girls I was with suddenly dropped her end of the rope and ran back to the canteen where many of the pupils were still having lunch. A cloud of black smoke rising from the town centre had scared her. We were all frightened. Sirens blared, and three roaring fire engines sped past the inch-thick upright iron bars of the school railings.

Two equally noisy ambulances and a police car followed. I was further alarmed by the antics of an eleven-year-old boy called Garth Howson. He fled across the infants' playground (where juniors such as Garth were not meant to go) and, clutching the school railings with both hands, peered after them as they headed towards the black smoke, which by now had red dots glowing within it. They were a bit like butterflies.

Mother had once told Daddy off for referring to Garth's daddy as a nutter because he went on about something called Armageddon. I didn't have a clue what it meant. Still, everybody knew about Mr Howson. He'd been a prisoner-of-war in Japan, and when normal people wore red poppies and marched through the town, he chained himself to the town-hall door knocker. Fifteen years would pass before I began to appreciate the purpose of CND activism.

'It's the Russians!' Garth screeched, swinging round to us all. His face was crimson and you could see he was terrified.

One of the dinner ladies went to him. By now he was now going purple and gasping for breath, but still, somehow, he ranted about how the special noiseless 'H-bomb' that had hit the town centre was the start of the Third World War. Fear swept the infant and junior areas of the playground. Child after child pointed to the approaching smoke and spread the word about the H-bomb, which had no bang. The panicked dinner lady shook Garth but he began a new rant about Armageddon.

At last I understood what Daddy had said to Mother about this. The Russians would come in old-fashioned armour and use swords to behead those of us who'd survived their H-bombs.

Garth Howson was dead right to worry. We were all going to die.

30

Barely a minute had passed before our head-mistress, Mrs Poulton, came outside and gave an extra long shake on the school's shiny brass bell. According to our teachers, it had been used a hundred years earlier by somebody called the town crier. I'd remembered this from our Jack's and my first day in Reception, two years before.

When our Jack had told Daddy about the bell, he'd retorted that if he'd had to make that damn racket every hour, he would have cried too. Daddy often had a bad head and didn't like noisy things, such as school bells.

Infants and juniors alike were quickly ushered by the teachers out of the smoky playground into the main hall. On normal days we were not allowed to sit on the herringbone floor, which had lost most of its varnish. That was because a girl from the year before had got a splinter in her bum and had had to go to hospital.

Now, however, we were told to park our backsides on the same wooden surface and be silent. Jack shuffled up beside me on his bum and heels. We each put an arm across the shoulders of the other. I saw that

Rachael and Craig had done the same where their class was sitting. That's twins for you. The armour-clad sword-wielding Russians might have been on their way, but for now I was relieved that my family had not been blown up.

One of the boys sitting nearby whispered that our school had been the target of the Russian bomb. Jack hissed at him to shut his face, then planted a kiss on the side of my head.

Some of the teachers were closing the high windows of the hall against the black smoke. They used long brown poles with brass hooks. It looked a tricky job. As they returned to their class groups, Mrs Poulton took her place before us all and smiled. Her eyes were violet, and I remembered Mother saying they were like Elizabeth Taylor's. Daddy had snorted.

All two hundred pupils felt the restfulness of the silence that had replaced the mayhem of minutes before. I wanted cuddly Mrs Poulton as a second mum. She'd stop Mother and Daddy fighting.

'Now then, children,' she began, 'there has been no outbreak of war today.' Her gaze coasted from class to class as she explained that there were lots of boys and girls just like us in Russia. Nobody in England wanted to blow them up and nobody in their country intended to blow us up.

Her voice became firmer. First and foremost, we had

to forget about bombs. The Silver Grid chip shop was on fire: Mr Livingstone, the school caretaker, had just come from the town centre and told her so. The brave firemen who'd rushed to help were no doubt already getting things under control. What we needed to do now, she concluded, was close our eyes and say a prayer for Garth Howson, who'd become overexcited and was being taken home by the deputy head, Mr Titley.

'And who else should we pray for, children?' she enquired.

'The people at the chip shop!' replied our Craig. Jack nudged me. We were proud of our baby brother. Even more so when Mrs Poulton praised him for being quick to think of those who specially needed our prayers.

'Dear Father God,' she began, as eyes closed throughout the hall.

'Dear Father God,' we repeated.

The deepening calm as the prayer got under way made me so happy that I put a return kiss upon the bowed head of our Jack. As he looked up, startled, Mrs Poulton smiled down at us. Her lovely eyes made a light shine in my heart. Maybe Jesus was somehow talking back to me as we prayed. Of course the Russians weren't coming. Garth Howson would have to go to the loony bin. That was all.

31

A French waiter, a scary Big Monster and a nuclear attack that turned out to be a chip-shop fire should have been enough for one day. But when we met up as usual by the school gates at the end of the afternoon, our Rachael pointed over the road to where Mother was waiting in the passenger seat of a stylish light green car. We normally walked home. Even the smallest children did in the mid-1960s. Mother picking us up was a surprise.

'Mr Mounsey's new Cortina!' declared our Craig, who, at five, already knew his cars by heart. Quite the little genius in his own way.

'A Mark Two 1500GT four door,' he added proudly, just to make the point.

The rest of us became glum. Mr Mounsey, the newsagent from up our street, craned forward in the driving seat to see around Mother's head. He continued looking our way while she gave an unusually tentative wave.

I didn't like them being together because Daddy had been angry about Mr Mounsey even before he had

WINSTON AND THE CANNY LASS

given Mother the magazines for our room. Jack had listened with me as our parents argued about him. Mother told Daddy not to be ridiculous about Mr Mounsey, who'd apparently left the big house where he lived with Mrs Mounsey in a posh part of town only temporarily.

Daddy had quietened down and had even taken our Craig outside with him to admire Mr Mounsey's car where it was parked at the kerb.

At supper that night, he'd told Mother that until then he hadn't actually seen the widely publicised replacement for the existing Cortina up close, and that the difference between the old and new designs was that the Mark 1 had circular back lights and the Mark 2's were rectangular.

'Modernism they call it!' he declared, with a wink at my baby brother, who'd lovingly hung on his every word.

Our Rachael giggled. 'You're wasted, you are, Daddy,' she said naughtily.

Mother had been cutting into the margarine in its open paper wrapper at the centre of the table. Her knife was still for the deadly quiet moment before Daddy laughed. Our cheeky little Rachael had copied something she occasionally said to him when his mood was good. We'd all long accepted from this that he was somehow 'wasted'.

We also knew that before the war he'd had an 'education'. Just like Mother had. This point had been made loud and clear during one of their fights about him not making enough money to clothe and feed us properly.

'But, Raymond!' Mother had wailed. 'The children cannot wear or eat church pews!' Luckily he'd been sober then and the whole family had ended up scoffing chocolates on Mother and Daddy's double bed.

Those were the days when Daddy's interests were still varied.

When we were out in one of his cars he'd made a detour to show us a newly built office block that really did look as if it'd been designed by the same person who'd thought up Mr Mounsey's sharp-edged Cortina. Modernism, Daddy playfully reminded us. His mood was great. Explaining that the glass and concrete building was where the dreaded taxman worked, he gave an exaggerated shudder. At that moment a briefcase-carrying man in a grey suit came out and passed where we were standing by Daddy's car. Pointing at the dapper stranger, our Rachael squealed in horror. 'Dreaded taxman, Daddy!' she cried.

Mother was quick to tick her off. Daddy nearly split his sides laughing. The man turned to wink at Rachael, then strode down a slope and into a wide rectangular tunnel. Daddy explained that this was an underground car park. A minute or two later the man tooted as he drove by in a gleaming gold car.

'Mark Four Ford Zodiac!' announced our Craig.

'Clever lad!' responded Daddy, who'd yet to start attacking him every time he opened his mouth. He added that while he liked the Mark 2 Cortina's compact lines, the new Zephyr-Zodiac was an 'outsized coffin on wheels'.

Had Mr Mounsey owned the bigger gold Ford of the taxman, those words would have suited the deadening slump I felt at seeing him keep an eye on Mother as she got out of his car. Because if anyone should have brought her to our school gates, it was Daddy, not the flipping newsagent from up the street. Even if he did own a spanking new Mark 2 Cortina GT.

32

When she got near to where we'd instinctively huddled closer together on the pavement, I saw that Mother's normally bright green eyes were dull. I thought of the dried peas I'd once spilled on the kitchen floor. What a noise they had made. Mother had been furious at the interruption to her cooking. Daddy had laughingly declared that he loved her precisely because she was always full of fire, eyes blazing. Now, on top of having dried peas instead of her eyes, her fiery ginger hair was muddy brown and flat. Something was drastically amiss. It was as if her fire had been put out. As she crouched down to embrace the four of us, her movements were oddly stiff. She held us so tightly against her that our Jack cried out.

'Ow, Mum!' He wriggled free.

The family settled into Mr Mounsey's car. Mother was in the front. When we'd got going, our Rachael asked why we were getting a ride home. Mr Mounsey glanced at Mother. No answer came.

Maybe she didn't hear Rachael's question. I could see

her face clearly reflected in the windscreen. Her right thumbnail was clenched between her teeth and she was peering ahead as if she wasn't seeing anything.

The back of Mr Mounsey's neck had a pink roll that bulged over his tight white collar. I thought of the fatty pork chops we sometimes had for tea. The droning car rode a bump and I stiffened. Nothing felt real, yet to this day, I remember certain things, as if I was still the little girl who would rather have walked home as usual.

1. The eyes of our Jack had also become dried peas.

2. My baby sister was glaring at me. No dried peas there.

And:

3. Our Craig was sitting forward on the seat beside me to watch Mr Mounsey's driving. As the car speeded and slowed, he made barely perceptible engine noises. He was in his own little world.

As we neared the junction with our road, a buckled reflection of the slowing green Cortina slid across the shop windows. I wanted to cry but didn't know why.

Mother came out of her reverie. 'Nearly home, children.'

She sighed heavily as Mr Mounsey stopped for the right turn. The loud click-click of the indicator was un-nerving. Car after car squeezed by to our left and carried on along the high street. Perhaps a lorry or bus would kill us from behind, I thought. A crash like that had once happened at this turning. For a long time there had been a sign saying 'Accident Black Spot'.

33

Mr Mounsey's Cortina whined as he backed up our street to where his rooming house was. He'd dropped us off outside our home. Rather than look at him while Mother said, 'Thank you, Horton,' I'd concentrated on our recently repainted front door. Daddy had done his nut when the council had insisted on dark blue, the same colour as the other council houses in the street.

When he'd further complained that he hadn't fought the Nazis only to be dictated to by little Hitlers at the town hall, Mother had thrown her head right back and laughed. Whenever she did that with him, I felt safe. When I got older, I saw that she'd understood his moods. The last remnant of his annoyance had gone when she had said that, if it had been up to her, the door would be every colour under the sun. She and Daddy were always on the same side against the outside world.

After we'd moved to number twenty Sea View Road, one of her first jobs was to paint the big old front door. She did the main part black, the four inset panels pink and the chunky mouldings around them blue-grey. Ours was the best front door in town. We kids dubbed it the Liquorice Allsort. First-timers to the house often said it made them smile.

You couldn't look at a boring blue door for long without getting sick of it. Besides, the shiny new council paint was reflecting the sun and I had to turn away from the dazzle. I found that my twin brother's dried peas were on me. Mother called, 'Thank you,' again over the gardens to 'Horton', who was now going into the rooming house. Compared to 'Raymond', 'Horton' was a stupid-sounding name.

Rachael needed a wee and Craig began babbling about the reverse gear whine on Mr Mounsey's Cortina. Daddy had explained to him about cogs going backwards making a different sound.

Mother told him to be quiet. She had a headache coming on. That was our Craig in a nutshell. Always getting it in the neck before anybody else. She must have felt the unfairness of this because then she stroked his hair. His face brightened and a spiral of love for him turned within me. Even then I knew what his strength was: recovering quickly.

Mother glanced at me as we went into the house. I wondered what I'd done wrong. Then she surprised me: 'You mustn't worry about Mr Mounsey, our Vanessa! He's married to a much younger, prettier lady than I!'

Had it been possible, I'm convinced she would have snaffled those words back. As it was, she looked at me with a smile that seemed to have been painted on her face. I didn't know what to do. It was like she wanted me to smile back but my lips wouldn't work.

Our downstairs bedroom was to the right of where we were standing. All of a sudden I was resentful that so many of the pictures on the walls and ceiling had been supplied by Horton. 'Did Mr Mounsey give us Muhammad Ali, then?' I asked. I found myself inching away from the now poisonous-seeming door to the colourful room in which we kids slept.

I didn't have to endure for long the sad look she was giving me: Jack reacted to the leaden atmosphere by twisting the ear of our poor Craig, who in turn stamped on his big brother's foot.

Then our Rachael innocently asked the very question that had hung in the air since she'd asked why we were getting a ride home with Mr Mounsey and been ignored.

'What's happened to Daddy, Mummy?'

Mother chose not to reply. Had the same question subsequently been put to Daddy, he would have been incapable of explaining. So disturbing would the day's events prove to be that they would be wiped from his mind for ever.

By the time I was twelve I'd developed a game inside

my head called Being Daddy. The idea was that whenever he hit Mother during one of their nastier fights, I would do my best to avoid hating him by trying to get into his shoes.

Now, I want you to experience what it meant for him to struggle on with his war-wounded mind. Take a big breath. You're poor old Daddy. And I'm your guide to his world …

34

Your moodiness, Daddy, really started when Mother suggested making a collage in our shared bunk-bedroom. I don't know: perhaps you felt that in using bits of magazine for wallpaper she was attempting to humiliate you because you hadn't provided enough housekeeping money. One thing I'm convinced of, though, is that you secretly admired her resourcefulness. Pity you couldn't show it.

It was wrong of you to blame her for Mr Mounsey moving into our street. As you might expect of a conscientious objector in the war, he was a calmer man than you'd ever be. That must really have grated. What could a man like him have known about living with a head full of death? It wasn't hard to understand why you might hate him. But surely it was obvious that, once he'd accepted he was on to a loser with Mother, Mr Mounsey would go home, tail between his legs. Meanwhile, he was just an amiable man who happened to be rooming temporarily up the street.

Enough of that!

It'd been your best morning for business in a while:

one 1956 Ford Consul, a 1955 Austin Cambridge, and a 1959 Rover 90 with unmarked red leather seats: all sold in less than three hours. If every morning was like this one, your money problems would soon be solved. Rather than trading fourth-hand cars from a bomb site that turned to mud whenever it rained, you might even have been able to afford a small showroom. No pipe dreams now, though. And, besides, even Mother knew you were right to quit teaching for the motor trade before your first year was done. Teenage boys and girls just know when something inside Sir has broken for ever. Nothing brings out their cruelty quite so well. And in your heart of hearts, Daddy, you realised it was risky for you to be in the classroom. Those blistering rages that wiped the smirks from your young tormentors' faces only made things harder the next day, didn't they?

You hadn't forgotten how much it hurt when Mother left in 1948, had you? Three years after the war ended. That must have taught you she had grit. Was she right to remarry you in 1958? Whether she was or not, she'd always loved you. Even your worst violence against her hadn't destroyed that.

Of course, we shouldn't forget that the psychiatrist who treated you during your first stay in hospital in the mid-1950s advised Mother that you were 'categorically over' your war trauma. No more rages. A brand new Raymond. That diagnosis might have been a seriously optimistic case of doctor-patient projection.

In the not-too-distant future you happened across an obituary in the *Daily Telegraph* while you were waiting your turn at the barber's. The barber supplied a nip of whisky to steady your nerves, and afterwards you went to the Horse and Groom and got very drunk.

You'd have read about how, after being haunted by guilt at escaping a shelled tank in which the rest of the crew perished, the psychiatrist who'd pronounced you fit for remarriage to Mother had taken his life. Two decades after the war had finished. Barbiturates, whisky and a razor blade in a nice warm bath. The least agonising way to do it, apparently.

War trauma, Daddy. It was everywhere. Even your old friend the barber had a shaky hand, which he steadied with constant nips of the same booze he'd give to you.

Despite your shock at the psychiatrist's suicide, you were compelled to read one sentence over and over: 'And so passes a gentleman-bachelor too at war with himself to have inflicted a difficult life upon a spouse whose misfortune it would have been to love him.' Bells ringing loud and clear, were they, Daddy?

Where would you have been but for Mother taking a second chance on you? I cannot think of another woman who would have been brave enough to do that. Anyway, you became our daddy. You were funny and we loved you. Even after you'd driven our little Rachael to defiance with your frightening Big Monster routine, had we not gone to school as a happy little gang?

Or, at least, that was how you needed to see it, unable as you were to admit to the deepening darkness that made you tell my baby sister the Big Monster was dead. That was when you became a murderer of sorts: killing the innocence of a five-year-old child who'd always adored her daddy's games. Some harm isn't obvious right away, though, is it? When breakfast was done, you lightened the atmosphere by twirling Mother in the air, and our little Rachael laughed along with the rest us.

But your renewed gaiety came with a powerful hankering for drink.

Business was business!

Helped by a sunny day that even made the bomb site seem welcoming to punters, you'd pulled off those three strong car sales. Good reason, then, to slake that ever-worsening thirst in the company of our next-door neighbour, kind-hearted Mr Napier, who for years had helped you prepare vehicles for display.

Twenty years older than you, Mr Napier had seen action in the First World War and had been a coal miner throughout the Second. What better company for a lunchtime session at the Horse and Groom than a man who had the same backbone as yourself? Forget Mr Pacifist Mounsey. Get the first round in, Daddy, why not?

35

You'd already had three beers and Edwin the barman – yet another little Hitler when the fancy took him – had been tetchy with you. That was because you got angry with a loudmouth who said Muhammad Ali was an uppity darkie whom the Ku Klux Klan should string up alongside Martin Luther King. 'Cheer up, Raymond, me lad!' cried Mr Napier, on seeing your long face as he returned from the bar. You shrugged and glanced to where Edwin was watching from the corner of his eye. It grated that, after you'd stood up to some thug's racism, you were still somehow in the wrong.

Alcoholics are never in the right, are they, Daddy? What could Edwin possibly understand about you being educated? His only knowledge was of a man in need of booze. And you usually got so drunk that you'd fall over in his car park. Try seeing it from his viewpoint. You were an old drunk. Of course he took your money when it was offered.

The good news was that Mr Napier was setting down two more pints and the whisky doubles, which you'd agreed must be your last round. It was Bell's, your favourite brand. You crushed a half-smoked cigarette into an emerald green glass ashtray. A non-smoker, Mother was often angry that so much of what you paid for was wasted. Half a cigarette sixty times a day. The ashtray was already nearly full.

Freddie Napier was one of your oldest friends. He was little and fat, with a round, friendly face. Whenever you were angry, as you were then, he smiled and waited. It was a game you both understood. You couldn't help it, Daddy: you had to grin back at him. 'Clever bastard, Freddie,' you said. His dark blue eyes widened as he laughed at the old refrain. He'd done it again, drawn you out of yourself. Looking at the mahogany swing door through which the man who spoke ill of Muhammad Ali and Dr King had left, you remembered how you'd threatened to break his effing neck. Maybe this time Edwin was right to scold you for going too far. Were you really so angry with that stupid, ignorant man? Or had something about your behaviour towards Mother and us kids at breakfast been eating away at you all morning? What would you have done to us if you'd become properly angry? That put a pain in your heart, didn't it? (Go on, Daddy: down another pint, quick as you can. See if that kills the hurt before you keel over with a full-blown coronary.) 'Cheers to the amber nectar, Freddie,' you said to Mr Napier, loud enough to irk Edwin, without giving him cause to boot you out. As had happened before.

Mr Napier raised his pint too. The glass resting upon your bottom lip was cool. Looking over the rim you met his smiling eyes. 'Here's to you, Raymond lad,' Mr Napier said.

It was good to drink. One long draught with Freddie, who burped as your empties were placed on the table. 'Clever bastard,' you told him again. He touched his upper lip, indicating that you had froth on your moustache. Something about the way he did it was funny. You laughed and wiped the back of your hand across your mouth. He slid the whisky across to you.

There was a new glint in his eye. He winked and mischievously said that 'Teddy Boy' was still watching. Your nagging worry about what had happened at home that morning was acquiring the slipperiness of a fish you were releasing back into water. That made you feel good. You would never have hurt us or Mother at breakfast, would you, Daddy? Not from where your drink-addled mind had got to now, anyway. On the other hand, maybe four beers in quick succession really had put you right again.

There was fun to be had with Mr Napier at the expense of the barman: Teddy Boy. This time, you stared directly at him. That got his full attention. Mr Napier was already sniggering. Tilting your head right back you looked to where the fellow had hung 149 potties from the exposed ceiling beams. You knew the exact number because you'd previously counted them. You set your right hand to your whisky glass. Mr Napier had already done likewise. It'd be sublime. Any second now he'd make the toast that would be loud enough for Teddy-Boy to hear. 'To the Piss and the Pot.'

Remember, Daddy, how Mother and Mrs Napier were amused when they heard that that was what you sometimes called the Horse and Groom? To be sure that the potty collection existed, they'd visited the bar themselves. That had made you laugh: Mother and tee-total Mrs Napier at a bar together! Counting potties!

But this, Daddy, was a day for the unexpected. Something had caught your eye through the large frosted window that faced the high street. 'What?' Mr Napier asked. He twisted in his seat to look at Edwin for some kind of explanation.

Your hands had closed tight on the rounded ends of the wooden chair arms. You half stood to get a direct view over Mr Napier's baldy head. Never mind a pain in your heart, your stomach was knotting.

The horror at what was happening was like being back in the war, when young men burned to death in seas that were on fire. You'd never got out of those waters, had you, Daddy? The screams of the dying were seared onto your soul.

Mr Napier and Edwin said something to you but you didn't hear them. And no wonder. It was taking all your concentration to peer through the clear 'Horse and Groom' script that was etched on the otherwise opaque window pane. You couldn't believe what you were seeing. It was just too shocking and unexpected. All you'd wanted was a lunchtime session with Freddie. A bit of fun to blow away the up-and-down moods that had lately taken an increasingly strong grip on you.

The whisky glasses were knocked from the table as you stood up. You strained harder to see through the curlicue lettering and across the high street to the far terrace of shops. Your eyes hadn't deceived you.

Mr and Mrs Lampredi, the well-liked middle-aged couple who owned the Silver Grid chip shop, were in distress. In the seconds that had passed since you saw them tumble through the black smoke billowing from the chip shop's door, a passer-by had used his jacket to smother the flames on the shoulders of Mr Lampredi's white smock. The Silver Grid was becoming an inferno.

36

Your brain, Daddy, had locked onto the fact that the Lampredis' sixteen-year-old son Milos had not followed his parents out of the shop to the safety of the pavement. Fearing he was trapped inside, you moved fast towards the mahogany swing door. You were hit by self-doubt.

After the war you'd had episodes in which you were surrounded by flames: the more you tried to save the screaming young men who were burning to death in the sea, the further they drifted beyond your reach. Haunted by what had happened then, you'd become an old drunk who terrified his little daughter at breakfast and fell over in the pub car park.

But suddenly you were as sober as a judge and Freddie Napier's urgent shout for Edwin the barman to dial 999 spurred you on. At the rate the chip shop was going up, young Milos Lampredi would be cinders long before the fire brigade arrived. It was essential that you acted now. As you shoved through the door into the smoky air, your sense of destiny was made all the more powerful by the knowledge that, if you weren't quick enough, another innocent boy would die by fire.

There was one young man in particular, wasn't there, Daddy? Twenty-two years old, the same age as you, and with whom, to your surprise, you'd tumbled into love. Mother let that cat out of the bag to me and our Jack when she was confused after her first mini-stroke. You should know that we agreed never to tell our Craig. Think what that would have done to his head. Attacked by you for being gay when you knew exactly what it meant for two young men to be in love. How much easier was it to let your wartime lover float into the fire, that terrible moment when you, too, were fighting for your life? Would rescuing Milos Lampredi make amends? There was only one way to find out.

37

The fire brigade had yet to arrive but passers-by had taken it upon themselves to stop the traffic in each direction. That at least made your dash across the high street safe. How ironic if you'd been flattened by a passing lorry, never to reach Milos. Still, you weren't thinking, you were doing, and you'd already scanned the Silver Grid frontage for access via a ladder to the upper storeys.

Flames were to be seen on the first floor and smoke was belching from an open attic window. That explained why the black fumes were no longer pouring so thickly from the open shop door. A draught was sucking the fire upwards, clean through the old building. The counter and the fat-fryer were fiercely ablaze. For a moment you gave up hope of rescuing Milos. Who could have been alive within an inferno such as that? Aware that the large plate-glass window where the Silver Grid prices were displayed might blow out, you backed off until you were standing on the white line that divided the road. The heat against your face was intense.

The desperate eyes of Mrs Lampredi were fixed on you, Daddy, as the potential saviour of her boy. She shouted, 'Milos is still inside, Mr Harrison! My only son!' You cast your eye about and upwards. Forty, maybe fifty onlookers had gathered and flames were breaking through the tiled roof around the attic. The black smoke drifting over the town now contained millions of red dots.

Mr Lampredi was struggling hard against his captors, cursing them in his native Italian. Nobody else was trying to move anywhere near the shop as you had done. Mrs Lampredi's wailing trounced the racket of the fire: 'My son! My only son is inside, Mr Harrison!'

All eyes turned your way. If anybody was trusted to rescue Milos, it was you. That was because so far you'd behaved with swiftness and certainty. Expectation had built up that you would go inside the Silver Grid. Mr Lampredi was too shocked to do anything, but if you hadn't got a move on he might have pulled free and run into the shop where he would have died. You threw out your hands in exasperation. Few people understood the capriciousness of fire as you did. If you entered the Silver Grid and attempted to bypass the blazing counter and fat-fryer, you would die. Then you had an idea.

'I'm running round the bloody back, Freddie!' you shouted to Mr Napier, who had followed you out of the pub. 'For the boy! Don't let Mr Lampredi inside the building!' you called to the people who were holding him back. As her husband ceased to struggle, Mrs Lampredi made the sign of the cross.

You took up smoking when you were on dead watch in the Arctic in the early 1940s. Sixty fags a day in the twenty years since hadn't done your lungs any favours. But you were running surprisingly fast, Daddy. You were determined to reach the Silver Grid before the fire destroyed the entire building. Milos Lampredi was going to be saved and you were going to do it. He was a bit simple and had a cheeky grin, which you'd once told Mother would make any half-decent man want to protect him against loudmouths in the chip-shop queue. Sometimes you were my true hero, Daddy.

38

As you swung sharp right into the potato delivery yard at the rear of the Silver Grid, Daddy, you shouted at the two women from the neighbouring flower shop to get out of your way. They moved aside and you dragged a galvanised metal dustbin across the concrete.

Milos Lampredi was standing at a window and, with your experience of young men and fire, you had only to glance at his blank eyes to know why he was ignoring the pleas of the women for him to climb out: he was paralysed by terror.

You also knew, from the flames billowing out of a lower side window, that the room below him was a mass of fire. If you were to save Milos, every second was critical. You hauled yourself off the bin and onto the wall that edged the roof, and took a moment to confirm that the corrugated sheets you were going to walk on were made of asbestos. Then, from the screws that held the sheeting down, you checked where the rafters were positioned that would bear your weight.

'Milos, laddie,' you bellowed, over the roar of the

blaze, 'stay right by that window!' With six big strides you were across the rafters. Beyond Milos's shoulder, you could see that the fire was already breaking through the floorboards from below. You gripped the lapels of his white cotton smock, took three backward strides, pulled him through the window and dropped him to the ground. Freddie Napier broke his fall as you crashed through the asbestos roofing – and landed, away from the fire, on a heap of potato sacks.

Thanks to you alone, Daddy, Milos was safe.

A cheer went up from the relieved office workers. Ignoring the pleas of Freddie and the two florists for you to stay, you fled. You'd hurt yourself during the rescue.

The sirens, which had been approaching for some minutes, were suddenly very loud. Mr Napier's statement to the press said that as you had disappeared out of sight at the far end of the lane the main roof of the Silver Grid caved in. But for the actions of Raymond Harrison, young Milos Lampredi would have been dead.

39

After you'd been running hard for about a quarter of a mile, you sat on a garden wall and struggled to breathe. A kindly traffic warden who'd been trained in first aid gave you a hanky for protection against the hideous black smoke. 'What on earth happened to you?' she asked, spluttering.

Your fall through the potato-store roof had left you dishevelled. It was also obvious that you were in pain.

'The damn chippie's gone up in smoke. I hauled the young laddie out.'

Avoiding her concerned eye, you touched your ribs and flinched. On lifting your shirt you were taken aback to discover a long, purple wound on your side: a jag on the asbestos sheeting had opened it. The traffic warden was alarmed.

'You need medical help,' she insisted, and pulled out her walkie-talkie. That was when you flipped, Daddy.

'For God's sake, woman! It's only a scratch!' you yelled.

Maybe, for a moment, you'd thought she was Mother. But you quickly apologised for your outburst.

'Please,' you added, 'the last thing I need is a damn ambulance.'

'Well, so long as no bones are broken, I'm sure you'll be fine.'

But she was clearly worried. Your eyes had been wild while you were shouting, but now they were blank. It seemed likely that you'd taken a blow to the head.

When you left the garden wall, she followed. Upon entering West End Park, you went through a gateway set in iron railings that had forbiddingly pointed tips. They were about six feet tall and bordered the concrete steps to an underground Gents where the traffic warden couldn't follow.

Her intention to radio for help was forestalled by the return of the toilet attendant, who'd nipped out to see which of the town-centre shops was on fire. Not only was he tidily dressed, his surprisingly educated tone inspired confidence. He identified you with ease. 'Raymond is an old friend who often pops below for discourse.'

He had a first aid certificate and would take care of your injury. If necessary, he would go to a phone box and call an ambulance. Lest the traffic warden now appears too trustful of a stranger, we should consider

1. The stress the toilet attendant placed on your mutual rapport as war veterans: the traffic

warden realised he understood your erratic moods better than she did.

And:

2. With only twenty minutes of her shift to go, she'd already decided to visit the fire scene and advise those present of your whereabouts.

Two people were incredibly courageous that day. You were the first, Daddy; Mother was the second. The traffic warden told Freddie Napier where you'd gone, and he passed on the information to her. She lost no time in setting about a lone rescue mission.

40

To Mother's surprise, the high supporting walls of the underground Gents had gleaming cream and burgundy tiles, which matched those of the urinal. Divided into six sections at each side, this spanking edifice had pride of place in the centre of the floor. As she stepped closer, each section was being cleansed with water that whooshed from the open jaws of a stunning brass iguana.

It made her laugh so much that she half expected a posse to exit the cubicles whose polished copper entry slots read 'Occupied'. Luckily, she had not been heard over the cascade, which quickly came to an end.

Mindful to be silent until she found the attendant Mr Napier had spoken of, she turned her gaze to where petunias, lobelia and nasturtiums flourished in metal baskets suspended from gold-painted chains. Each mini-garden had been positioned so that it was reflected in the iron mirrors above a row of gleaming hand-basins. Somebody, she realised, had made it their mission to turn the underground toilet into a haven.

Tilting her head back to discover the source of light

that had enabled the flowering baskets to thrive, she saw the dual function of the pointy black railings. Not only did they protect walkers against the concrete stairwell, they were a deterrent to Peeping Toms. Many small squares of thick glass comprised large sections of the otherwise white-painted roof.

Delighted by the Victorian engineering that had made the underground space as light as the park above, she forgot herself again. 'Well, I do say! Isn't that simply a wonder?'

This time, there had been no watery cascade at the urinal to drown her words. Harrumphing echoed from within the cubicles. The most significant thing, though, to note about this particular moment, Daddy, was that she'd expected you to snarl at her as an effing bitch who'd plagued him to the bowels of the earth. To her relief, the calm statement that came was from somebody else.

'I'm afraid your husband departed to drown his sorrows some fifteen minutes ago, Mrs Harrison.' It was the attendant. He'd spoken from behind her back.

41

His voice had been familiar. So, too, was his striking mix of dark blue eyes and walnut skin. With his height of around five feet, she was left in no doubt that the silver-haired man before her was the former principal of the college where she'd taught art during the war. It was quite a secret you'd kept, Daddy, knowing all along that they'd once been colleagues.

'Why, Dr Pimento!' she cried.

Her mind whirled. Before he'd been pensioned off with ill-health in the early 1950s, he'd been in the papers for throwing an egg at Sir Winston Churchill. 'Welcome to my palace!' he said now.

Mother understood that he felt no awkwardness about his changed life. Looking him square in the eye, she was swift to respond. 'You've made it beautiful down here, Dr Pimento,' she declared. 'Really.'

Dr Pimento bowed his head slightly, his way of saying, 'Thank you.' She remembered that his courtly manners were said to come from his Anglo-Indian heritage. They had made him widely liked in education circles.

'If you'll kindly excuse me,' he said, 'I have discerned a smudge.'

Stepping aside he took a tin of Brasso and two cloths from his pea-green council overalls. The traffic warden had told Mr Napier he was smartly presented. Recalling that he had always been a natty dresser, Mother concluded that he probably never went above ground in his work clothes.

Seeing she was intrigued, he set a finger to the spiked back of the offending iguana.

'You see here?' he said. 'We most certainly have a smudge!'

As he poured a generous measure of the caramel-coloured polish onto one of the rags, the tip of his tongue appeared between his lips. Subtly, he was becoming more serious. The air cooled and the room darkened. Mother looked to the glass squares in the roof. Surprisingly, on a glorious day, a cloud was blocking the sun.

Shuffling could be heard within one of the cubicles. Two men whispered something she could not make out. When she looked back to Dr Pimento, he was on his knees, polishing the iguana as if his life depended upon its absolute cleanliness. Later she would consider this notion to be bang on the mark.

'Dr Pimento,' she protested, eager that he should become his merry self again, 'you'll rub the thing away if you keep going like that!'

Looking up at her, he responded with indignation: 'But a smudge, my dear, has no place in the palace!'

His face shone with the sweat that was falling from his brow in big drops.

After twenty years of dealing with your crazy ways, Daddy, Mother knew better than to say anything until he was done with the iguana.

The Brasso, which had already dried, was drab green now. As Dr Pimento took up the second cloth, the warm sunlight returned. Mother knew before she looked up to the glass squares that the cloud had gone. Returning her eyes to Dr Pimento, she found he was rubbing even harder than before. Suddenly he was talking fast too.

'I was twenty when I went over the top. That was the spring of 1918. The shell that dismembered the boy ahead of me also took my private parts.'

Mother bit her lip. Everybody at the college in the 1940s had known that his genitals had been blown off in the First World War. Yet while his body was incomplete, his sense of humour was intact. 'So is it any wonder,' he asked, upon standing away from the now gleaming iguana, 'that I should be custodian of the finest urinal in England?'

That was when they shared a good laugh. Still, she couldn't resist offering something of a challenge.

'Good old England,' she quipped.

'Oh, but England isn't so bad,' he chided, and added that where the likes of him and you were concerned, Daddy, it was war that had smudged your lives.

That galled her. 'Then why, Dr Pimento,' she demanded, 'did you throw an egg at Sir Winston Churchill?'

His eyes hardened. 'I believe it's well documented that I was in the midst of a mental collapse.'

Unfazed by his severity, Mother spoke the truth as she knew it from her long experience of your problems, Daddy. 'Whenever my husband becomes agitated, it's usually because he's remembering how badly you men were treated.' That was a reminder of her unhappy, perhaps even dangerous, purpose in visiting the palace.

Dr Pimento broke away from her eyes. Fastidiously he screwed the top back upon the tin of Brasso. He returned it and the two polishing cloths to his overalls. When he faced her again, he was relaxed. 'You're quite right, of course,' he conceded. 'Those of us who survived France were largely ignored by the government. I was lucky. I'd merely lost my privates. Those who'd lost their minds were either shoved out of sight or left to create hell for their loved ones.'

It struck her that telling the truth suited him well.

'Indeed, Dr Pimento', she promptly agreed. That, of course, was a direct allusion to you, Daddy. The college-principal-turned-lavvy attendant bowed his head in acknowledgement and resumed: 'Twenty years later your generation endured the same God-awful fight.'

Mother made to interrupt. Her intent was to observe that she hardly needed a history lesson on the Second World War but he urgently waved a hand for her to be silent. Despite her annoyance, she obeyed. There had been something about their talk she hadn't quite got. His eyes were fixed on hers, suggesting that they were in cahoots. This was puzzling but she was willing to trust him. He tilted his head upwards and sideways at the occupied cubicles, in effect throwing his voice to the unseen men.

'And just where,' he asked, in ringing tones, 'has the official help been for those who went through all that? Men like our friend Raymond.'

The penny didn't so much drop as clang within Mother's mind. The palace wasn't only out of bounds because it was a Gents. It was also a place of secrets. Dr Pimento needed the blessing of the others to speak openly with her about you, Daddy. Otherwise his role would be undermined.

'Good old England,' he said drily to Mother, while cocking an ear for a response from the cubicles.

42

The shiny copper slot clicked on the door where the cistern had earlier been flushed. Two men, who'd been inside together, came out. They were in their twenties.

The first set a hand to the side of his face and darted for the concrete steps. His companion, however, went to the nearest mirror. Having taken a comb from his jacket, he rearranged his slicked-back hair. Unfazed by the watchfulness of Mother and Dr Pimento, he sauntered to the stairs. He began to whistle tunefully as he climbed to the park above.

Mother turned upon Dr Pimento. 'What exactly is my husband's purpose in coming here?' she demanded.

Dr Pimento paced the ultra-smooth strip of concrete in front of the cubicles. 'Well, now, let's just say that gentlemen of all ages visit the palace for all kinds of reasons. So long as no harm is done, my role is not to pass judgement.'

Setting a finger to his lips, he held her gaze.

No harrumphing came from the unseen men. She realised this amounted to their consent for Dr Pimento to be open about your time in the underground toilet, Daddy. Dr Pimento's dark blue eyes were firm but friendly. 'But rest assured,' he said, 'that Raymond does not come here for carnal reasons.' His candour made her laugh, but not happily. At least if you had been having sex, Daddy, it would have been different from the same old war problem. Unwittingly, Dr Pimento emphasised this.

'I'm a veteran of the First World War. Your husband is a veteran of the Second. He comes to the palace when he needs to talk with an older survivor, that's all.'

Incensed, Mother replied, 'Funny how you wretched men will share every detail between yourselves while divulging precious little to your long-suffering wives.'

In short, Daddy, your sharing of your pain at the palace hurt her greatly. I know this because it was said after your death.

Dr Pimento stepped up to her and laid his hands upon her shoulders. 'There are things we cannot say to those we love most,' he told her.

She remembered that at the time of his egg-throwing disgrace Mrs Pimento had reportedly been unaware that he'd even gone to London. Not long after he'd lost his prestigious job, she'd developed cancer and died. It didn't take much to conclude that the palace was all he'd got left. True to the big heart that you've always said she had, Daddy, she offered him what reassurance she could. 'Well, maybe if it wasn't for your palace, Dr Pimento, Raymond would be even more destructive at home.'

Mother had expected him to tip his head graciously, as he had before, but he winced. She pressed him as to why. When he was further evasive, her thoughts raced to the likely harm the Silver Grid fire had wreaked upon your fragile mind. In all probability, most of the listening men had been at the palace when you'd earlier visited. It was her turn to address them. She did so frantically.

'How bad is he? I need to be told. Please, somebody in this place, just how bad is my husband?'

No sooner had Dr Pimento put his hands out in a gesture of helplessness than the man in the nearest cubicle answered her: 'He's not in a good way today, Mrs Harrison.'

Mother judged him to be in his mid-fifties, same as you were, Daddy. That meant he was almost certainly a veteran too. Powerlessness briefly overwhelmed her.

'Then what should I do?' she asked, of the unseen stranger.

To her own ears, she'd sounded like a little lost girl. With her attention focused elsewhere, Dr Pimento slipped aside.

'Bring your four children from school and get the house settled.' Clearly that stranger knew stuff from you about our family, Daddy. 'Let Raymond sleep a very black day off in peace,' he stressed. 'Or,' he added, as his voice hardened, 'call the police and get him sectioned.'

Her situation was stark. Give you a chance, at great risk to herself, or have you locked up? The silence from the cubicles thickened. Her later observation was that she could have trampolined upon it.

'The last thing I want,' she explained to all of her listeners, 'is to see my husband put away.'

Unable to bear any more of their silence, she turned to Dr Pimento. The tip of his tongue showed between his lips. He was about to polish a copper pipe that was screwed to the wall.

As she went up the steps to the park, she heard water whooshing from the wide-open mouth of the brass iguanas.

She was more scared of you now than ever before, Daddy, but she still didn't want to see you banged up. No wonder she was subdued when Mr Mounsey took us home from school in his snazzy green Cortina. By then, she was terrified.

43

She sent us to bed early but, after all that'd happened, sleep was impossible. 'I know!' declared our Jack. 'We'll have a boy-girl pillow fight!' That meant him and Craig against Rachael and me. It was great fun until one of the pillows burst. We feared that Mother would go bananas. But on seeing the feathers, which were all over our room, she sighed heavily and left us to Mrs Napier.

Mrs Napier was plump. She had big eyes, which Craig called her gobstoppers. She could be strict and kind at the same time. I loved being calmed down by people who didn't need to be loud. This time, however, we'd made such a mess that even Mrs Napier's voice was raised.

'Dearie me, children!' she exclaimed. 'Anyone would think it's been snowing in here!'

We had gone quiet. If the others felt like I did, Daddy, they wanted to cry. My twin brother spoke for us all. He was barely six years old. The contrition in his voice still touches me.

'We were only playing, Mrs Napier,' he explained.

'We didn't mean to make Mummy sadder.'

Mrs Napier smiled. Years later I realised that she loved us. 'Of course you were only playing, darling,' she reassured Jack. At that, our Rachael stepped forward to be held against her waist. Looking towards my unhappy baby brother, as their embrace went on, Mrs Napier made her eyes bulge even more than usual. 'Craig will be first to do horizontal hold,' she decided. That made us all happy again.

His job was to keep our grainy black and white Radio Rentals telly in focus while the rest of us watched and gave instructions. When I got older I realised that the horizontal-hold knob had been overly sensitive, Daddy. You and Mother had devised a way of managing us when we were too lively for bed. Mrs Napier was using a proven method to calm us down.

Mother remained alone in the kitchen. She was waiting for you to return. In my own funny little way I became competitive over this. Even in the midst of our pillow fight I'd had a feeling that, of us all, I was the one who should open the door to you.

Wasn't ours always a special bond, Daddy?

I needed to make you happy again. You'll never remember things as they were after you finally came rolling home, booze-addled. Let me help. I know the facts better than anyone.

44

Your mile-long stagger from the Horse and Groom was witnessed by many locals. One would later claim that, but for reluctance to interfere in our family business, she and her husband would have taken you inside for some sobering coffee. Mother's exclamation to Mrs Napier was blunt: 'Pooh! All they saw was a drunkard who'd got himself into a worse state than usual!'

Ironically, in the late edition of the evening paper you were hailed as a hero for saving Milos Lampredi. That might have changed the opinions of some. But for now even Freddie Napier couldn't help you. He'd got angina pains after the Silver Grid fire and was told to rest by his GP.

Edwin the barman justified allowing you to drink so much by protesting that you were a hardened boozer who knew his limits. The cash from the three cars you'd flogged that morning had filled the Horse and Groom till. In the several hours since Dr Pimento had dressed your side, you'd been buying rounds for the entire bar, Daddy.

Still, at least you made it home without tumbling off a kerb or harming yourself in one of the other ways that us kids earlier heard Mother worriedly discussing with Mrs Napier. I'd slipped away from where the others were engrossed in the horizontal-hold game and only I realised that you were at last back.

Unable to make your front door key work, you slurred the same word over and over. 'Damn, damn, damn . . . Damn, damn, damn.' That drew me from where I'd been waiting upon the stairs. Unfortunately the Yale lock was too stiff for me to turn it and I dared not call to you through the door. Mother would have come running and you'd have started fighting.

I stole through the house in my thin yellow nightie. My heart was thudding. The last time you couldn't unlock our front door you'd gone down the side path. If I was lucky, I'd catch you outside before Mother realised you were there. It'd become my mission to throw myself into your arms.

To my surprise, you'd gone beyond the house and were now lopsidedly planted upon the lawn. That changed things. If I'd been a little bit scared of you at breakfast that morning, I was a lot more so now. You weren't my daddy. You were the Big Monster turned real. There was sick on your shirt and a big wet patch at the top of your legs.

Unsure what to do, I hovered at the edge of the lawn.

When you looked up to the early-evening sky, I wondered if you were searching for God. You looked as if you needed him. Suddenly your bleary eyes were set upon me. I shivered. Clearly you were too drunk to know which of the four twins I was. I felt empty.

Mother's surprised voice carried from inside: 'Why, there you are, Raymond!' If she sees me , I thought, I'll be in big trouble.

Thankfully she hadn't yet because I was to one side of the big window that let the sun pour in when we were at breakfast. Aware that she'd be coming out to the garden, I backed into a space between a bush and the end wall of the kitchen extension, which the council had recently added. I set my bum against the sharp serrations of the bricks.

Mother called again: 'Raymond! I say, Raymond?'

She was outside now but not yet in the garden. I could tell she was frightened. Her voice was too high and oddly jolly. Like it belonged to somebody else. On any other day she would already have been scolding you for being drunk.

45

I pressed my bum harder against the ridged bricks. As I did so, Mother strode onto the lawn where you were. She put her hands on her hips and took a deep breath. 'Oh, for Heaven's sake!' she cried. Her normal voice was back but that was no comfort to me. Something bad was coming and I knew it.

I tried to pray but my eyes wouldn't close. In assembly Mrs Poulton said God wouldn't listen if your eyes were open. I tried Jesus instead. Being younger, He was probably not so strict. 'Please, Jesus, help my mummy and daddy.'

You faced her, clearly puzzled, and your right hand made a fist at your side. The brick serrations had now cut through my nightie. I didn't need to see her to know that her cheeks were crimson. Or that her eyes were blazing with fury.

'Thousands of men, Raymond, returned from the war,' she screeched, 'and are not drunkards with such unreliable incomes that the bedrooms of their children are decorated with magazines!'

I thought again of Mr Mounsey supplying the

Muhammed Ali picture and shuddered. Very quickly the newsagent was gone from my mind. Things on the lawn looked scary.

You were swaying, Daddy. Too drunk for shouting, your body language was saying it all. Still, Mother was not cowed.

'You're not a proper husband! You're not a proper father! You're an embarrassment! It would have been better for all concerned if you'd drowned at sea!'

I pressed my bum against the bricks with all my strength.

When I dared to look again you were holding your fist close to your face as if it disgusted you. It certainly should have. Mother's right hand was cupped to her nose, blood oozing through her fingers. I screamed.

Her head flipped up and you exchanged a mutually shocked look. 'My God, Raymond!' she cried. You turned clumsily to where I was hidden and called something I couldn't understand. It was a pathetic slur. Mother had shaken the blood from her fingers.

She rushed over to me. As she grasped my hand, I felt the warm stickiness of the blood. She knelt on the grass and kissed my forehead. 'Oh, Vanessa. You silly, silly little girl, coming out here.'

Seeing her up close was horrible. Even the corners of her eyes had blood leaking from them. She knew what I was thinking. 'Daddy didn't mean to hurt me, lovie,' she said. 'One day you'll understand that he's not well today.'

It was then, Daddy, that your terrible roaring began. You roared and roared and roared. Then you began the wild staggering that went on until the authorities took you away, the Big Sick Monster who flattened Mummy's nose. I didn't bother praying to Jesus. He never listened. Neither did God.

46

It was a bright Saturday morning a month later when the other three twins went next door for their breakfast. Mrs Napier was making something called French toast. Evidently I was not to be included. I began to cry. That was when Mother surprised me. 'Don't you want to see Daddy now that he's better, darling?' she asked.

My tears stopped. I watched as she sat upon a squishy old chair that was in a corner of the kitchen. She smiled and patted for me to come close. She stroked the side of my face as she spoke.

'You've been such a good girl lately, Vanessa, that I want you to come to the hospital with me.' Her eyes widened a fraction. They were gentle and shiny. 'I get so lonely going each week by myself.'

I wanted to be happy but my insides were heavy. Having her big bent nose so close was making me feel worse. It was ugly and I wanted it to be straight again. I'd been feeling guilty about what you'd done with your fist, Daddy.

From the moment you were taken from our house

in the ambulance I'd known I was the cause of your violence. What had happened was my fault. I'd been a sneak hiding in the garden. That was why you'd hit Mother. I was an evil little spy. You wouldn't want to see me at the hospital. I was sure of that.

Mother looked at me closely. The green of her eyes had tiny amber dots that circled the pupils. I'd never noticed them before. She watched me looking at her and then, very carefully, spoke again. 'Do you know, Vanessa, that our eyes are the windows of the soul?'

I only half understood this, but it was lovely. 'Have you been looking at my soul?' I asked.

Her reply suggested that she had: 'You did nothing wrong on the day when Daddy became ill, darling.'

My eyes had gone so wide they were beginning to hurt.

'Nothing that happened was your fault,' she added firmly.

Before I knew what I was doing, I planted a kiss upon her face. None of us kids had been allowed to do that while she'd been healing. It wasn't only because of her nose: our Jack had overheard her telling Mrs Napier that her cheekbones were cracked too, Father.

Pulling away from her, I wanted to cry again. The tears felt like stone blocks that were trapped inside me. She looked at me even more closely. I'd never known her to be so calm. It was like being comforted by Mrs

Poulton or Mrs Napier. When they were kind, as Mother was now being, I felt as if my heart was being stroked by a feather.

'You will always be Daddy's special little girl,' she promised. 'Always.'

That made me feel dizzy. I loved you so much, Father. With you gone from the house there was a gaping hole inside me. Even so, I was scared of what you'd done to Mother's face. That was the day when you'd been the Big Monster at breakfast. You were only playing then. A shudder went through me as I made a sudden connection. 'Did a real-life monster take Daddy over?' I asked.

Mother bit her lower lip and thought for a moment. As she replied, her skinny right eyebrow went up. 'Yes, Vanessa,' she answered. 'Clever girl. A real-life monster took your daddy over for a while.'

I didn't need to ask if the monster was gone. She would not have been taking me to see you if he was still there. Truly happy for the first time since you had been away from us, I shoved my face forward and kissed her again.

'Mind my sore nose!' she protested playfully. That was more like her old self. I loved it when she was fun. Another thought came to me and I said it out loud.

'Daddy's better because he's been eating the currants, Mother.'

She frowned and asked what I meant.

'Our Jack said that the doctors at the loony bin have been feeding him currants,' I explained. That bemused her even more. 'But you do know about the currants,' I objected. 'You do, Mummy.'

She was getting the look of one who was beginning to understand so I pressed on. 'You told Mrs Napier that currants were helping Daddy to become "thoroughly dried out". That,' I proudly concluded, 'means "not full of damn booze"!'

Her eyebrows had lifted to the top of her head. 'Your twin brother'll get himself into big trouble, earwigging at the kitchen door when I'm talking to Mrs Napier!' she retorted.

I knew better than to ask how currants could be electric, Daddy. And, besides, our little talk was evidently over.

'Come along,' she said crisply, standing up. 'It's quite a way and we've a train to catch.'

47

Where the railway followed the coast at a slight height for several miles, the sea looked vast, blue and magnificently shiny. You'd taken us to the beach but I had never seen such a panorama. My utter wonderment made Mother laugh.

It was then I realised she was becoming properly happy again. I also saw that the ginger was coming back to her hair. For weeks it had been the dull brown I'd noticed when Mr Mounsey had driven us home from school. Not her proper shade at all. Now the sun that was pouring through the carriage window caught its returning redness. Looking directly at her over the slim Formica table between us, I said loudly, 'Mother, you're getting all colourful again!'

She stopped laughing and her eyes shrank, Daddy. It was only natural for me to fear that I'd upset her. The misery this brought on must have shown in my face. Wherever her mind had briefly got to, she quickly refocused on me. 'Thank you, Vanessa, darling,' she said.

Upon seeing that this had cheered me up again, she smiled broadly. Also, her eyes were back to their proper size. I hadn't said anything really bad after all. Becoming thoughtful, she clasped her hands together upon the table. It seemed that she was going to say something important. I waited. The clattery rhythm of the carriage wheels was comforting.

'Would you like to live by the sea, Vanessa?' she asked.

That made me squirm and giggle: she was teasing me and it was fun. 'It would be magic!' I replied, not thinking it could ever happen.

She smiled again and sat back. Even her funny new nose no longer seemed ugly. I didn't want her eyes to shrivel again so I kept that thought to myself.

As the railway turned inland we jolted in our seats. Mother explained that we'd crossed some bumpy things called points. Twisting my head as far as it would turn, I watched the sea until it was out of sight. It was the bluest thing I'd ever set my eyes upon. 'Not too far to the hospital now,' she remarked. It was as if I was being wrapped in blanket after blanket of her love. Soon the hole inside me that you'd left would be filled, Daddy. We were going to be so happy.

48

I hadn't expected the hospital to be the size of a village, or that it would have a huge brick chimney tapering at its heart.

'It's a giant's ice cream!' I told Mother. 'Only upside down!'

We'd walked hand in hand from the nearby town where the station was. Many of the houses and shops had been built of distinctive reddish-purple bricks. There had been a time, she now explained, when the patients had made the bricks for the local builders. That chimney had been part of the hospital's brick kiln.

'Were bricks always made in loony bins?' I wanted to know.

I'd already been told not to say 'loony' or 'loony bin'. Briefly tightening her grip on my hand, Mother reminded me of this. My increasing nervousness at getting nearer to you, Daddy, made me defiant.

'But Daddy said it!' I protested. She sighed.

When the ambulance men had carted you off, you'd been shouting at the top of your lungs about the 'damn loony bin'. The whole street had heard. Mr Mounsey for one must have been really upset: the next day he went home to Mrs Mounsey. Mother pointed out that you'd done a lot of shouting that evening, Daddy.

To my surprise, the men and women walking in the hospital grounds were deathly quiet. I wondered if they'd lost their voices. Aptly, they had rubbery lips, which stayed slightly open. Also, when I looked into their eyes, they didn't react at all. It was like I wasn't even there. I found it very creepy.

Mother squeezed my hand. 'For heaven's sake, stop gawping, Vanessa! It's rude to stare.'

I knew that was true. I also knew that she, too, was uneasy. An unwelcome thought pressed itself upon me. I had to raise it with her. 'Will Daddy have wobbly lips and dead eyes?'

It scared me that her answer would be yes. That would have explained why she was becoming edgy. Stopping in her stride, she looked down at me. 'I would never let them do that to your father.'

I wondered how she could have stopped them. Our Jack had heard her telling Mrs Napier that you were only released when somebody called your consultant said you could go home.

As we walked on I thought of the currants that had apparently helped to make you better, Daddy. I still didn't understand how they could have been electric. Upon smelling boiled cabbage in the air, I asked if all types of fruit and vegetables got used for curing people at the hospital.

Although I hadn't intended to be funny, I was pleased that this made Mother laugh again. She explained that a building a little way off from where we were was the canteen. I knew what that meant because we had one across the yard at school. It, too, often sent out a smell of boiled vegetables. Our walk had been speeding up.

When she brought us to a halt, we were facing a row of old houses that had peaked attics. They were spooky and a shiver went down my back. Mother must have felt it. 'No need to be scared, Vanessa,' she said kindly. 'These are special houses for people who are ready to go home.'

I don't know why exactly, but suddenly I didn't trust her judgement.

When you saw that it was me who'd come visiting with her, Daddy, you were going to become the Big Monster again. I was so frightened I could have peed my knickers.

Our Rachael had once wet herself when you were only pretending to be a monster. But I'd seen the real thing. It was impossible to believe it had gone. You were that monster, Daddy.

'Mummy' I asked, 'can we go home now?'

My voice had been whiny. When she didn't respond I looked up. There was no delay between the meeting of our eyes and what she had to say next.

'I promise you, Vanessa, that your daddy is completely better.'

She looked and sounded so sure that I felt okay again. That was a relief. I'd really wanted to see you, Daddy, but I'd got scared on the way. Angling her head towards the houses, she smiled and said gently, 'Daddy's here for you right now, darling.'

That was when I saw you standing at the front door of the second house in the row. Metal chains could not have stopped me tearing across to you, and you picked me up in your strong arms. Your blue eyes were gorgeous and you didn't even have a tiny, residual smell of booze.

What Mother had promised was quite correct. The monster I'd seen in our garden was gone. My daddy was back and perfectly well.

49

Barely had we begun the short walk back into town than I was having a tantrum. 'I hate you both!' I screamed, meaning it. 'I hate you!' You held my wrists while I kicked out at you, Daddy.

This wasn't a lovely special day that meant we were all going to be happy again. It was a truly nasty day. Even the sun had been a liar with its brightness. You and Mother had tricked me into leaving the others. It was as if the lorry or bus I'd feared would crash into the back of Mr Mounsey's car had now driven over our Jack, Rachael and Craig. I was never going to see them again. They were going to stay with Mr and Mrs Napier while we lived by the sea.

Or, at least, that's what I'd misunderstood you as saying, Daddy. Mother's apparently out-of-the-blue question on the train, 'Would you like to live by the sea?', had come back with horribly confusing power.

I was being kidnapped because I might tell people what I'd really seen in the garden. If I did, Daddy, you would be locked up in the loony bin until you died. Between you and Mother, you'd probably fibbed that she fell on a rock and hurt her nose. Adults were always fibbing. Every child knew that. You two were the biggest, fattest liars ever. Plus Mother, too, was a loony cos only someone like that would steal a little girl away from home.

Hurt showed in your eyes as I continued to kick and scream. You were a loony, loony, loony! You'd punched Mother's face. I didn't want you anywhere near me. If you stayed at the loony bin, she could marry a proper man, like Mr Mounsey. Even as it came out of my mouth, this last bit astonished me. I'd only ever been conscious of wanting Mr Mounsey to go home to Mrs Mounsey.

Mother was purple with fury. 'Out of the way, Raymond!' she ordered, and waded in.

The slap to my face shocked me into listening to her.

'Stop this nonsense now, our Vanessa!' she instructed. 'Your father did not say that we're going to the seaside without the others! We're all moving to the seaside! It's a new start for us all!'

My crying had ended. I didn't know what to say or do. She was now on one knee before me and, though I was aware of you looking on, Daddy, I could not tear my gaze from her big green eyes.

Soon, however, the anger that had blazed within her turned to concern. She lightly shook my shoulders, which she'd been gripping. 'Oh, Vanessa,' she said, 'what on earth made you think we would ever take you away from the others?' Drawing me forward she held me tight.

That was when your face twisted, which told me how deeply my tantrum had cut into your heart, Daddy. Many times over the years to come Mother would screech at you for being self-pitying. I always knew what she meant. I was a confused child. You were an adult and your twisted face made me feel guilt for your pain. Even today it occasionally troubles me.

Still, I was thrilled to learn that a big old house by the sea was being given to us by your twin sister, our never-to-be-seen auntie Vera, who was emigrating with Uncle Derek. They were going to South Africa.

'Come along!' cried Mother, now that our crisis was over. 'Let's get to where we're going before it's time for me to take Vanessa home!'

That got me happily excited again. I'd already been told something special was waiting for me at the end of our walk.

50

You led us onto a track, which had sun-baked tyre ruts made by vehicles that went in and out of a cobbled yard. Arty workshops were all around this. Mother guessed that they had once been stables. Your footsteps had quickened so you didn't hear our chatter, Daddy.

'Come along,' she urged. 'Let's not keep your father's friend waiting.' That surprised me. Nothing had been mentioned about us going to visit somebody.

Looking ahead, I saw a lanky man in overalls sand-papering a large brown wardrobe at the entrance to his premises. He shook your hand, Daddy, as you drew level with him, and quickly peered our way. It was clear that he was expecting us. My next impression was that his long straight hair was like a girl's, partly because of its light colour. As we stopped a few paces away, you set a hand upon his upper arm, Daddy, and looked to Mother.

'Barbara dear,' you announced, 'this is Nigel.'

Instinctively I snuggled against Mother's side. As she drew a breath in readiness to speak, her left hand rested upon my head. 'Delighted to make your acquaintance at last,' she informed Nigel. For some moments I felt all queer. Though I managed not to giggle, I was embarrassed. Her suddenly posh voice had been like a dress that was too flashy for her. It simply didn't suit. To my shame, I squirmed free and stood aside. As her hand fell away from my head, it clipped my shoulder. Fortunately I wasn't the one she was concentrating on.

Nigel had accepted her extended right hand. 'And a pleasure to meet you too.'

His voice was deep, loud and clear. Even I could tell that its poshness was not put on. It was like those of the newsreaders on our telly at home.

Until then I didn't think that a skinny man with scruffy overalls and a girl's hair could talk like that. I knew from the blush in Mother's cheeks that she was thrown. It seemed unfair that you were allowed to chuckle at her mild embarrassment, Daddy.

No sooner had he finished replying to her than Nigel's piercing grey eyes were resting upon me. 'So this,' he said grandly, as you and Mother also looked my way, 'is your number-one little girl, Raymond!'

Frankly, it was like being held under a magnifying glass by three exceptionally nosy giants. 'Stop gawping!' I felt like screaming, to Mother in particular. She was the one who'd earlier insisted that gawping was rude. Needless to say, Daddy, that would not have gone down well. I'd already been slapped for having a tantrum. A repeat was the very last thing I wanted. Our silence dragged on until she finally broke it.

'Say hello to Nigel, please, Vanessa,' she cajoled. At least her posh tone was gone. Had it still been there, I would have giggled, no matter what. Unable to utter a syllable, I concentrated hard on the six eyes that were set upon me.

Nigel's had become amused and expectant. He knew I'd have to say something eventually. Yours, Daddy, were shiny and kind. You just wanted to make me happy. Mother's, too, were kind . . . and becoming angry. She'd always taught us to be polite. It was a golden rule and I was breaking it.

'Say hello, Vanessa,' she pressed, firmly.

That was when my tongue suddenly got the better of me again. 'Nigel's not a proper man's name,' I said.

You burst out laughing and clapped your hand upon Nigel's back, Daddy. Shortly before you'd been taken away from us for punching Mother, the dreaded taxman had been investigating your car business. Thanks to you, it had become a running joke between us four twins that 'Nigel was just the right name for a nosy penpushing ponce!'

Mother was now looking at me in a way that signalled another slap might be on its way. Luckily for me, Nigel had apparently found my outburst even funnier than you did. He laughed heartily and loftily fixed his gaze upon her.

'Oh, but Raymond here advised that young Vanessa brimmed with vim,' he explained. I knew from the tightness and brevity of her smile that she wasn't best pleased. Nigel had blocked her from getting her ha'pennyworth in before him.

Turning my way, he now offered a grin, which came at me like a bouncing beach ball. 'And, by gum,' he added, 'she's a young lady who certainly doesn't disappoint!' I was near bowled over with pleasure by that.

Years later I would see his astuteness. In making it clear to Mother that he wasn't annoyed, Nigel had turned me into his ally. The brains behind those striking dark grey eyes missed nothing, Daddy.

Mother ruefully shook her head. She rarely let go bad behaviour by any of us kids. But that was an exceptional day. Switching her attention back to Nigel, she brightened again. 'I wanted to thank you for teaching my husband to do french polishing while he's been receiving treatment,' she said. Later, when I'd grown up, I would realise she had been reasserting herself in the conversation.

For now, however, Daddy, I was thrilled to see you grinning with boyish pride at your new skill in making old furniture look good. Nigel waved his hand your way. 'Ah, but Raymond was a five-star apprentice!' he declared. Nobody could have sounded or looked more kingly than Nigel did right then.

Disturbingly, Mother acquired a drawn look that made her injured nose seem ugly again. Dragging her eyes from Nigel to you, Daddy, she let out a weary sigh. 'Isn't it time we got on with things, Ray?' she queried. That was when regret at upsetting her wiped the happiness from your own face, Daddy. Before you could reply, Nigel was already agreeing that it was indeed time to 'get on'.

I'd never understood until this nifty intervention that part of what people meant came from the way they said it. I distinctly heard Nigel apologising to Mother for being arrogant, yet no one said, 'Sorry.' I marvelled at how he'd done that. You did pretty much the same thing. 'But of course, Barbara, dear, we should get on,' you added, when Nigel had stopped speaking.

It was like a cloud had come and gone from over your heads. Mother was gay with you both again. Our merry mission was back on track.

Nigel wrapped his long, thin fingers around my hand and led me inside to a carpeted area, which faced onto his messy workshop. You and Mother followed. Something special was happening and I was at the heart of it. I felt as if I'd known upper-crust Nigel for ever. He seemed like an uncle. That was ironic, because our uncle Derek and auntie Vera had always kept away from us on account of your drinking, Daddy.

'Bear with me for just one minute,' Nigel said, then ducked into a cubby-hole beneath some stairs. That minute might as well have been a year. It yawned before me.

'Where's he gone?' I pestered Mother. 'Where's he gone?' I fretted.

She smiled knowingly at you, Daddy. You were watching me very closely. Your blue eyes were so calm that I quickly understood you were reading my soul. Only you and Mother were allowed to do that.

51

Nigel emerged with a large, heavy office file that had several chrome rings at its spine. Only when Mother tapped my shoulder did I realise that my excitement was making me fidget upon the spot. 'If you need the loo, Vanessa,' she cautioned, 'do tell me before you pee yourself.'

That didn't impress me. It was only little girls, like our Rachael, who became so excited that they wet their knickers. Unless, that was, something really bad was happening. Such as you punching Mother on the day of the Silver Grid fire, Daddy. I'd wet my knickers then, all right. And cut my bum on the sharp bricks of the extension wall.

Still, my wounds were not deep and everybody thought them to have been accidental anyway. Not surprisingly, the happenings within my head had been far more complicated. I was still easily upset by the slightest thing.

To her credit, Mother understood that her warning about the loo had upset me. 'I'm only asking for your own good, darling,' she reassured me. As she spoke, she glanced to you for support, Daddy.

Cocking your head at me, you winked as if to confirm that all you wanted was for me to be happy. I loved you even more for that. If ever there was a day for topsy-turviness that was it. My mood improved again.

By now Nigel had placed the mystery file upon a highly polished coffee-table, which was positioned before a two-seater sofa of burgundy leather. He patted the cushion for me to sit at his side, then looked at Mother for her consent to proceed. I followed his gaze to her eyes. Their unusual stillness showed that she did not want to unsettle me again. Nevertheless, she was equally determined that an 'accident' must be avoided.

'So long as you're absolutely certain you don't need to spend a penny first, Vanessa,' she said, with a smile. She had barely finished her sentence before I was gleefully taking my place to Nigel's left.

'Well, now,' he said, stroking the file, 'let's see what's in here, shall we?'

My heart thudded. Craning forward and slightly to my right, I fully expected the contents of the bulging file to become clear without delay.

Frustratingly, his big hand stilled with the cover just half open.

'Open it properly!' I cried, bouncing up and down upon my backside.

Nigel was not a man to be hurried.

Perplexed and silenced, I found that he was concentrating on where you and Mother were now standing slightly apart, Daddy. 'I'd rather expected,' he observed, 'that this was to be a shared event.'

I marvelled at him again. Somehow he'd ticked you and Mother off for not being together when the contents of the file were going to be revealed to me. This made the whole thing seem even more important. I loved it that you each readily accepted this mild rebuke as your cue to get close and link arms.

Had somebody informed me then that Nigel was a therapist I would have been confounded by the term, but not by his actions. At last, looking at me, he batted his blond eyelashes. Dust from the brown wardrobe he'd been sanding tumbled to his right cheek. I was all but mesmerised by him.

'That's better, Vanessa,' he concluded. 'We're all together now.'

I nearly told him I loved his kind grey eyes. He certainly had a knack for imparting a look that made me feel special. Your eyes and Mother's were also set upon me. This time you didn't seem like three nosy giants. To be the centre of attention when you were calm soothed me and made me happy.

'Please show me what's inside the book, Nigel.'

It was now his turn to cock his head, as you'd done earlier, Daddy.

'But of course,' he promised, with a smile.

True to his word, he lowered the cover until it was resting flat upon the table. Several seconds passed before he set his mouth close to my ear and whispered, 'It's fine to be excited, if that's how you feel.'

He'd read me well. Upon glimpsing the hilarious image displayed to the right of the file cover, I'd wanted to cry out in happiness. Scared of being scolded for breaking the unusual calm, I'd held back. This was so difficult that it had actually hurt my throat.

Now I looked to you, Daddy, for added encouragement. Your eyes were smiling. Mother's too.

'Well, Vee, darling?' you asked, with a nod at the open file. Cleverly, you'd used my pet name. The effect was that of a claw hammer levering a last obstinate nail out of wood. Now I knew for sure that it was okay for me to show how excited I was at the picture.

'It's a big cheeky monkey!' I cried.

That cleared the pain from my throat.

All three of you laughed heartily, Daddy. It was the happiest sound I'd heard in ages. Sliding from the slippery leather cushion I'd been sitting upon, I stood at the table edge. That gave me a bcttcr view of the file. Just to make things easier, Nigel raised his left arm for me to manoeuvre into the space in front of his knees. That done, he tapped his finger upon the image before us. 'Ah, but it's a gorilla, not a monkey,' he said.

'A silverback,' he added, upon looking to you, Daddy.

Mother exclaimed, 'Pooh!' and you all laughed some more. Missing the joke wasn't a problem for me. It was funny enough that the grinning gorilla was joyously scratching both armpits.

'He's lovely!' I cried.

To my added delight, you and Mother now hugged each other.

If it had been down to any of us four twins, our home would have been a menagerie. Had I not adored the gorilla on sight, maybe you would've concluded that the bad event in our garden had been even more harmful to me than was apparent.

52

As Nigel went to turn to the next image, I realised that the 'pages' were not made of card or paper. You explained that I was looking at lino samples, Daddy. Seeing my bemusement, Mother revealed that you'd specially wanted me to choose the flooring for the kitchen of our new house by the sea. Ingenious Nigel, she disclosed, was the designer of the lino patterns.

Any lingering notion that I was an evil child who'd driven you into thumping Mother died there and then. You wouldn't have asked me to choose the lino if I was a bad person. I wanted to speak but I couldn't. That was because I was relieved at not being wicked. I was sort of winded but in a good way.

Also, I knew, from the look you and Mother were giving me, that something very special was about to come. I wasn't disappointed. 'Your daddy and I both love you very dearly, Vanessa, darling,' Mother explained. That simple message, so clearly put, was all I'd needed to hear.

Often her voice was like a saw being drawn across

your nerves. It had sometimes helped to trigger your worst rows. Now it was as gentle as a soft kiss. Yet it was strong enough to enter my heart for ever. Hardly a moment slipped by before you said, 'Very, very dearly.'

Your eyes were filled with tenderness, Daddy. You were beautiful and so was Mother. Nothing could have been at a greater remove from when you were in a rage.

I silently thanked the hospital for giving you currants. The other three would be amazed when they saw how happy you and Mother were together. I truly brimmed with love for you both. Had I tried to speak, I probably would have wet my knickers. Nigel placed a reassuring hand upon my left shoulder and I calmed down. Instinctively, I knew whom I needed to thank for helping to make our family well again.

Spinning to face Nigel, I plonked a big kiss upon his lined forehead. That astonished him and banished any further likelihood of my knickers getting wet. I was back in charge of my feelings.

'Oh, Vanessa!' cried Mother, but not disapprovingly.

My attention, however, had already moved on. 'Show me the next pattern!' I urged.

Nigel deftly turned to the next cut of colourful lino.

I was thrilled by the horse that cleared a five-bar gate while the exasperated man who'd fallen off was running behind. I adored the markings of the giraffe that was sticking its head inside a car with a woman escaping out the other side. All of Nigel's designs were fun. I was laughing from within my heart again.

In the end, of course, he tapped his watch. Time to make my mind up. Otherwise it would be too late to ring the factory and get them started on our lino right away. The decision was easy. I went for lovely yellow seahorses, which bobbed within a turquoise ocean because that was where we were going to live. By the sea.

Almost as excited as I was, Nigel remarked that the seahorse was the only species where the male was known to give birth. You and Mother laughed when I said I'd show my twin that happening in rock pools, Daddy. I already knew that the beach was at the bottom of our new road.

Letting me choose the lino that day was one of the best things you ever did to make me feel good about myself, Daddy. It was also why, despite all that was to come, I never stopped loving you.

53

The Canny Lass loomed over Vanessa and Zenon, and the troubled eyes of Raymond the spook were fixed upon me, Brucie-Dog. He began to sob. This was new to me. What he hadn't forgotten after years of alcoholism had since been buried deep within his ghostly soul. Vanessa's memories had brought his many sins against Ginger and the family to the surface.

I started to itch where my mange had been worst. Soon it was as if maggots were eating my skin. If only to end the discomfort, I wanted to lick his hairy face. That usually brought a smile to humans who were in similar misery. Spooks, of course, were impossible to touch. I did my best to cheer him up, wagging my tail and barking loudly.

'Oh, do be quiet, our Brucie!' snapped Vanessa, turning her annoyed green eyes on me. That was amusing. She'd sounded just like Ginger. Perhaps that was what prompted Raymond to clamber aboard the steamroller and settle his bum upon the driver's seat.

I'd used my second sight for so long without a break

that I was weary. I lay down on the patch of red-painted concrete in front of the Canny Lass. Resting my nose between my paws, I summoned my biggest blue moons for Vanessa. Her yellow and red ladybird shoes shone as she moved towards me.

'Artful bugger,' she quipped, upon stopping at my side.

That made the itching stop. She'd deliberately echoed her mum's decade-long description of me as being 'artful'. The fond green eyes looking down upon me could have been Ginger's too.

Seemingly entertained by our antics, Zenon brought two folding chairs from where they'd been tucked into a gap at the end of the workbench. He set them up so that they were facing each other, sat in one and gestured Vanessa to the other. 'Please,' he implored her, 'finish your story.'

I thought even more highly of him. Not only was he a genius at maths and stuff, he also understood when a tale needed to be concluded. On a less happy note, I grasped that, as Vanessa's story went on, the lurking spook would have to endure more pain.

Rolling onto my back, I peered at him, still atop the Canny Lass. Somehow it was right for him to be near the many overhead strip lights that were making the dark blue machine glisten all over. 'It's okay, Brucie-Dog,' he called. 'I have to hear it all from Vanessa.'

I was so relieved his misery had eased for now that my tail thump-thumped upon the ground. It had a mind of its own, but often it did exactly the right thing.

Aptly, in light of the spook's emboldened mood, Zenon's blue and green eyes were in perfect focus. An endlessly patient young human, he was waiting for Vanessa to resume. I, too, was prepared for the rest of her story. It had to be told and heard.

54

She spoke clearly and quickly. A month after his happy return from hospital Raymond had travelled a day ahead of Ginger and the kids to the new house. Primarily, this was so he could lay the seahorse lino. His big promise was that it would be in situ when they arrived.

Upon completing the short walk from the town-centre railway station, the family encountered him kneeling in the middle of the kitchen at number twenty Sea View Road. Purple-faced and otherwise disarrayed, he was sweating. Ignoring Ginger's pointed question as to why the lino job wasn't completed, he'd kept his bloodshot eyes on where the four children were clustered upon the step from the hallway.

The bright turquoise lino that covered the floorboards was thickly decorated with golden-yellow seahorses. A few tacks remained to be hammered into place where the hearth was. Raymond, Vanessa explained to Zenon, quickly set about doing this.

Drawing a deep breath, she tilted her head back until the crown was pointing through the outer garage towards the sea. She was gathering her thoughts and, un-surprisingly, Zenon did not interrupt. The intensely watchful spook, though, was troubled again. He threw his upper body forward and rested the side of his head on his forearms, which made bars across the metal steering-wheel of the Canny Lass. 'For God's sake, Bruce,' he grumbled. 'If only Vanessa would just get on with telling the ruddy tale.'

I thought of his hero, Muhammad Ali. Taking the next blow would have been easier for Raymond than waiting for it, as he was now being forced to do. I stood up and noisily shook myself. That brought Vanessa's head zooming forward again.

'What's up, Brucie?' she quizzed. Despite the pain I knew it would cause me, I made my ears into the sharpest possible points for her.

Zenon clicked his fingers. 'Brucie wants you to get on with it!' he cried.

Vanessa's right caterpillar eyebrow rose high. It wasn't taking him long to grasp my idiosyncratic ways.

Parking my bum next to his seat, I kept my blue moons upon her. Maybe from this she would feel my deepening pride at her courage in making herself so open to Zenon's love.

Now Raymond wielded some particularly sharp in-tuition. 'Yes, Brucie,' he mused, lifting his head from his arms. 'My daughter's a plucky young lassie, all right.'

That really spooked me. He had accurately read my doggie-mind. I began to wonder who really had the second sight.

At the most gentle of urgings from Zenon, Vanessa resumed talking. 'Daddy wasn't actually drunk, Zenon, but even us four twins could smell whisky from where we were at the kitchen door. To be fair, he'd worked hard with the lino and the pong was probably so strong because his shirt was literally soaked in sweat.'

She might have added that after two dry months Raymond's body would have been working overtime to purge the alcohol he had poured down his neck some hours before. His sweat would have been smelt by canines for miles around.

'Mother,' she continued, 'was adamant that he'd been out boozing hard with the removal men the night before. Naturally he denied it, but we all knew it was true. The way he hammered the next couple of tacks in worried me for his fingers.'

The silence that came this time was thick as concrete. As it dragged on, the spook sat up, ramrod straight, and gripped the Canny Lass's steering-wheel in both hands. It was as if at any moment he might drive the mighty machine clean through the outer garage and into the night.

What with the powerful strip lights turning his shaggy grey hair and beard silver, it was almost funny.

Not only was he God-like in appearance, his altar was the vintage steamroller, which had been restored by Grandfather Kalaknowski and Zenon.

Zenon cleared his throat and made a far grimmer observation to Vanessa. 'And, of course, you all feared your dad would hit your mum again, right?'

The speed and certainty with which she rejected this appeared to startle even her. There was no similarity, she insisted, between Raymond when he was crazy and her daddy when he was 'merely a little hung-over'. She loyally claimed that the struggle to make the seahorse lino fit the tricky corners of the old room had wound him up. My tail swept gentle arcs upon the inner-garage floor.

Zenon opined that laying the lino would have been far easier if Raymond had been sober. I noticed long spaces between his words. Incapable of not honouring the truth as and when he felt it, he was still wary of bad-mouthing Vanessa's long-deceased father. Little did he know that Raymond himself was in full agreement with him.

Leaning back as far as he could go upon the driver's seat of the Canny Lass without toppling against her coal bunker, he smacked his palms to his forehead. Getting plastered with the removal men on the eve of the family's arrival at their new home was one of his bigger regrets. In light of his violent behaviour, the offence seemed minor to me. Perhaps to Vanessa also. When she picked up the tale, her tone was matter-of-fact.

'I remember that as he looked at our little Rachael, he was all set to hammer the very last tack in. I didn't need to see them to know that her eyes were the most accusing of us all. In the next instant he'd clouted his thumb.'

My tail was wagging hard. Partly this was because Zenon had involuntarily cried, 'Ouch!' As a hands-on techno-geek, he knew all about such painful slips.

'You might just think,' Vanessa went on, while looking him square in the eye, 'that Daddy's bruised thumb said it all about our new life by the sea.'

55

Folding his right leg across his left thigh, Zenon sat back in his chair and thoughtfully returned her gaze. 'So what you're implying,' he shrewdly remarked, 'is that your old man's hurt digit was no big deal.'

'Exactly!' confirmed Vanessa, who then launched into a description of how Raymond had busily swept the gleaming blue and yellow lino of stray tacks and welcomed the family onto it. Her arms were thrown wide and she laughed.

'Unknown even to Mother, he'd done flipping anger-management sessions with Nigel! For once,' she continued, as her eyes flashed with love for Raymond, 'he wasn't going to let a bloody great row happen between them!'

Plonking his right foot back upon the crimson concrete, Zenon craned his upper half forward to where she was now doing the same thing. Very quickly, they kissed, laughed, and sat back for the completion of her tale. Before she got under way, a few yaps escaped my barking box. I had good reason to be excited.

While the red haze that had earlier started at the front of the Canny Lass's boiler was now spreading, warm turquoise-coloured water was deepening upon the garage floor. It was as if a new ocean were being created. Within this I glimpsed a shoal of golden-yellow seahorses swimming in a large circle.

'Daddy was simply wonderful with us,' continued Vanessa. 'Even our scowly Rachael was happy again. He led this game in which we were each a seahorse bobbing upon the lino. Round and round we went. Eventually even Mother forgot she was annoyed and joined in!'

By now I, Brucie-Dog, was doggie-paddling in the wake of all the bobbing humans, perhaps the oddest thing being that each time one of Nigel's seahorses overtook me its beady eye was that of Picasso, the baldy old family parrot.

'Keep swimming, children!' Ginger urged her four very young twins.

'We are, Mother, we are!' they chorused, with love that made me go faster to stay with them.

Noting that the spook had disappeared, I wondered where he'd got to. The answer soon arrived. He paddled up in a leather canoe. Really this was the moccasin he'd been making on the distant day of the ladybird swarm. Years before he had lost it and its partner. After his death, he'd evidently found them again. They'd become much bigger than any human foot.

A few feet to his left was the second giant moccasin. Nobody needed to tell me that the human within it was none other than Grandfather Kalaknowski. It couldn't have been anybody else. He was certainly impressive. Massive grey sideburns bracketed his craggy face. They were like wings.

Following Raymond's gaze, he looked to where the Canny Lass was very close, yet also miles away. My eyes popped. I was in the inner garage where Zenon and Vanessa were sitting upon the folding chairs, yet they were standing as one upon the driver's deck of the steamroller.

With a sideways glance at his fellow spook, Raymond declaimed, 'They're in love, my Vanessa and your Zenon! In love!'

With his hand over his brow to shield his eyes against the glare of the redness that was now all around the Canny Lass, Grandfather Kalaknowski thought for some moments. 'In love very much,' he proudly agreed.

Those four words amounted to a triumphant rejection of Dr Hopeless's prediction that Zenon's life would be loveless. I wanted to bark, yap, wag my tail, prick my ears and do my blue moons all at once. The current, however, was strong and it was all I could do to keep paddling. As I did so, I became aware that the spooks had turned their smiling faces upon me.

It was Grandfather Kalaknowski who spoke.'Brucie-Wucie-Lucie-Darling!' he exclaimed, in his thick Polish accent. 'Old Artful!' he added, with a glance at his ethereal companion.

Raymond sat back in his gently rocking canoe and roared with laughter. He must have been telling Grandfather Kalaknowski all about my role within Ginger's family. I didn't mind. It was flattering to be counted in.

Of much greater interest to me, though, were the mixed colours of Grandfather Kalaknowski's perfectly focused eyes. Bright blue to one side. Vivid green to the other. Exactly the same as his grandson's.

'Come now, Raymond!' he barked, turning away from where Zenon and Vanessa were now passionately kissing upon the Canny Lass's deck. 'We leave young lovers to their loving.'

Throwing a last glance my way, Raymond paddled after him. Upon looking back to the Canny Lass, I found her extraordinary redness so strong that I was temporarily blinded. I also began twitching, as if my first human had returned to set his special electric cable against my spine.

56

The redness that had hurt my eyes was also the glare of Ginger's lovely bright hair. Her arms were cranked upon the now well-worn seahorse lino and her spinach-green eyes were peering right into mine. 'Oh, dearie me! Vanessa! Rachael!' she cried in alarm. 'You're both quite correct! He has! He has! Old Artful's been taking a fit!'

I'd been sleeping at her feet while Vanessa revealed all about Zenon and the Canny Lass. The mid-morning sun was pouring through the side window and reflecting against the oval mirror upon the kitchen chimney breast. Picasso had a particularly beady eye fixed upon me. I swear that, for a fraction of a second, a seahorse watched me from deep within its centre.

'Taking a fit!' the baldy old parrot squawked.

That brought a swift end to my twitching. I was being mocked. All avian creatures regard canines as fools for becoming too engaged with human emotion. Still, it was a relief to see the worry leave Ginger's face. Licking her big, battered nose, I wished I had the power to mend it.

'He loves you, Mother,' remarked Vanessa, who was now standing beside Rachael, smiling down upon me.

'Course he does,' added her sister, who quickly went to get some water.

'Dear old Artful,' cooed Ginger, as I basked in their love.

57

When I'd joined Ginger's family my water bowl was an old glass dish. After that got broken, they gave me a soup bowl, which lasted until Craig dropped it. An unbreakable metal pan took over. One day, having drunk it dry, I padded into the yard and splashed against one of the galvanised dustbins Ginger had planted ferns in. I'd picked my target carefully. It was the one with '20' painted on its side – the bin I'd cheekily wetted after I was rescued from the kennels in 1976. Ginger had called me an artful bugger then. Now I was Old Artful to her. I, Brucie-Dog, had become part of the family's history and it felt great.

Upon returning to the kitchen I flopped down on the tatty seahorse lino and made big blue moons of my eyes. It was important that my three humans understood I was okay: the focus needed to remain with them. The question as to why Vanessa had kept her engagement a big secret was yet to be answered. I could smell Ginger's hurt at this. She was hiding it as best she could. Reassured that I was fine, she settled on her knees at my side. Vanessa knelt to the other side of me. Rachael stayed by the sink, watching her mum and big sister.

Very soon I rolled onto my spine. Ginger and Vanessa smiled. They thought I was playing one of my doggie-games. I suppose I was. Primarily I wanted a clear view of them as they spoke.

My front limbs were in the way so I lowered them, kinking my forelegs. They all laughed, which was fine by me. I felt as if I was helping them prepare for a difficult conversation. Ginger was the first to speak.

'Why didn't you tell me about your engagement, lovie?' she asked plaintively.

Vanessa shrugged. It was clear that she would explain, but not quite yet.

Ginger's lumpy old hand, which had painted thousands of pictures over fifty years, rested upon my belly. I'd always loved her touch. She'd chosen me to come into the family and help her with the kids. Nothing could ever diminish my love for her. Now Vanessa's hand settled beside her mum's. I groaned with delight.

Out the corner of my eye I saw Picasso beadily watching me again. I didn't care what he thought. I was doing my best to prevent a serious rift opening between Ginger and Vanessa. When I groaned a second time the two hands gave me the slightest of tickles. I knew from this that they were not angry as such with each other.

Ginger repeated her question. 'Why didn't you tell me you'd been engaged all this while?'

Vanessa lifted her face from me and looked squarely at her. 'I would have told you, Mother, but you had a stroke and began talking in a French accent.'

That left Ginger nonplussed. For the first time ever, I saw a white mist around her. The same non-colour had shrouded Craig when I'd first seen him. It's the sign of a human who is feeling lost. There was a long silence.

Vanessa broke it. 'I'd fallen in love,' she explained. 'You and Daddy were always in love. He punched you and look what happened to you both.' She was trying not to cry.

Ginger had been observing her very closely. The white mist was going. She understood what her daughter was telling her. Or, at least, she thought that was the case. 'But, Vanessa darling,' she exclaimed, 'you mustn't judge Zenon by Raymond's behaviour!'

Vanessa tensed. Her fingers became hard sticks against my ribcage. Red and black swirled around her. 'That is not what I'm saying, Mother!' she snapped. Her eyes were balls of fury.

Ginger flinched in shock. Rachael asked her big sister to mind her temper, but nobody was listening to her. I thought it wise to remain dead still.

'Then what on earth are you saying?' cried Ginger. Her scent had become acrid. She feared that the conversation was going somewhere very difficult. Vanessa had lowered her face to me again. The dismay in her eyes was so deep that I could've plunged into it and sunk endlessly down. Of course, the big danger was that this might happen to her. If she didn't speak now she might be harmed for ever. I wagged my tail once. Its thump upon the seahorse lino was the cue for her to face Ginger again.

'I saw what really happened in the garden, Mother, on the day of the Silver Grid fire,' she said bluntly. 'When Daddy was drunk, you got into his face and tormented him, and tormented him, and tormented him!'

She was sobbing now. This time I smelt her terrible despair. Was she blaming Ginger for Raymond's violence? Rachael's brow was crinkled in worry but she said nothing. She must have realised this was a conversation that had to take place.

I wasn't keeping dead still out of choice any more. I was rigid with alarm. Ginger might easily do one of her nuclear blasts. It wasn't that in itself that scared me. I was terrified that if she became powerfully angry she might have another stroke – there was already a touch of Frenchness in her voice. Something very different happened, though.

Her skin had been particularly grey and wrinkly. That was part of the despair I'd smelt. As she drew a deep breath, in readiness to respond to Vanessa, her pinkness came back and most of the wrinkles went. Her bad smell was also gone. I realised that her fingers, too, had been hard sticks upon my belly. A far gentler touch equalling Vanessa's now returned.

'When I first married your father he was a good man,' she began. 'When he came home from the war, he was still a good man, but he was also an alcohol-sodden brute.' Vanessa had stopped crying. Ginger's measured tone was soothing her. She changed position on the floor so that she was on the side of her hip, mermaid-style, beside me.

'Why did you marry him twice, Mother?' Evidently this had long been a riddle to Vanessa.

Ginger, too, found a more comfortable position upon the seahorse lino. Rachael moved from the sink and parked her bum on one of the breakfast chairs. Ginger occasionally glanced to her as she spoke.

'I loved Raymond. I missed Raymond after we parted in the late nineteen forties. Before I remarried him I was advised by his psychiatrist that he was categorically over his war trauma.' Lowering her head, she shrugged and sighed. When she looked up again, she was matter-of-fact. 'Years later that psychiatrist killed himself because he wasn't over his own damn war trauma.'

Rachael chuckled. Her sense of humour had always been dark. People respected her for it. She dared to laugh at the bits where others feared they shouldn't.

Ginger and Vanessa shook their heads at her. Holding her hands out in a mock-protestation of innocence, she asked, 'What?' The big green eyes that I adored were bigger than usual and loaded with cheek. Her furry caterpillars had gone up nearly to her hair. Lowering them and her hands, she laughed at herself. It was Vanessa's turn to speak again.

'What I'm really scared of, Mother,' she confessed, 'is becoming you.'

This, too, might have been a nuclear blast moment. Ginger sucked in a much deeper breath than before and shook her head. Whatever she was thinking now, Vanessa didn't give her time to say it. I saw that she was pressing on while her nerve held. 'That last time he hit you, when the statue was being unveiled,' she said, 'he was so drunk and just needed to go to bed.'

I knew all about that later incident. Raymond had been staggering drunk and naked in the front street. A hundred yards down the road the Salvation Army was unveiling the new statue of Sir Winston Churchill. Maybe he was so drunk because the ceremony had stirred up the war in his head. Fifteen-year-old Jack had talked him into coming inside. It might have ended peacefully. Ginger was in a rage because Raymond had spent the housekeeping money on booze. Standing upon the high stone step at her exotic front door, she'd blocked Raymond's path. Spit flew into his face as she'd screeched at him: 'Oh no you don't! You don't! You don't come into this house in that state! Pathetic, sozzled spendthrift!' she added, and went on with more of the same, drowning Jack's pleas for her not to antagonise his dad.

Vanessa was staring at her. Nobody had ever dared suggest to Ginger that she'd had a hand in Raymond's violence. Rachael was white with anxiety. I could feel the tremor in Vanessa's fingertips. She'd said the unsayable. When she spoke next it was with slow emphasis.

'I don't want to make the victim responsible here, Mother, but—'

She was cut off with a derisory snort. Nothing in a million years would make Ginger accept the status of victim. Biting her lower lip, Vanessa clearly realised this. Her mother allowed a few seconds to pass, then said angrily, 'I remarried your father because I believed the violence was over, Vanessa. I believed he was cured,' she insisted. Her eyes blazed and she was very red. Rachael and Vanessa exchanged worried looks. Never mind a mini-stroke, a major haemorrhage could have killed their mum. But all dogs know there's a time in human relationships when things have to be aired. Ginger probably understood this more than most.

'Was I supposed to be his convenient punchbag?' she demanded.

Vanessa bit her lip again. She was preparing to vent the accusation that had been with her ever since the day of the Silver Grid fire. She had been a little girl then. But she knew what she'd seen in the garden. 'You bloody well provoked him!' she yelled into Ginger's face, directly over my body.

That infuriated Rachael, who claimed Vanessa was almost making it sound like it was acceptable for Raymond to have hit their mum. Like, if Ginger had wound him up, it was reasonable for her to be thumped.

'No man should ever hit a woman, ever!' she hotly concluded.

Getting to her feet, Ginger promptly advised her to mind her own damn business. I remained where I was. Vanessa's hand briefly tickled my belly. Her glass-hard eyes had not left Ginger. They both knew that the accusation she'd made needed to be answered.

Ginger had been standing with her hands on her hips, her back to Vanessa and Rachael. They waited. I waited. Picasso's beady eye had become so big, it was a wonder it didn't pop out. What with his scrawny baldness, a dangling eye would have been the perfect finishing touch. Ginger turned. No longer angry, she had the look of one who'd gathered her thoughts and was ready to carry on.

'Of course I knew that hitting me made him feel dreadful afterwards,' she conceded. She'd said that to

Rachael as an apology for scolding her. For what was to come, her eyes returned to Vanessa.

'And you're right. I damn well did provoke him. If he thought he could thump me anytime he liked, I made sure it was when he did not like.' Her thin lips were drawn tight. Once more I wanted to go to her and lick her nose. That would have been wrong. Most mutts are shrewd enough to know when to hold back. The sun was still streaming into the kitchen but its normal weightlessness was absent. You could not have cut the atmosphere with an axe. Its steel head would have shattered, like glass, and its shaft would have splintered.

Suddenly Vanessa spoke. 'Mother!' she said boldly. 'You became addicted to the fight with Father!'

To my great surprise Ginger took that on the chin. Now it was her turn to be candid. 'If you want to make that your excuse for not having the courage to trust in your and Zenon's love, then more fool you,' she said.

Vanessa flinched again. Now she was the one to hide her feelings. Her sweat reeked. My nostrils were working overtime. She got up and sat upon a breakfast chair. Ginger faced both daughters from where she was standing in the middle of the room.

'You bloody know-it-all young people!' she expostulated. 'You have no idea what I went through. You have no idea what your father went through. You know absolutely nothing about absolutely anything!' Rachael and Vanessa turned to each other in shock. If their mum had been shouting like usual, they would have laughed her words off. But Ginger was not over-wrought, and her firm voice had lost the hint of French. They were being told the truth and they knew it. Their miffed expressions were funny. My tail started its thump-thump-thump malarkey but I stopped it before it got going properly. The three whacks it had made upon the lino appeared to have gone unheard. If the seahorses were real, though, I would have concussed at least a hundred of them. Any pregnant males would have been sent into premature delivery. The thought al-most set off my tail again. Humans will never know how difficult tails are to manage.

Ginger sighed wearily. 'Don't you see that your father and I must never be your excuse for not trying? What-ever we became, the war started it. We damn well did our best with the rotten hand dealt to us.' At that the sisters began to protest that they knew this already. I saw a danger that the talk would lose its power. Ginger held up a hand for them to be quiet.

'Please!' she cried. 'For once will you listen to me?'

Good old Ginger. A vital moment had been rescued. They were listening. I was listening. Picasso was listen-ing.

'You both have a duty,' she insisted. I whimpered at that. It was like hearing Her Hoityness when I'd given

---

up all hope at the kennels. I was very young. It was at her cajoling – her insistence – that I'd fought harder for my life. It was my duty to survive, she'd said. Without her, I would have been long dead and forgotten. A troublesome abuse victim, conveniently offed by Psycho-Vet. A shudder went through me and I whimpered again. My three humans looked my way, but I must have appeared to be okay. And, besides, I don't think anything would have stopped Ginger now.

'You.' She eyeballed Rachael.

'You.' She eyeballed Vanessa.

'Both you girls and your brothers,' she continued, 'you each have a duty to trust in love.'

Vanessa and Rachael had their ears back so hard you would have thought rivets had been used to do the job. This was their mother speaking to them from her heart. Ginger looked at the elder of the pair and pressed her advantage. 'Big sacrifices have been made for you,' she said.

That hit Vanessa like a wet kipper across the cheek. It had long been the view of the family that Raymond had killed himself to spare them the chaos he was fated to cause.

The sunlight in the kitchen had regained its weightlessness. The two sisters had been struck silent. A faint red mist surrounded Vanessa. Now I understood why she'd needed this showdown. Ginger's blessing was essential to her. The argument had proved beyond doubt that her mother still believed in love. Finally she was free of doubt and able to seal her commitment to Zenon. Their love was new. The shadow of Raymond and Ginger could not darken it. They needed to be brave. It was down to them to make their future work without trading emotional and physical blows.

'There is one more thing.'

Ginger had said this. I was up and sitting on my bum now. Rachael's brow rose in time with her sister's green and purple caterpillars. They waited. Ginger tried to keep a straight face. 'Just don't buy heavy saucepans, darling,' she advised Vanessa.

Rachael and Ginger burst into laughter. Picasso squawked and I barked. Vanessa was never going to be allowed to forget that she'd once concussed her twin brother Jack with a preserving pan.

58

Jack and Craig were astonished to learn about their sister's secret engagement. Everybody now wanted to meet Zenon. Vanessa agreed to fix up a family drink at the Gay Hussar. She affected that she was being pressured into it but they all knew otherwise. A year of subterfuge was over. Introducing Zenon to the family was exactly what she needed to do next. Her excitement shone through. They were all touched that she was in love.

A little after lunchtime she slipped out of the house. It amused me that she was once again wearing her yellow ladybird shoes. At any key moment in her life, they were her choice of footwear. I'd come to think of them as her talisman. Only the week before she'd meticulously redone the many hand-painted insects with bright red Humbrol paint. Jack had lent her one of his smaller brushes for the job. Ginger had admired her talent. Each ladybird was so well painted it looked real. Jack commented that if they all flapped their wings at once, Vanessa would have been borne aloft, like the Virgin Mary. She snorted, then told him he should stop doing cocaine while he was working in his studio.

Ginger concluded that because she'd been in the swarm with Raymond – and had even got a ladybird trapped in her sinuses – her elder daughter had the species in her blood.

Late in the afternoon Vanessa informed Ginger and her sister of an invitation for a drink at the Gay Hussar with Zenon. Rachael made a rare call into the workshop to advise her twin brother Craig of their date, and Vanessa told Jack. The event was set for that evening. Nobody laughed at the apparent urgency. Nobody teased. Nobody was spiteful. That was the loyalty of my young humans for you.

The publican at the Gay Hussar was an old friend of Ginger's. When Raymond had been drinking heavily in his last months, he had rung the house to warn her that he was coming home. Ginger's attitude towards the Gay Hussar had been that if her husband was going to 'drink like a damn newt' it was best he should do it 'in a pond where he was well known'. The publican's enduring fondness for the family led him to bend his no-dogs rule: I was allowed into the saloon bar for the special occasion.

Zenon's blue eye had gone to its right and his green eye was like jelly. This time it was his sweat that reeked. He was incredibly nervous about meeting everybody. Vanessa, too, was on hot coals. The passionate steamroller-loving fiancé, to whom she was devoted, had been usurped by a reticent young man who couldn't say boo to a ghost.

Neither Raymond nor Grandfather Kalaknowski was anywhere to be seen. That made the hairs along my spine go up Ridgeback-style. Vanessa would need all the assistance she could get. Maybe the moccasin canoes of the absent spooks had sunk, I thought.

Ginger insisted on buying two rounds of drinks. Zenon was already reacting to the family's runaway conversational style by putting more and more full stops between his words. I made a point of keeping my biggest blue moons upon Vanessa. She needed my reassurance. Nobody in the gathering knew how to respond to Zenon's increasing awkwardness. Not even Vanessa, it seemed.

If the air in the kitchen that morning would have shattered a swinging axe head, the atmosphere at the Gay Hussar would have resisted a full-on nuclear attack. Even Garth Howson's ban-the-bomb dad might have agreed that, if it was rolled out nationwide, the UK would have been impervious to Russian attack.

My beloved humans were not entirely insensitive to Zenon's anguish. Jack later quipped that meeting the family en masse must have been like entering a lion's den. Things would not have been so difficult, though, if Zenon hadn't allowed the others, one by one, to buy a round of drinks; and then, in spite of some severe looks, from Rachael in particular, to empty their pockets on the next rounds.

Zenon was judged by all as being tight with money. Meanness was a trait the family was united in loathing. My young humans were generous to a fault. When Zenon went to the Gents, and it appeared he was avoiding a trip to the bar, Jack rested his eyes firmly upon Vanessa's.

Vanessa's unhappy scent was now stronger than her fiancé's. Her twin brother had always been extremely generous. She'd once legendarily given her only twenty pounds to a tramp known as Smoky Joe. Willingness to give to others was part of their shared nature as twins. Jack didn't need to articulate the question that glowered in his eyes. How could she have become engaged to a mean man?

I, Brucie-Dog, saw that his judgement of Zenon was unfair. I also knew from the change in his smell when he returned from the Gents that he'd vomited hard. Loving Vanessa and her zaniness was one thing. Meeting her entire family in one go had been too much for him. It wasn't that he didn't want to go to the bar and spend his money: it would have been a nightmare for him. He needed to sit in a corner. He needed to recuperate.

Things got worse for him when the atmosphere finally lightened. The family had instinctively dismissed him. Everything was random. Jack and Craig were arguing about who should replace Michael Foot as leader of the Labour Party. They swore. They cut off each other's sentences. They even reached over the table and gave slaps. Not hard. And not without love. But from where I was curled a little way off by the open fire, which the publican had lit specially for Ginger, Zenon had the demeanour of one who'd tumbled into very rough waves. He was in danger of drowning and nobody could throw him a lifeline.

Matters grew worse when Ginger began speaking in a heavy French accent. Trying his hardest to reconnect with the family, Zenon asked what part of France she was originally from. All heads turned accusingly towards him. The hairs along my spine were up again. Instead of helplessly thrashing around in company he couldn't handle, poor Zenon needed to be checking his Del Monte cans or adding finishing touches to the Canny Lass. He was so out of his depth that I yelped and clambered to my paws.

That was Rachael's cue to announce that last orders had been called. Zenon exhaled a sigh of relief that could have cracked the Gay Hussar's mock-Tudor walls. Everybody heard it. His need to escape the family resonated loud and clear.

The evening had been a disaster. Jack looked especially worried when Zenon insisted to Vanessa that he needed to go home alone. The seafront walk back to Ginger's was quiet and miserable. Ginger, Jack, Craig, Rachael and even Vanessa were all thinking the same thing. Her engagement was going to be cancelled. Zenon and the family were chalk and cheese.

Every millimetre of my skin that had been mangy since my first human had electrocuted me itched again. Maybe I'd deserved that punishment. I wanted to scratch myself hard, ripping the skin and drawing blood with my claws. Just like Her Hoityness had done before Psycho-Vet offed her for being unstable. I'd been totally useless to Vanessa. Above all, I'd let Ginger down and Her Hoityness would have been ashamed of me to boot. I'd always been a worthless runt. I still was a worthless runt.

59

Vanessa and Rachael sat up late talking in the kitchen. Ashamed of myself for being a useless mutt, I lay beneath the table. The rusty old fridge hummed quietly and Picasso was asleep with his head tucked into one of his near-featherless wings. At least he was getting some rest. I continued to itch all over. Still, I'd thought better of clawing myself. Her Hoityness had made long deep wounds in her sides doing that. My fur was nicer than hers and spoiling it would have been a betrayal of Ginger and the kids. Their love had transformed me from a scabby mongrel into a canine whose appearance drew compliments from strangers. When push came to shove, I was vain about my handsome looks.

Rachael confided in Vanessa that she, too, was in love. Her fiancé was called Ernest and he was in his late twenties. After he'd left school, he'd been a miner at the pits up the coast. But he was bright and determined. After doing A levels at night classes, his trade union had sponsored him to go to Cambridge where he'd won a first in maths. Vanessa gasped. The four twins were hopeless at sums. Craig had once been caned for protesting that simultaneous equations should be called simultaneous disasters. Jack had empathised with him. The brothers were even worse at numbers than their sisters.

My ears were again pricked to the point of hurting. Ernest was now the boss of a multi-million-pound firm that made seatbelts for cars all over the world. Rachael proudly added that when he went to meetings abroad, he was flown there in a private jet. She was marrying an extremely wealthy man. I thought back to the day when the family had rescued me. She'd done two hundred and fifty press-ups and could easily have done five thousand. Her determination to make a success of life had always been absolute. Nothing could diminish her. Despite my shock at another great failure by my second sight – how could I not have known about Ernest? – my happiness was such that most of my itching was gone. I didn't need to hear more to be convinced that Rachael had found the right person to love and share her life with. It crossed my mind that some humans fare better without canine guidance.

Vanessa asked why she had kept Ernest a secret. Seeing the irony of her own question, she joined in with Rachael's incredulous laughter. It was rare for them to be so close. The disastrous meeting with Zenon had had the unlikely effect of strengthening their relationship. Rachael said she would introduce Ernest to her mum first. The sisters agreed that even the toughest of characters would find the whole family too much in one go. My tail thumped the seahorse lino. They lowered their heads and looked to where I was still beneath the table. I loved their funny chins, skinny lips, big noses, spinach-green eyes and furry caterpillars more than I'd ever done before. Their faces were the human equivalent of a Greyhound's. They shouldn't have been beautiful but they were.

'Brucie-Wucie-Lucie-Darling,' crowed Rachael. My tail went like crazy and Vanessa laughed. Craig's twin sister had never imitated his pet line for me before. When they'd argued in the past, she'd even been cruel about it. It was pathetic and ridiculous, she'd sniped. I saw that falling in love with Ernest was the best thing that had ever happened to her.

Vanessa was becoming happier again. She'd done the wrong thing in arranging for Zenon to meet everybody in one go. It would all come right in the end, she concluded. Rachael agreed. 'All come right,' squawked Picasso. At some point he had woken up and tuned into their talk. I don't know. Call me a sentimental old mutt, but maybe sometimes parrots do care about their humans.

60

I had free run of the house at night. Sometimes I would sleep at the bottom of a bed. My humans usually grumbled but soon a hand would pat the duvet. That was the signal for me to shuffle up and be close as they fell asleep. If the day had been demanding, I would seek my rest elsewhere. To have your second sight opening to human dreams when your head is already full of daytime drama is too much. Dogs, too, need recuperation. Setting aside the risk of death, those that do not get this may go mad and bite their humans. Nothing would have made me readily use my teeth but I knew when it was time to rest.

Slumbering under the table was fine. Stretching full length upon the sofa with my legs in the air was luxury. Unusually, though, the door to the front room was closed. I contented myself with the carpet at the bottom of the stairs. It was a draught-free spot and my spine fitted neatly into the inch-wide over-lip of the step. My weary eyes closed.

I was hopelessly wrong to anticipate restorative sleep. My second sight instantly opened to Zenon. That was what the itching had been about. The human who was new to the family was in distress. Resistance would have been an act of betrayal. My only option was to surrender to it. Zenon's experience was now my experience.

As Zenon, I was desperate to rectify the cock-up I'd made at the Gay Hussar. I'd thrown up in the Gents. At times my breathing was so shallow and quick that it was all I could do to avoid panting. The family thought I was odd. They were bloody odd. I wish I'd said that. They would have laughed. My tongue had a knot in it that made me think Dr Hope's prediction was coming true. I was supposed to be in love with Vanessa but I couldn't let her family see it. I'd let her down. I'd let myself down. If I didn't make up for it without delay, she would inevitably reject me as a freaky geek. Naturally, she was closest to her twin brother, Jack. Once he'd got a drink or two down his neck, he'd looked across the table at me like I was a zoo exhibit.

My strategy to correct all of this included the Canny Lass.

I'd already formulated a plan when I'd insisted that Vanessa should go home with her family. That had been hard. There was anguish in her eyes I'd never seen before. She'd probably thought I was going to flee her and them for ever. To ease the misery this caused me, I ran the full length of the seafront back to my house.

The day before had been momentous. With the help

of half a dozen neighbours the Canny Lass had been wheeled onto my short garden drive, where a Ministry of Transport engineer had pressure-tested her boiler. She'd passed with flying colours. That had been a big relief.

When she had crashed into a wall in the mid-1960s she'd suffered big cracks to her boiler. The merest pin-hole in one of Grandfather's welds, and she would've been classified as dangerously unfit for use. I could understand why they were so strict. If a steamroller's boiler blows up, anyone close by stands a chance of death. The human skull is no match for cast-iron shrapnel.

My two-mile run from the Gay Hussar had left me breathless, but there was no time to care about what my lungs were doing. When the man from the ministry had departed, I'd been reluctant to wheel the Canny Lass back into the garage. This had been her first foray into the open since Grandfather and his mates had used a lorry to tow her home twenty years earlier. It was only right that those who were walking the links or passing in cars should witness her beauty. Appropriately, her name had recently been reinstated in yellow curlicue lettering upon her canopy frame. Recalling that Vanessa had done this was like an extra-hard kick in my pants. I had to save our engagement from disaster.

It was nearing midnight and the boiler needed three

hours at least to be hot enough for what I had in mind. I needed to work like the devil. Fortunately the Canny Lass was brimming with water and her bunker was crammed with lumps of coal the size of breeze blocks. She was returning to the road earlier than I'd expected. And all because of my love for Vanessa.

61

As soon as I'd got the blaze going in her fire-hole, I tore off the shirt and tie I'd worn to go to the Gay Hussar. I was far more comfortable in overalls. Far more me. And, besides, it was likely to get very hot in the driver's seat.

The neighbour to the right of my house was called Alec. He was a small plump man who wore round spectacles. We hadn't always got on, and the day before he'd moaned about being asked to move his car while the ministry man did the pressure test.

Still, if he was angry at a twelve-and-a-half-ton steamroller being fired up in the early hours, he would have had a fair point. When he came outside, I looked him square in the eye. The words that came put my predicament in a nutshell: 'If I don't get this bloody beast of a steamroller to Vanessa's, Alec, mate, she won't marry me and I'll live my life alone.'

He removed his glasses and cleaned them slowly with his hanky. I braced myself for cross words. When he finally looked at me, through the newly polished lenses, he broke into a huge grin.

'In that case, young man,' he said, 'we'd best be getting you and your steamroller on the road!'

More neighbours came out to help. It was suggested that it would speed things up if the Canny Lass was wheeled from my drive to the far side of the dual carriageway. That took twelve men and a good hour of hard toil. The boiler pressure was climbing but more heat was needed. Alec made it his purpose to feed the breeze-block-sized coals into the fire-hole.

The canvas driver's canopy was clipped into place and the space below was bathed in fiery gold. Smoke belched from her chimney. Steam began to whoosh from valves and pipe connections but the boiler held firm. It was as if a dinosaur that had been perfectly preserved in permafrost was coming back to life. The slickly oiled slide bars, which would soon propel her rear wheels, glinted in the moonlight. I'd anticipated this moment since I was eight. My heart pounded. I knew exactly what I was doing.

People I'd known all my life came out of their homes to watch. The Canny Lass was ready to roll again, and word went round that I was on a mission to repair a rift with my fiancée. Families even came from the estate behind our seafront houses. Dr Hope had said I would be a loner. I was drunk on the company I now had. Every eye that I looked into shone with merriment.

Dr Hope would never have embraced a rusting

steamroller and brought it back to life as Grandfather had. Dr Hope was the loner. Dr Hope would probably have called the police and complained that some maniac with a steamroller was creating a disturbance in the middle of the night. Good cheer played, like exquisite music, in the air. Above all else, I realised, since I'd fallen in love with Vanessa, my perception of humanity had reversed. Most people were more like Grandfather than they were like Dr Hope. My hand rested on the long iron brake handle. The pressure was up and I was ready to roll.

'Three cheers!' cried good old Alec.

'Hip-hip-hooray!' roared the crowd of fifty or so, as I released the brake. 'Hip-hip-hooray!' they hollered twice more.

For the first time in twenty-five years the Canny Lass rolled under her own steam. Kids, aged thirteen, fourteen and fifteen or so, were outside too. Urged on by the adults, they ran alongside while the heat from the blazing coals all but seared my face. I closed the fire-hole door and set my sights firmly ahead. There was no speedometer to accompany the white-faced pressure gauge but I felt the acceleration. Two miles an hour. Two point five miles an hour. A gentle wind in my face now. Three miles an hour, and soon we'd be flat out at four miles an hour. One by one, the laughing youngsters returned to their parents.

Three times Formula One world champion Jackie Stewart couldn't have overtaken me. It was all I could do not to pull the chain of the trumpet-shaped whistle that Grandfather had rescued from a scrap locomotive in Wales. Its magnificent howl would have woken everybody within a five-mile radius.

The Canny Lass was reborn and ready for me to share with Vanessa. I, too, was renewed. The nerve I'd lost at the Gay Hussar was back. If only a quarter of what she'd told me about her family applied, I knew they would accept me for the man I was. It delighted me that I was wearing overalls and steel-capped work-boots. Hopefully, my face was smudged with coal and soot. There's makeup for you, high fashion Zenon Kala-knowski-style.

62

I was a hundred yards short of Churchill's Promontory when I became aware that Grandfather was also upon the small iron deck, slightly behind the driver's seat. This was no surprise. It was only right that he should be present for the inaugural run of the restored Canny Lass. He came forward and stood to my left. I noted he was gripping a tin of Del Monte fruit cocktail in his right hand.

The shiny silver top of the tin had two triangular punctures, directly opposite each other. That was how he'd always done it. He'd delegated to me the bigger task of cutting off the tops to make storage cans. The Del Monte collection was one of many threads that had bound us close. Having him at my side emboldened me.

Peering ahead to where we were due to make the sharp right-hand turn onto Sea View Road, he took a long draught of the juice. I got a feeling that if I stared at him he would be gone. He was beside me and that was enough. From the corner of my eye I saw that his flaring grey sideburns were as impressive as ever. I'd loved him so much that, since his death two years before, he'd become mythical to me. When I'd told Vanessa that Grandfather was my Zeus (although I didn't believe in any deity), she'd taken it as final confirmation that I was nutty enough for her family. Compliments don't come bigger than that.

A protester stood in the middle of the road directly ahead. I knew, from his silver hair, that it was Dr Hopeless. He held a placard aloft. It was similar to a 'No Entry' road sign, except that the words were 'No Love'. Fury and resentment burned in his eyes as we got closer. I'd fallen in love with Vanessa and she'd fallen in love with me. His cruel judgement upon an eight-year-old boy had been overturned. The Canny Lass crushed him. Neither Grandfather nor I flinched. I'd often wondered how many other young lives Dr Hope had damaged with his predictions. It seemed just that he was flattened upon the road.

The Canny Lass had excelled herself.

Dividing the distance we'd come by the precise time we'd been travelling told me we'd averaged an astounding five point one miles per hour. Never mind Jackie Stewart with his racing cars, I was now Captain Smith pushing the *Titanic* on her maiden voyage, a legendary act of folly that ended in disaster. Since meeting Vanessa, though, I'd accepted that some risks had to be taken.

Grandfather was clutching the nearside front strut, which supported the canvas canopy over my head. The chain for the gleaming brass trumpet was close to his left hand. Pulling the brake lever to its halfway point, I slowed in preparation for our turn. Aiming slightly to our left, I gained as much road space as possible. That was a tricky thing to do. An inch too far and the roller would have clipped the granite kerb. But the bigger the potential arc, the easier the turn would be.

We were down to one mile an hour. The Canny Lass was shuddering as if desperate to surge forward. Any faster for the manoeuvre, though, and she might have toppled onto her side. I hauled her metal-rimmed steering-wheel through several clockwise circles. Her front end began majestically to turn.

The bottom fifteen yards of Sea View Road was the steepest bit. Grandfather bristled in response to a groan that came from deep within the boiler. It seemed to me that the Canny Lass was protesting at the incline that confronted her: a daunting blood-red boulevard soaring up the side of Everest.

At eighty-four years old, she was being made to perform like a brand new creation from Aveling and Porter. I was struck with fear that she was going to fail. Here was my Captain Smith moment. The load was too great for her. The strain was too much. Grandfather's welds might blow at any moment. My skull would be no hardier match for hot iron than that of anyone else. I was on a suicide run.

She faltered for seconds that seemed like hours. Twenty-five years earlier she'd crashed dramatically not far from this very spot. The accident had come about after her regular driver had died at her wheel from an aneurysm. He'd felt no terror as she'd trundled out of control. I was alive and aghast.

Vibrations were travelling through every millimetre of her iron body. If she didn't actually blow apart, we were going to roll backwards, smash the granite kerb, clear the promontory, and plunge into the sea. Sir Winston Churchill might even go with us.

Briefly I believed that Fate could not be bucked. The Canny Lass had been meant to die when she first crashed. Dr Hope had been right. I would not be sharing my life with Vanessa. His revenge on us for defying his prediction and crushing him, like an insect, on the seafront road was about to manifest itself. The Canny Lass had passed her pressure test the day before but something was now seriously amiss with the boiler. It groaned again. The sound was haunting. A whale calling to a lost calf through the deep. The pressure gauge was to the limit of its red sector. Another second or two and she would blow apart or lose all power and begin an unstoppable backward roll. I did not know what to do.

That was when Grandfather pulled the whistle chain. Huge amounts of steam billowed into the night air and formed a swirling shroud over the Canny Lass. The long howl was so piercingly shrill that the pressure with which I clamped my hands over my ears all but crushed my skull.

Grandfather was not yet done.

He reopened the fire-hole door and the flames therein roared with increased life. This action could have been disastrous. To my incredulity the combined release of steam and increase in fire power sent a surge that brought the pressure gauge back to its safe zone. A sticky valve had been blasted into working properly. We had already cleared the steepest part of the hill.

The Canny Lass had shown her mettle. Fate could be bucked. Lights were coming on in all the houses. Number twenty was just fifteen yards ahead. It was four in the morning, and if the family didn't appreciate the call I was making, I'd misjudged everything. The temptation to give another toot on the whistle was enormous, but I resisted. I knew that somebody would already have phoned the police. All I really cared about, though, was seeing Vanessa again. Life without her had become incomprehensible to me.

63

Excited voices carried from the upper landings to where I, Brucie-Dog, was standing to attention in darkness at the bottom of the stairs. The hall light was switched on from above. 'Out of the way, dog!' cried Vanessa, as she hurtled down, two steps at a time.

As she tore past me and into the porch, my tail went like the clappers. Her nightgown was a glitzy kimono, which Ginger had bought at a posh charity sale. It left dizzyingly bright streaks in her wake. Turning the lock of number twenty's colourful front door, she exclaimed, 'I just knew he would come!'

Adrenalin must have been giving her extra strength. The old door was heavy and had always dragged against the frame. Vanessa effortlessly pulled it wide. Within a trice, she was down the garden path. Catching the wonderful scents of Ginger's garden, I followed her to the pavement. That was when I smelt soot too.

Smoke was belching from the Canny Lass's chimney as she came to a halt outside the house. She was a vision. Smoking. Steaming. Gleaming. Proud. Magnificent.

Fortunately, for once, there were no cars at the kerb and I saw Zenon pull a long lever, which held her steady in the middle of the road. His waving fiancée was eager to clamber aboard. 'I'm here, Zenon!' she called. 'I'm here!'

He checked the all-important pressure gauge and reached down to where Vanessa was hopping about upon the red tarmac. As he did so, a huge grin cracked his bearded face.

Nothing touches a canine heart like the happiness of young lovers who are repairing a rift.

Their hands connected and my tail thumped the gatepost. There would be consequences from that but, at the time, I didn't feel pain. Bringing the Canny Lass to Sea View Road had been Zenon's master-stroke. Now the family would overlook his seeming miserliness at the Gay Hussar. 'Mind you don't get burned!' he cautioned Vanessa.

In her rush to be aboard the iron deck she'd forgotten her feet were bare. 'And watch your nightie doesn't go up in flames!' he added. Even in the midst of their great excitement, he was looking out for her.

The fire-hole door was wide and they were bathed in a golden glow. Vanessa's multi-coloured kimono shone like treasure. So, too, did her spiky bright blue hair. Their shared life would be filled with enviable richness.

Ginger had ordered Vanessa to trust in love. If

Zenon's confidence in himself had now been proved, then so had her willingness to share her heart. She'd been correct in telling Rachael that everything would come right in the end.

Zenon gave her a shovel, which had a wide pan that had been made to fit the fire-hole. 'Heap the coal on for the pull up the hill!' he instructed. Already they were working as one at the controls of the Canny Lass.

Seeing the size of the lumps in the bunker, Vanessa used her hands instead. It didn't matter that her purple-varnished nails would be broken and the kimono smudged. They were together again, which was all that counted.

The fire crackled and sparked ferociously. Ginger's front room had an open grate but I'd never seen coals burn like that. I wondered if Grandfather Kalaknowski was blowing upon them. Maybe Raymond, too. Or perhaps it was just that the sea breeze was flowing in the right direction for a potent blaze.

Releasing the brake lever, Zenon cast an eye over the side to ensure a satisfactory take-up by the massively heavy roller at the front. 'More coal!' he roared to Vanessa, as the slide bars began to make the gigantic rear wheels turn. Steam whooshed from pipe connections.

The Canny Lass wasn't a machine. She was alive. She was breathing. She had a soul. Grandfather Kalaknowski would have known this. Dr Hope would have called for men in white coats to remove any human who expressed such a notion.

64

Despite the noise of twelve and a half tons of Victorian cast-iron getting under way, a familiar clunk brought my ears back to their sharpest points. Ginger had flung open the large square bay window in the middle of the upper floor. A stunning redness swirled around her. She, too, was thrilled. I'd never seen her so happy.

'Oh, I do say!' she cried, as the Canny Lass's rumble up the steep hill gathered pace. 'Oh, my word! Oh, Jack! Oh, Craig! I really do say!'

The brothers were now leaning out to either side of her. Seeing the three of them together, laughing with happiness for Vanessa, set off my barking box. It didn't matter a fig about the neighbours. The lights had come on in every house, and loads of humans were coming outside in pyjamas.

One or two shouted complaints, but when Ginger declared that her daughter was in love with the young man whose steamroller it was, a round of applause filled the air. Not for the first time that night, I was reminded that most humans are truly good-hearted.

Rachael strode outside and stood on the pavement near me. She was surrounded by redness, too, and her eyes had a sparkle that made them exceptionally green. The Canny Lass was now about twenty yards up the hill from the house.

'I hope Zenon's paid the road tax on that thing or the police'll be after him good and proper!' Jack shouted.

'Hey! Mr Zeppity, mate!' Craig bellowed. 'Ya may have cobwebs on ya wallet, but ya loony enough for this mad family!'

The neighbours burst into another round of applause but Ginger looked a tad miffed. She was soon laughing again, though, when Rachael yelled, 'I hope you know what you're letting yourself in for, Zenon! She once brained our Jack with a jam-making pan!'

There was another tide of laughter. Even the complainers were now joining in with the spirit of things.

The departing Canny Lass was the QE2 of the road. Majestic. Glorious. A triumph. Standing on my hind legs at the gatepost, I barked into the night. Looking down upon me, Ginger shouted, 'Oh, do be quiet, damn dog!'

Back upon my four paws, I saw Vanessa's left hand reach to the Canny Lass's steam whistle. Zenon flicked a backward glance down the street. I could see that they were laughing hard. When she pulled upon the chain the howl that followed was even louder than Grandfather Kalaknowski's, and the mighty Canny Lass was bathed in steam.

At last whiteness signified something other than being lost. Vanessa was now the most found of my young humans and my optimism for the others was un-limited. I sent up a prayer of thanks to Her Hoityness.

65

Before Rachael had come outside she'd pulled on her red tracksuit and white sports shoes. Excitedly stepping onto the road for a better view of the Canny Lass, now that she was well up the street, she trod on a loose lace and tumbled over. That was a big surprise for Craig and Jack. Their sporty sister was the nimblest member of the family. Certainly I'd never seen her fall over before. As she was getting back to her feet, her eyes rested upon me. Maybe she'd sensed the mischief that was stirring in my heart. Before she could grab my collar, I was off, tail high, as I gained on Zenon's steamroller. I wasn't a middle-aged mutt. My front legs weren't dodgy. I was a stunning dog – humans on the beach were always saying so – and here was proof that I could still run like a Greyhound.

'Brucie, come back!' hollered Rachael. The Canny Lass's whistle was no longer blowing and I heard that cry repeated with the addition of 'Right now!' I guessed that, before chasing after me, she was tying her shoelaces.

'Hoi, Brucie!' bellowed Craig.

'Brucie!' That was Jack.

Then Ginger shrieked that I was a damn nuisance, and would somebody please stop me? A couple of doddery old neighbours were easily avoided. I hadn't enjoyed an escape so much in years. If there was an Olympic race for canines, I would have been the gold medal champion.

'Run, Brucie, run!' exclaimed another onlooker. Others laughed. I felt more impressive than Lassie ever was. And to think I'd once been a mangy mutt that nobody had admired! Psycho-Vet would have been amazed to see me now.

My paws barely made contact with the road as I passed between the Canny Lass and the cars parked to my left. The noise and danger were exhilarating. If my front legs gave way and I toppled to my right, I would have been flattened. This run wasn't only about teasing the family. It was also about denying that I was getting older. The steam that came from the lower workings kept me hidden from Zenon and Vanessa.

The devil was in my blood. I was in the mood to outrun anything. Drawing level with the huge roller at the front, I felt the Canny Lass slowing for her big right turn onto the high street. Cutting as close as he dared to the parked cars, Zenon gained extra space for the manoeuvre. For some moments I feared that even if my legs stayed strong, I would still become a mess of bloodied fur upon the tarmac. It was a tight squeeze. My left flank swept the length of a parked car. The Canny Lass actually brushed the longer hairs that stuck out from my right ear. Now the road really was vibrating beneath my paws.

There was no time for panic. I was elated. I ran even faster. Zenon and Vanessa must have spotted me because I heard urgent cries for me to get out of the way. Nothing would have made me drop back. They were journeying into a new life of love and, whether they liked it or not, I would accompany them on the first stretch.

Ginger had asked me to help her with the kids on day one. I'd done my best, and now the emotional load was lighter for her. It would have been appropriate if the Canny Lass's whistle had woken the whole damn nation. My crazy run was a marker of something wonderful.

Outpacing the Canny Lass, I took a big arc onto the high street. Fortunately no cars were coming or I would have been hit. I pounded along the middle of the main road. The plate-glass windows of the shops gleamed to either side. I knew by my reflection that I looked good. Turning right again onto the long and curvy road that came next, I glimpsed a police car ahead.

Rather than follow as it swung into a side-street that met Sea View Road at its halfway point, I aimed for the promenade. The last thing I needed was some bobby I didn't know taking me to the station. That had happened before. I'd gleefully outrun the exasperated kids and got picked up by a human who'd thought I needed rescuing. Ginger had sent away the young policeman who'd asked to see her dog licence with a flea in his ear.

I was mildly surprised that Rachael hadn't followed me to the town centre. Slowing to a trot, I crossed the seafront road, cleared the high granite kerb to the far pavement and headed for the promontory.

The air was salty and fresh. Sir Winston Churchill gleamed in the starlight. I would cap my celebratory run by lifting a leg against his plinth. I'd been splashing at that spot for years. One corner was my favourite. Another corner was frequented by a big black Labrador with a self-important air. That didn't bother me. He knew not to splash on my spot and I knew not to splash on his. The scent of other dogs didn't concern either of us. It was just an ego thing between him and me.

A long doggy splash, such as the one I now took, normally ends in restfulness. No sooner had I finished, though, than I heard movements from on high. Sir Winston had spoken to me several times before. On each occasion I'd been sickening for something. All dogs are accustomed to spooks, but talking statues and suchlike can be a worry. Humans aren't the only ones who lose their marbles, and I didn't intend to let go of mine. Leastways, not when my seven-plus doggy years made me the equivalent of a human who was only fifty-three. Still, the statue was in the mood to talk.

'Stop pissing on me, dog,' it ordered.

The voice was gravelly and the downward-set eye scary. My tail went between my rear legs. I feared a return of the arrogant black Labrador. He was connected to Sir Winston somehow, and if there was a scrap, I didn't fancy my chances. To my surprise, though, when the statue spoke again, it sounded hurt.

'And do stop blaming me for everything!' it moaned.

Winston Churchill might have been the cleverest prime minister in history, but he'd certainly got that bit wrong. All I wanted him to know was that, despite what the war had done to their mum and dad, my four young humans were set to enjoy lives free of crazy violence.

Sir Winston cleared his throat and looked back to the sea. He'd been staring over the water towards Norway for seven years. Suddenly I didn't care about his authority, his big black dog, or his easily wounded feelings. He needed to know that everything was beginning to turn out all right. It further struck me that the person who would want say this to him most of all was Raymond.

No sooner had I thought this than Young Raymond and Old Raymond climbed over the rail from the seaward side. Sitting side by side upon the top bar at the point where Raymond's suicide had occurred, they braced themselves with their hands and inclined back-wards towards the water.

I watched as they stared up at Sir Winston. My impression was that he would never deign to talk to them. This saddened me. Poor tortured Raymond was being denied the chance to say his piece directly to the one he most needed to hear it. He looked to me as he never had before. 'You make him understand how everything is, Brucie,' he instructed.

He wanted to balance an old accusation. Just before he'd thrown himself into the sea, he'd ranted at the statue, blaming Sir Winston for all that had gone wrong in his life. Now was the time to help him understand that the family was at last beginning to get over the worst of its wounds. Raymond and Ginger had suffered horribly but the four twins would be fine.

'Tell him, Brucie!' Old Raymond snapped. I started. There was a savage urgency in him that could be frightening even when he was sober. Young Raymond saw my fear. My first human had frequently terrified me and I'd never forgotten it. 'Tell him please, Brucie-Dog,' he said calmly.

The warmth of his smile made me happy again. My tail was no longer lost between my rear legs.

I loved Ginger even more than I did Craig. Raymond had beaten her. But over time I'd come to love him, too. It wasn't my message that had to be conveyed to Sir

Winston. I was just the conduit. It was Old Raymond's message. Maybe this would help him find the peace he needed. Young Raymond wasn't sitting in judgement of his angry older self: there was no reason why I should either.

I took off like a bullet, barking as I ran in circles around Sir Winston's plinth. In the midst of this, the large black Labrador arrived. His arrogance was gone and I saw that, in common with Her Hoityness, he was just a little stuck-up. That's pedigrees for you. Noses in the air, hearts of gold (well, most anyway). His presence encouraged me.

Maybe I was delivering a message on behalf of all the humans who'd suffered like Raymond and Ginger. The war had been hell but evil had been trounced. Those who were born to the humans that had suffered were now finding their feet. Most of the damage was not being passed down the line.

I barked, barked and barked.

'Thank you, Sir Winston!

'Thank you, Sir Winston!

'Thank you, Sir Winston!'

Young Raymond was gone. Old Raymond had come off the railing and Sir Winston's now immense black dog was standing upright with his front paws to his chest. As the long-troubled spook wept tears of relief, the dog licked his face. The Labrador was a spook too.

I ran faster and barked more. At last a totally sober Raymond was becoming reconciled to his dreadful war. Days would pass before I was given penicillin for the infection that would soon spread from my injured tail to my spine. For now, though, I still wasn't feeling pain where I'd whacked it hard against the garden gatepost.

What I saw next was real to me.

Raymond's wartime lover was sitting on the railing where Young Raymond had earlier been. He looked up at Sir Winston, who was now facing downwards again. The handsome young man smiled. It was perhaps the saddest smile that any mutt has ever seen. But it was a smile. A large tear formed in the corner of Sir Winston's eye and fell. It landed in the exact spot where I'd earlier done my splash. Raymond did not see the young man but, with Sir Winston's black dog now departed, he jiggled his spine and threw his arms wide. If the weight on his shoulders had not completely gone – there was still so much to reconcile with Craig – then it was much reduced. Raymond could not be blamed for everything that had happened to Ginger and the family. Nobody was one hundred per cent guilty.

66

A strong hand closed on the scruff of my neck. 'Aha!' cried Craig. 'Got ya, bloody bad mutt! Got ya!' Drawing upon an old trick that he must have thought I couldn't do any more, I locked my paws and set my body backwards, making him stumble. His astonishment was so funny that I did another circle around the promontory. The statue wasn't talking now, but if Sir Winston knew what was going on directly below his white marble feet, he must have been amused.

'Get a proper hold of him, our Craig!' shouted Rachael. She was sprinting towards us along the curvy road I'd come from. She must have followed my route through the town centre. 'Grab his frigging tail!' she added, as I evaded a new lunge from the now furious-looking kid.

Jack was also there. He and Craig had obviously come straight from Sea View Road. 'Bruce,' he commanded, looking square at me and pointing at the ground to show he was deadly serious. 'You bloody come here!' I was having none of it. If Jack wanted to make me stop running, he'd have to catch me first.

I dodged into the gap between the sea rail and the bench where Vanessa had sat with her father on the day of the ladybirds and where she'd met Zenon on their first date. It was also the spot where Raymond had asked Big Eddie to look out for Craig: he regretted bullying his son for being queer. He must have known then that he was going to take his life. Perhaps he was already planning to jump from the railing that was directly before them.

Rachael and Craig were very young when their dad had died, and Rachael had said resolutely that his suicide was the coward's way out. But it was a long time now since she'd argued against her older brother or sister when they had commented that Raymond had actually been very brave. It didn't take much to see that her view on the matter was mixed now. She'd been more brazen than the others but no less loving for it.

I had made a tactical error in going to the front of the bench.

Rachael was closing in and her brothers were readying to block any escape from either end. There was no time to ponder about whether or not my front legs could take more hard action. Pressing my rear quarters to the lower part of the sea rail, I crouched like a tiger and leaped with all the strength I possessed.

'Wow!' exclaimed Jackie. 'Will ya just look at that!'

I'd cleared the bench and made a perfect landing on the paving before the plinth where my earlier splash had taken place. Purely for the fun of it, I lifted my leg and gave a fresh squirt. That set my three humans laughing. I'd won the game and they wouldn't pursue me now. Standing a little way off, I adopted a sideways stance and wagged my tail at them.

'You cheeky old thing!' cried Rachael. In common with Craig and Jack, her cheeks were flushed and her eyes were large and shiny. I made my biggest blue moons at her.

'Go on, go home!' laughed her older brother. He'd obviously got a stitch and didn't want to run any more.

'Yeah, Brucie-Wucie-Lucie-Darling!' Craig added. 'Find Mum!'

I gave them a few cheeky barks and padded towards Sea View Road. It was still early enough to be dark and there was no traffic for them to worry about. It felt good to be the victor. I'd outrun my young humans and proved beyond doubt that fire still burned in my belly. As I neared the gate where Ginger was standing in her nightie, Bill the copper was getting into the police car I'd earlier noted. I'd never seen a deep red glow around him before. 'Do give Pammie my love,' Ginger called to him, before he drove off.

I didn't have a clue who Pammie was. Many different colours swirled around Ginger as the panda car headed up the hill towards the town centre. Something lovely had happened and once again I wasn't in on the details. I didn't care. I stood on my hind legs, as Sir Winston's black dog had done to Raymond on the promontory, and licked Ginger's face. By now Jack, Craig and Rachael were approaching the gate. 'My word, do I have news for you three!' declared their mum. Her happiness stirred the cheek in me again: on four legs now, I lifted a back one high and splashed her irises. 'Oh, you artful bugger!'

I scarpered into the house as quickly as I could.

Ginger revealed that Bill the copper had married a woman who'd previously been a student at one of the night classes where she'd taught art. Now I understood who Pammie was. Bill had been a widower for a long time, and while the family was pleased that he would no longer be lonely, they were equally happy that he was back on good terms with their mum. Ginger had wounded him in turning down his marriage proposal but now the hurt was forgotten. The other good news was that, so long as the Canny Lass's whistle didn't sound again, he didn't give a hoot about Zenon and Vanessa waking the town. Ginger and the kids appreciated that. Bill had always looked out for the family and was still doing so. Zenon would escape with a ticking off that had to be given for form's sake.

First Craig, then Rachael and finally Jack slipped off

to bed. Picasso was asleep with his head tucked into his wing. Ginger had always made sure he had enough water and food. Careful not to wake him, she replenished his water butt and its matching plastic food container. I never resented it when she tended him rather than me. Picasso was a pain in the bum, but a good one.

'Come with me, Brucie,' she whispered. 'Come with me.'

67

We went to the front room where she closed the curtains, which Rachael had opened when the Canny Lass arrived. She positioned a free-standing lamp behind the old sofa, turned it on and switched off the main light. She took the wartime photograph of herself and Young Raymond from the marble mantelpiece, then sat within the cocoon of light on the sofa. Patting the empty cushion to her side, she made it clear that she wanted me to be with her. I leaped up and shuffled along until my front was slumped across her thighs. The base of the photograph came to rest between my haunches. For the next hour she told her long-dead husband all about Vanessa, Zenon and the Canny Lass. And also that, no matter how wrong her own and Raymond's marriage had gone, she would always love him. I hoped that Vanessa properly understood that, even when life had dealt her its worst blows, Ginger had never lost faith in love itself. That was what made her special. Her heart brimmed with love. Raymond had always known that better than anybody.

68

When the family came back to Sea View Road after the wedding ceremony, there was much merriment. The newly qualified vicar had been so nervous, he'd unwittingly declared 'Zephyr and Vanessa' to be man and wife. That had brought to Craig's mind Raymond's abhorrence of the outsize 1960s Ford Zephyr, and he had quipped that super-slim Zenon had better not put on weight or he'd end up like that: a bloated, undesirable lump. He went on to observe that his dad had been proved right about the last of the Zephyr-Zodiacs. The range was almost as unsuccessful as the early-1960s Ford Classic-Capri models. Even Zenon's eyes were glazing.

There was no denying that Craig, too, could be a full-on geek. Rachael helped him out of the hole he was digging by recalling the cheeriness of 'the dreaded taxman', the dapper office worker who'd been at the wheel of the gold Zodiac when Raymond had taken the family to see the new glass and concrete building shaped like the boxy car. That had been sixteen years earlier. The twins' dad had still been a capable human with interests other than his next boozing session. Jack used his first finger to turn a circle upon the side of his head at his younger brother. Craig laughed. He'd tried to be clever about the nervy young vicar and it'd come out sounding crazy. In common with his brother and sisters, he'd grown more able to poke fun at himself. I, Brucie-Dog, was proud of them for that.

As might have been expected of Vanessa and Zenon, the wedding was an unusual occasion. Vanessa had decided upon a Victorian dress code. After the ceremony, the colourful congregation had walked from the church to number twenty. It was a beautiful Saturday in mid-September and friends had come from far and wide. The sea was a glorious spectacle at the bottom of the road. Vanessa's glowing happiness was silently understood as a triumph over the darker parts of her early life: her father had experienced a mental breakdown, thumped her mother, and she'd seen it all. Hardly the stuff of happy families.

Bill the copper tended the Canny Lass where she gleamed in the sun on the red road outside Ginger's garden wall. She was the perfect oven for the ten sacks of potatoes that Rachael had scrubbed and wrapped in foil. It had been her idea to make the steamroller the focus of the reception. Bill had fixed it so that, as long as the whistle wasn't blown, nobody in authority would object. His new wife, Pammie, came early in the day to help with the preparations. I was constantly being patted and stroked. Many humans I'd never seen before called me a handsome dog. With such a consensus it was hard to believe otherwise. My first human had been wrong: I'd never been a runt; I was a beautiful canine. The Cary Grant of dogs. My tail was high in the air.

The stocks Ginger had planted six weeks before were prolific. Wonderful colours swirled everywhere I looked, and even Craig showed traces of red. That made me even more optimistic. All he had to do to find the same joy as his big sister was accept his queerness. It was the way of humans to make this into a problem. For now, though, I didn't want to think too deeply about it. Craig was in fine fettle.

Bill the copper thought the Canny Lass was magnificent. At his instigation, Zenon had recently used her at a charity event at which thousands of pounds were raised for a young man who'd been disabled when serving in the Falklands War. The money had bought prosthetic legs that were superior to the clunky NHS ones. It was important to Bill that the steamroller should look her very best for Vanessa's big day. He'd been attached to the family for so long that it was almost as if his daughter was getting married. The huge blue boiler was too hot to touch, but otherwise he wiped away every smudge, every speck of soot, every ooze of grease. As for the potatoes, Pammie laughingly remarked that, with his lousy cooking, Bill was best leaving them to Jack and Craig.

Hence the busyness of both brothers with hot spuds.

They used the Canny Lass's extra-wide coal shovel to roast twenty King Edwards at a time. As each freshly cooked batch arrived, a wave of excitement went through the throng. The mood could not have been happier. To Ginger's delight, the thirty-plus man who'd been a terrified sixteen-year-old when her husband had rescued him from the Silver Grid fire produced a gleaming flugelhorn and played Dvořák's *New World Symphony*.

Milos Lampredi, too, had triumphed over the hand life had dealt him. Now nobody would consider him to be simple in the head. The Lampredis had cancelled a Spanish holiday so they could be at the wedding, and the hauntingly beautiful music that he played was their shared gift. There wasn't a dry human eye to be seen. Each of the kids and Zenon hugged Milos, who spoke about Raymond's bravery in crossing the fragile roof to pull him to safety. Maybe for the first time, they really understood what their father had been through in rescuing the teenager, who'd been paralysed with fear.

Upon hearing a hint of French in Ginger's voice, I stayed close to her. It was a wonderful day but a great deal was happening, and it didn't take much doggie-instinct to know that her nerves were fraying. Sensitive to this, Milos switched his attention to helping Rachael, who was serving drinks. He was a gentle human. No amount of alcohol would have turned his hand into a violent fist. Something in Raymond had responded too easily to provocation. Probably that was what he'd hated most about himself.

Mr and Mrs Napier had travelled with Milos and his parents in their big late-1970s Vauxhall estate car. The two households had been friends since the fire and they had last visited for Raymond's funeral. Wry humour was had at Mr Napier's expense when he revealed that he no longer drank alcohol. He was now eighty-five and confided to Ginger that Raymond had been an errant and much-loved son to him. This had been true of Dr Pimento, too, he said. Those who'd understood Raymond's torment had loved him despite his faults.

Noting the past tense in reference to the college-principal-turned-underground-lavvy-king, Ginger enquired as to his well-being. Mr Napier was surprised that she hadn't heard. Dr Pimento had suffered a fatal heart attack while polishing one of the brass iguanas in the Gents. He had turned a grimy underground bog into a palace, he concluded. A loose shoelace had caused Rachael to topple when Zenon had first brought the Canny Lass to number twenty. As the party progressed, I had a deepening sense of old laces being tied up everywhere.

69

Craig and his brother worked fast to keep up the supply of cooked potatoes. Leaving the driver's deck uncluttered for them, Bill the copper continued his endless polishing of the Canny Lass's not-too-hot bits. She was a gleaming testament to twenty years' hard work by Grandfather Kalaknowski and Zenon. Wedding guests agreed on her splendour and were fascinated to hear that she had even rolled the striking crimson surface of Sea View Road. I thought that, in common with Craig, Vanessa knew how to tell a good story.

There was a moan from deep within the Canny Lass's boiler. The last time this had happened, Zenon had likened it to a whale calling a lost calf. This time, however, the pitch was too high for human ears and even I wasn't sure that I'd heard it. I was prepared to bark in warning to the partying humans but, quick as it had come, the noise was gone. The last thing I wanted to do was create an unnecessary racket when they were all so happy. For once I overruled my barking box.

After the first near-disaster, Zenon had sent every

steam valve away for reconditioning by a specialist firm. Grandfather Kalaknowski had had them done, but the Canny Lass's restoration had taken so long that several were sticky through lack of use. Wisest to have the whole lot done again, decided Zenon. Since then, the Canny Lass had performed faultlessly at several shows and, of course, there'd been the fundraiser for the Falklands soldier. There was no reason for Zenon to be paying particularly close attention to the pressure gauge. He'd instructed Jack and Craig as to the correct reading – which was obvious anyway – and that was enough.

My ears remained pricked. The cry of the whale in the boiler was not repeated. She must have found her lost calf. Another neatly tied lace. Aside from the tiredness that was making Ginger a little tetchy, the day was perfect. I had never been happier for my humans.

Until Craig suddenly swore loudly. When I looked his way, he was tapping the glass front of the big pressure gauge. For all that the warm air was drenched with the mouth-watering smell of cooked potatoes, the stench of his fear hit my nostrils.

Jack also studied the gauge. If anything, his terror stung my nose even more than the kid's had. So busy had they been in keeping the fire up and making sure the spuds didn't burn that they'd forgotten to take pressure readings. Jack rapped the dial exactly as Craig had.

The needle remained upon the uppermost part of the red zone.

Some guests were giving them quizzical looks. Everything was happening quickly. The second after Ginger herself realised something was amiss, I alone saw her eyes accusingly rivet upon Craig. That was when I got a massive shock. Old humans frequently lose their marbles. After their deaths, those who have loved them realise that their behaviour had been changing for years before the illness had become obvious.

Extremes of anger. Extremes of joy. Black-and-white judgements where previously they had been more subtle analysts of life's daily challenges. There's no other way to say it. Something new and complex was happening to poor old Ginger's stroke-ravaged brain. Whatever transpired next, she was going to blame Craig. I could smell that above all else. Humans have no awareness of how terrible the burden of canine intuition may be. We see dementia before it manifests. We know. It's a larger-scale version of being tuned into an imminent epileptic fit. The wedding day was about to misfire in spectacular style, and Ginger would blame the kid. Worse, she was readying herself to enjoy it. He didn't have a clue as to what was about to hit him. Having the savvy to sell cars was one thing. In all other respects he was utterly naïve. That was down to his long fight against queerness. It had prevented him learning about the contrary workings of the human heart. In essence, he was still a child. Hence the increasing aptness of my old moniker for him: the Kid.

Zenon was moving in fast from where Milos Lampredi had been showing him the flugelhorn and its beautifully crafted case. I'd overheard Milos explain that the instrument was as old as the Canny Lass and that he'd inherited it from Mrs Lampredi's dad, who'd been a miner and a brass-band member. Unlike her husband, Mrs Lampredi was not of Italian extraction. Learning to play the flugelhorn had been the best thing ever for Milos. It reminded me of Zenon and his steamroller, and the endless creativity of the household I'd been rescued into.

Ginger's creative approach had always been right. Each of the four twins had been strengthened by the passion she'd encouraged them to follow. This, of course, had happened long before bad things had begun to manifest in her head. The Canny Lass might have been about to blow up for all I knew, but my overwhelming worry was that, in her coming confusion, Ginger would set out to destroy Craig.

The clarity of this perception shocked me. Ginger was a fighter. In battling to keep her marbles she would need an antagonist. On some primal level, the kid reminded her of Raymond's deepest betrayal. Ginger had been his young bride in the early 1940s, and he'd fallen in love with a young sailor. Now there was a lace that had never been tied. However much she loved her youngest son, his queerness meant that he'd long been drifting into her sights. I began to itch all over. I could see that she was about to blast him with both barrels. It was a conflict that had been on the cards ever since Ginger had seen Craig and Marcus Wright together at the kennels. In rescuing me from Psycho-Vet the whole family had witnessed the flirtatious encounter, which had openly confirmed Craig's sexuality. He'd tried to be aloof with Marcus because he hadn't wanted his family to know the strength of his feelings for the kennel lad. The Canny Lass's pressure gauge was stuck on high. Something between Ginger and Craig was going to blow.

70

The whale might have found her calf, but when she called again from the depths of the Canny Lass's boiler, all the humans heard her. Zenon moved fast to where Jack and Craig were facing each other. Their stance echoed that of Milos when he had been stymied by fear at the Silver Grid fire. Something was dangerously wrong with the Canny Lass and they were incapable of responding. They, too, were paralysed. Zenon kept his cool. 'You'd best be getting off this thing now,' he advised the brothers. Coming to their senses, they dismounted the tread plate and joined the crowd, which was instinctively backing away from the steamroller. Now she sounded like a dying whale. I knew exactly what Zenon was about to do. Grandfather Kalaknowski's quick-wittedness in blowing the whistle to release a similar build-up of pressure had prevented an earlier explosion.

'Cover your ears, everybody!' Zenon shouted. He pulled the chain. My ears felt as if explosions were going off within them. A dense cloud of steam billowed from where the highly polished brass whistle, which resembled a trumpet, was mounted on the Canny Lass's weather canopy. Because the steamroller was pointing up Sea View Road, the whistle was side-on to the front of Ginger's house. Ideal positioning for what was soon to happen.

I dived over the garden wall. The soil in which the stocks were bedded was soft and this time my front legs gave way. In the midst of all the steam and confusion, I was thankful that no human saw my loss of style. My chin was briefly buried in the garden, and so much juicy scent geysered into my nose from the crushed flowers that I fell to my side. Now I really was like Raymond. Drunk, and destroying Ginger's plants. Maybe Her Hoityness or even Raymond himself was looking after me, though. If I hadn't been flattened amid the stocks, with the brick wall beside me, I would have been killed outright.

The force that had erupted from the Canny Lass shattered all twelve panes in the double-storey bay window. Any glass that wasn't blasted into the house soon fell to the garden. Cries of alarm filled the air. My ears and head hurt as they'd never done before. The steam cleared quickly. I was now the one to be paralysed by fear. Such was the force of the explosion that I believed the Canny Lass's iron boiler had been blown into a zillion pieces. The sad old whale hadn't been calling to a lost calf at all. She'd been crying out in warning to

Zenon and the others. A terrible disaster had been on its way and they hadn't understood her effort to prevent it. The wrecked Canny Lass would be surrounded by human carnage. Despite the horrible ringing in my ears – which would last for weeks – I had to leave the garden.

In my heart I believed that Ginger, the four twins and Zenon were all dead. Terrible images of hot iron lumps smashing the skulls of my beloved family came to me. It was the worst moment of my life. Not even a nuclear bomb could have done more harm, so far as I was concerned. I, Brucie-Dog, had become akin to young Garth Howson, who'd feared the Russian attack when the kids were little. My Armageddon had come. The mighty Canny Lass had been its bearer. My only option was to lie down and die.

71

*Z*enon would always speak about his error in not sending the ex-locomotive whistle to the same specialist firm that had reconditioned the rest of the Canny Lass's steam valves. The whistle itself had been far too shiny and perfect-looking to fall under suspicion. Also, the fault that had made its entire side break away and damage the front of Ginger's house was an intermittent one. In other words, hard to pin down.

Grandfather Kalaknowski had created a bespoke safety valve for the boiler via the whistle and it had been inclined to stick. When this had happened at Vanessa's wedding reception, it had closed so tightly that Zenon's tug upon the chain had made things worse. Massive pressures were exerted and the hundred-year-old brass metalwork could not take the strain. I saw almost straight away that my Armageddon fears were unfounded. The Canny Lass was undamaged and no humans had been harmed.

Still, it had been a shocking event and I was shaking so hard that Bill the copper's new wife Pammie got down low and hugged me. Her body was soft like I imagined puffy clouds to be. 'There now,' she said, 'it was just a bang.' As I twisted my head to lick her chin, I saw she had huge brown eyes. When Big Eddie from across the back lane had first encountered me in the kid's workshop in 1976, he'd advised that I was a dog with eyes to be trusted. That was my instinct about Pammie. She was a human being whose good nature could be relied upon. I lavished more licks on her. After the powerful scent that had gone up my nose in the garden, her perfume didn't bother me.

A nervy silence was giving way to widespread laughter from the wedding-goers. Vanessa said something about Zenon's eyes being so far apart they might meet at the back of his head. Then she kissed him and declared that nobody was hurt and that his insurance would cover the cost of the windows. The three other twins were also quick to reassure Zenon. I loved that. He was one of them now. My post-explosion jitters were calming by the second.

To everybody's surprise, the broken whistle let out a long, high-pitched wail. It was a dying sound that soon had many of the guests laughing hard. Ginger did not share in this fun. Furious about her windows and the interruption to the party, she had focused her eyes on Craig. He was still blissfully unaware that he was about to be turned upon. I was itching with a vengeance. It seemed that Ginger was wilfully exploiting a moment in which nobody was paying attention to her or Craig.

She strode up to him and seized his wrists. He was wiry and strong but would never have used his strength to resist her. His eyes went wide with shock. Dragging him into the house, she hissed that he was a useless bastard who'd maliciously spoilt Vanessa's big day by overloading the steamroller fire.

Only Pammie saw and heard it. Her eyes were now big pools of unhappiness. I wagged my tail and briefly made blue moons for her. The war getting under way between Ginger and Craig was so ugly that even I almost wasn't up to dealing with it. It was the deepening sadness in Pammie's eyes that made me shake myself down and go inside. Perhaps Bill had told her that I'd always been Craig's protector. My momentary neglect of him shamed me. I still shudder to think what Her Hoityness would have said about it.

I got into the house in time to witness what was happening at the far end of the corridor. Ginger hurled Craig from the step to where he landed on his feet upon the tattered seahorse lino. He began to protest, trying to laugh off her attack. She brutally overrode him. He was a parasite who hadn't even left home. He was jealous because the others were falling in love. He was worthless, just like his father. He was lazy. He was this. He was that. It was exactly as I'd feared.

The onslaught drew me along the corridor. I couldn't

help it. For the first time ever, I lifted my leg and splashed inside the house. Poor old Ginger really was on a mission to destroy. Craig was gawping at her in disbelief. Listening to the tirade, I found it hard not to believe that she truly despised him. Raymond had done this to him when he was a boy. School had done it to him because he was queer. Ginger was doing it because she was losing her marbles and he was the unwitting personification of Raymond's betrayal in loving the young sailor. Thirty-seven years had passed, and now her anger was pouring out. Had she launched the same attack upon Rachael, Vanessa or Jack, it would have rebounded upon her tenfold. Craig's biggest weakness: he was the kindest of the kids.

For the first time ever I saw that if he'd loved his mum less, she might have respected him more. He'd always been resilient, but her turning on him might be the final straw. My hopes had been falsely raised. I'd believed that, in order to be happy, he'd needed only to accept his queerness. Now he had also to surmount Ginger's rage. I was filled with fear for them both.

72

lack! Black! Black! Black! For the first time ever, that was what I saw all around Ginger. Black! The first onslaught over, she drew a deep breath, looked to the floor, then confronted Craig again.

'Bastard!' she spat, eyes ablaze.

'Bastard!' she repeated, getting right up close to his face.

He shrugged and stared bleakly at her. If she truly intended to make him believe he was worthless and unlovable, she was doing a good job of it. The worst of what she was saying was down to a problem with her marbles. He knew that. 'Are you okay, Mum?' he asked.

Ginger slapped his face hard. My front legs suddenly became so weak that I had to lie on the seahorse lino. Hearing me, she glanced my way. I wagged my tail. The unhappiness that flickered in her eyes confirmed what I already knew. She didn't understand why she was going for the kid. Her only certainty was the attack. That was when she was in control. Turning back to him, she told him once more that he was just like his father. Trying to make out she was unwell was his devious way of shifting to her the blame for ruining the party. The kid shrugged again. His eyes had gone small as pinheads. Ginger could seemingly do what she liked to him and get away with it. He had become her punchbag.

Old Raymond was back. He and Picasso now had something in common. Where the parrot kept tucking his head under his wing, the spook continually placed his hands over his eyes. Neither wanted to watch but each had to. I knew precisely how they felt. The dynamic between Ginger and Craig was grim but compelling. She had attacked every aspect of his personality and I wondered what she would come up with next. Perhaps he thought that if he let her continue, the words would simply bounce off him. That was what had happened in the past. This was different. Every nasty accusation was like a knife going into him. Ginger held nothing back. Still, he didn't respond.

It became too much for me. I barked in real anger at her. That was a first. If she had been in her right mind, she would have approved of me doing so. Craig was a loving son and she was out to make him into something different. It was glaringly obvious that she needed him to be a bad son.

I got back to my paws and barked more. If Picasso thought my aim was to redirect Ginger's fury at me, he was right. Gamely colluding with my plan to take the heat off Craig, he squawked loudly and flapped his tattered wings against his cage.

Ginger scolded the parrot and snapped that I was a god-awful dog that she wished had never joined the family. She faced the kid again. Attacking me was a new way of getting at him. There had been a vet at the kennels who'd wanted to put me to sleep, she screeched. I'd been such a lousy dog it would have been better if she'd done it. Suffering from distemper when I was young had fried my brain. I was a stupid, ridiculous dog, she claimed. Now I felt as if I were being stabbed. My instinct was to go to her and lick her hand. Before I could do so, blackness flared where Craig had previously been surrounded by white. Ginger's onslaught had been relentless and deliberately cruel. Furthermore, she understood that in traducing me she was mauling his heart. I feared now, more than I'd ever feared anything in my life before, that he would hit her. Raymond must have been dreading the same outcome. His hands were pressed so tightly over his face that he would have needed X-ray eyes to see anything. Picasso tucked his head firmly under his wing. I was rooted to the spot.

The kid's faced zoomed forward and stopped perilously close to his mum's vulnerable nose. She flinched but held firm. No longer pinheads, his eyes were large and black. He didn't speak. He snarled. It wasn't his fucking fault if the antique whistle on Zenon's steamroller had blown apart. Without a moment's hesitation she reacted by punching his chest. Raymond was observing again and pulling anxiously at his hair. My right flank itched so badly that I scratched it hard. I wanted to draw blood. If I could show them I was hurting, maybe the nightmare would stop. When Ginger spoke, she was calm and withering. Of her two sons, she pointedly claimed, she'd always known that Craig would be the one to inherit his father's violent streak. It was just as well that he was queer or he would have become a cowardly wife-beater too.

Nothing could have smashed the marble-hard atmosphere in the room. Ginger had said her worst. Craig had once described how, after being baited at the car auctions when he was drunk, Raymond was like a wounded old dog, bitten and bleeding. Something similar had now been done to him. Ginger steeled herself and proffered her face as she used to do when Raymond was drunk and roaring. Craig sighed. If he was young and naïve for his years, he was also learning fast.

'Mum,' he explained, 'I'm not Dad, and even if I was pissed as a rat, I wouldn't punch you.'

Ginger flinched, then relaxed. At the far side of the room Raymond was quietly sobbing in relief. Realising that Ginger had been as frightened as she was angry, Craig added that she would never have reason to be scared of his fist.

'Now,' he smiled, 'instead of wasting time fighting with you, ya mad old bat, I should be outside helping with broken windows.'

Placing a hand upon each of her shoulders, he kissed her forehead and turned for the hallway. I thought that was it. I thought the war between them was going to be brief and a lot less ugly than it might have been. Ginger was biting her lower lip as if deep in thought. Before Craig was out of the room, she asked him to come back for a moment. Raymond, Picasso and I saw her hands close around the inch-thick wooden handle of the mop, which was kept in a bucket by the rear door. I barked. Picasso squawked. Raymond gnashed his teeth. The ever-trusting Craig turned to face her.

73

Before he knew what was happening, his face was hit. He cried out in pain, then was quiet and still. Raymond the spook was aghast. Picasso slowly side-stepped to the far side of his cage. I itched as if on fire. The heavily sodden end of the mop had caused it to collide at a slant to the left of his big nose. He stared at Ginger, who suddenly seemed tiny and vulnerable. His right hand remained firmly at his side. It was going to be several years before he would kick his way out of the closet, but here was a moment to resonate. Although painful in every possible respect, he began to grow up. What stronger message does a young human need that he must carve a life in his own identity than an assault by his loving mother?

Craig went on staring at her. The mop slowly slid through her fingers until the wet end was resting upon the hearth. All her black was gone. She was surrounded by white. If that whiteness had been water, she would have drowned in it. Never had I seen such a clear expression of shame. It was all that Ginger could do to stop her head lowering in the way of a fourteen-year-

old-human who'd been caught out in some misde-
meanour. She hated herself for what she had done and
it twisted my heart. Finally the kid spoke.

'I've already told you, Mum. I'm not Dad. Nothing
would make me hit you. Or,' he added, 'any other
woman.'

Ginger seemed even smaller. It was almost too much
for her to face him at all. She drew a deep breath and
adopted a pretence of cheer. 'I didn't mean to hit you,
Craig, lovie,' she protested. 'I just wanted to make you
jump.' He went on staring. His mother was desperate.
If Craig didn't go along with the falsehood she was now
creating, she would be sunk. The many party-goers
would wonder why he'd been attacked. Under normal
circumstances, nobody would think she was losing her
marbles. Even when she spoke with a French accent she
wasn't loopy. It was within Craig's power to help or destroy her. His left hand went to where his cheek must
have been hurting. I thought he would turn on his heel
and announce to the family and guests that she was
having dangerous moments of insanity.

Raymond had been watching closely. He cleared his
spook-throat. Craig flicked a glance at the apparently
empty corner where his father was. Raymond shivered.
Spookily for me, when Craig's eyes returned to Ginger,
he shivered too. I thought his mum might fear he was
going into shock, which often happens with humans

after they've been hit. Nobody knew this better than Ginger. Craig was proving strong, though. It wasn't often that I'd seen green around him – that was Jack's prime colour – but I did now. Green meant strength, and now Craig showed he had it.

'Are you sure you're okay, Mum?' he pressed gently. Whatever damage had been done to his face was not the issue. He loved Ginger. If it would be some time before he fully understood that her actions were slipping beyond her control, he had sensed enough to be extra-protective of her. Maybe at that moment he loved her more than he'd ever done. Picasso warily shuffled back along his cage. Raymond had clasped his hands in prayer and was mumbling thanks to God. I barked several times and my tail wagged unstoppably. Laughing and crying at once, Ginger apologised to the kid for being mean about me. She loved me, she reassured him. That was her way of telling him she knew he would never hit her as Raymond had. Her attempt to prove to him that he would had been wrong and cruel. Sometimes human beings don't need to say the most important bits. Redness swirled around them. That was enough for me. I leaped up and licked her nose and cheeks.

'Oh, you artful old bugger!' she cried. 'Oh, you artful old bugger!'

As she stroked my haunches I rejoiced that this time

her returning good cheer was real. Ginger's marbles were not so much lost as inconveniently scattered. Still, her attack on the kid had been real enough. From the corner of my eye, I caught him eyeing her warily. It was afterwards that I wondered what might have happened if she'd been holding a knife instead of a mop. I loved Ginger, but after that I never quite trusted her as safe. Especially around the kid. Had she been an old collie-cross from a difficult family, Psycho-Vet would have offed her for being unstable. Look what had happened to Her Hoityness. The treachery of those thoughts briefly made me itch again. Fortunately the kid came speedily to my rescue.

'See, Mum?' he cried. 'Even Brucie-Wucie-Lucie-Darling still loves ya!'

I licked her face more. She was crying again and I wanted to do away with the tears.

'Go on, Brucie!' cajoled the kid. 'Show her she's loved to bits!' He had more green around him now. Some good had come from their near-catastrophe. Craig was stronger.

74

'Well, of course he still loves her, our Craig!' Vanessa insisted. She'd arrived unnoticed from the wedding party out front and was standing upon the step from the hall to the kitchen. Framed in the doorway, she resembled a photograph from Victorian times. Her lace-trimmed silver-green silk dress had been made by Ginger's grandmother and complemented the colour of her eyes. Back to their natural tone, her furry caterpillars were the same black as her crisply styled hair. If less zany in appearance than usual, she still looked striking. When she saw Craig's bruised cheek and blackening eye, she gasped. Misunderstanding, she asked why they hadn't told her he'd been hurt by the explosion.

Ginger and Craig were caught unawares. Had they been on the ball they could have bluffed their way out of it. Nobody, except Pammie, who wouldn't have said a thing, could have questioned that Craig's injury had been caused by shrapnel from the Canny Lass. Looking closer, I saw there was even a cut where the broom had whacked his left furry caterpillar. It was just the sort of mark to have been left by sharp metal. Ginger would have been the heroine who'd whisked him from the garden to confirm his sight wasn't harmed. In the moments of puzzlement that passed between her and Craig, Vanessa divined that something very different had occurred.

'Well, if it wasn't the whistle, what did happen?' she asked. A fearful note in her voice showed she didn't want to hear the honest answer. It was her wedding day and the last thing she needed, on top of the Canny Lass incident, was family trouble. Nonetheless, she eyeballed Craig, then Ginger. If there was something to be dealt with, they might as well get on with it. A silence dragged until Picasso gave a squawk, which cued some impromptu acting from the beleaguered mother and son.

Craig did a playful simulation of a tumble to the floor and told a fib about tripping from the very step where his big sister was now standing.

Ginger put equal gusto into demonstrating that, on turning too quickly from where she was cleaning up a spilled drink on the seahorse lino, the kid's face had been caught by the mop handle.

It took a moment for them to realise they had told contrary tales. Vanessa laughed at their confusion. If she'd been empowered to see spooks, as I could, she would have been touched by Raymond's response. I could see that he was proud of her because she hadn't instantly snapped at them for telling ridiculous stories. Her kindness gave them space to refine what they had said. Unsurprisingly, it was Craig who gathered his wits the quickest.

'Sorry, our Vee,' he said, glancing at his mum. In common with Vanessa, she raised a quizzical eyebrow and waited. Everybody knew that he was about to tell a whopping fib. That was a good thing. The truth would have been destructive for them all. What counted was the quality of the fib. If he made it sound plausible, they could all go along with it. Just for a second he looked to me. I, too, was watching him avidly. My upright ears were hurting again, and I knew that I was giving him gobstopper-sized blue moons. A laugh broke out of Craig. My tail wagged hard in response. The delay was too much for Ginger. 'For God's sake, get on with it, our Craig!' she cried. Even Vanessa laughed at that.

A strange happiness was developing. It reminded me of my first days with the family. They squabbled, shouted and fibbed but everything was driven by love. The funniest thing of all was that, as he set his large green eyes upon Vanessa's identical peepers, Craig was being challenged to prove that he could still cut the mustard. If he cocked up the lie, the family would be left to deal with the horrible truth of what had been done to him. Nobody wanted that to be acknowledged.

Vanessa had only to breathe in the air to know that something had already been resolved for the better between Craig and Ginger. The nasty details were insignificant. Fortunately her brother now lied ingeniously.

Each story was correct in its own way, he explained. Vanessa suppressed another laugh and said, 'Oh?' Her arched furry caterpillar was even higher up. Ginger was rapt. It clearly hadn't occurred to her that Craig might take this line. She appeared impressed. Raymond folded his arms and clamped his hands into his armpits. I doubted he'd ever believed Craig lacked brains. More likely he'd been upstaged by the kid's relentlessly inquisitive mind. It was obvious now that his bullying actions, too, had been beyond his control. Alcoholic confusion combined with jealousy of a lively-minded son had overwhelmed him. Humans get like that. It's why they need us dogs to help them through. Any mutt could see that the spook burned with the desire for his younger son's life to come good. Vanessa was now openly enjoying herself.

'Come on then, Pinocchio,' she teased. 'Convince me how both explanations can be right.'

Craig smirked. Their game was on.

Both stories were true because he'd tumbled off the hallway step when it just so happened that Ginger was mopping the floor to prevent somebody slipping on a drink that Milos Lampredi had slopped. Milos, he cheekily reminded Vanessa, was helping Rachael to serve the drinks. Amused, Vanessa nodded for him to continue. The rest, he laconically stated, was obvious. Startled by his fall, Ginger had turned quickly and accidentally whopped him in the face with the handle of the mop. The combined force of their actions had left him heavily bruised. It was a bit like cars in a head-on collision, he elaborated. If both were doing thirty, then the impact speed was sixty.

Craig was pleased with himself. There was no doubt that he'd spun a plausible yarn. Vanessa continued to stare at him. I waited for her to laugh. But something brittle had entered the air. Craig's face was badly bruised and, in facing him square-on as he'd spoken, she'd been forced to acknowledge that he must have been clobbered hard. The head-on collision scenario had backfired. Her mother's intent to hurt him had been strong and couldn't be overlooked. Maybe Vanessa was obliged to pursue the truth, after all. Ginger began to look small and ashamed again. Forestalling the question that his sister might have put, Craig set his right forefinger very close to the bruising around his left eye and spoke with a firmness that was more Jack's than his own.

'You're not saying Mother did this deliberately, are you?' he demanded. His green eyes were set but not glassy and unkind in the way that Jack's could be. I'd never seen him challenge Vanessa like this before. Now it was down to her to help Ginger out or to let everybody know what she'd done. She shrugged. If Craig deserved an Oscar for acting, she was about to merit one for irony.

Of course he'd been accidentally hit with the mop. Nobody in their right mind would suspect it'd been done on purpose, she concurred, giving Ginger a pointed look. But since the bruising was bad enough to make it look non-accidental, wouldn't it be wisest to go along with a fib about the Canny Lass's whistle?

Craig drew a deep breath. I knew what he was thinking. For Pammie, who'd seen Ginger bustling him inside from the garden, there would now be an explanation. Even if she'd heard Ginger's hissed accusation that he'd deliberately caused the explosion, Ginger might still have been reacting out of panicked concern for his eye. This wasn't about bluffing or not bluffing. This was about the best possible bluffing.

Ginger was watching him keenly. As he began to nod in agreement with Vanessa, she chipped in, 'Oh, I say, our Vanessa, what a very good idea! There's absolutely no point perplexing people on your big day!'

For an instant, Vanessa appeared stricken. I realised she was beginning to determine what Craig had already half grasped. Where the four twins were fast relinquishing childishness, Ginger was going the opposite way. Little wonder that she'd been hanging her head like a naughty fourteen-year-old.

The kid was swift to jolly his sister out of her sudden gloom. 'Get back outside now, our Vanessa!' he ordered. 'Otherwise Zenon'll think ya've dumped him already!'

Vanessa stared at him in an all-new light. He wasn't her baby brother any more. He was her brother. Ignoring his instruction would be foolish. Still, it wasn't in her nature to comply too quickly. 'Since when did you become headmaster?' she teased.

Craig laughed. It was a compliment of sorts. Vanessa had tacitly agreed that he was right. She should be outside with Zenon and the wedding guests. Ginger understood this too. 'Shoo, Vanessa!' she crazily ordered. 'Shoo!' She'd never said that before, and it carried a hint that she knew the fight for her marbles was getting under way.

Her gameness touched the kid. Placing an arm about her waist, he hugged her to his side. As he did so, my head was trapped between their legs. I like to think it was this that helped Vanessa to concede.

'Well, hurry up and come outside yourselves before you squash poor old Brucie-Dog to death!' she retorted.

So much happy redness came into the air that I was forced to half shut my eyes.

Before stepping from the kitchen to the hallway she paused to look back at them. 'I love you both,' she commented. The kid hugged Ginger tighter to his side as they watched her go. 'She's a gem, our Vee is, Mum,' he remarked. 'A complete gem.'

Ginger daubed a purple ointment called gentian violet on Craig's face. They laughed like scheming children. The bruising became so exaggerated that you might have thought he'd been run over by the Canny Lass. Nobody could have suspected that Ginger had inflicted it. She would have required a sledgehammer.

'Oh, but good Lord, our Craig!' she exclaimed, when it was done. 'The guests will think you've gone ten rounds with Muhammad Ali!'

If the kid saw anything ironic in that, he didn't show it. Pausing to check that my water was topped up, he plonked a kiss on my head and purposefully crossed the seahorse lino towards the hall. 'C'mon, funny old woman!' he cried, over his shoulder, while striding from the kitchen to the front of the house. 'Hitch ya dress! Let's see what's happening with this mad wedding do!'

Ginger held back. Perhaps she was nervous that everybody would know what had gone on. I trusted Craig to carry things off. No guest would be allowed to make his mum feel bad. For a long time now she'd been nagging him but he hadn't let on how bad it had got.

In truth, he'd been protecting her more than anyone knew. I sniffed her hand as it dangled by her side. Steeling herself, she whispered, 'Come along, Old Artful. Let's face the merry mob.'

That was my beloved Ginger. She was imperfect. She was vulnerable. She loved and needed me. I wouldn't have had it any other way.

75

Craig had gone outside and I was nearing the glass door of the porch when I passed Pammie lurking within the downstairs front room. As I stopped to look back at her, she came serenely from the open doorway into Ginger's path. I realised she had been waiting for this moment.

'Now then, dearie,' she began, 'before you rejoin the party I want you to be aware that in light of the explosion the police have visited the scene. But with my husband being a senior officer, everything is nicely sorted, and even as we speak the emergency glazier is on his way to attend to your windows.'

My tail wagged and a yap escaped me. Craig had earlier said that his sister Vanessa was a gem and it was clear that Pammie was another. Her tenderness cast a warm light throughout the normally gloomy hallway.

'Oh, thank you, Pammie, thank you kindly,' Ginger responded.

Pammie embraced her and I understood that, after all her years of bringing the kids up on her own, Ginger was now the one in need of motherly love. For half a minute she was like a long-lost little girl who was being found. Bill the copper had married one of the kindest human beings outside the family I'd ever encountered. I parked my bum on the carpet and watched, fascinated. Never had I seen Ginger as submissive as she was now. Carefully stepping back again, Pammie revealed that at the 'most excellent suggestion of young Rachael', who was apparently working with several guests to clear the glass that had been blown into the upstairs front room, the wedding celebration was being moved to the promontory.

If anyone else had said this, Ginger might have been angry. It was her daughter's wedding party and the change in location should have been run past her before it was agreed. As it was, she seemed relieved. Pammie's tact had worked wonders. Plus, there was a timely intervention from Craig, who came back inside, laughter carrying from the garden. 'Hey up, Mum, are you coming or what?' he asked. 'People think my purple face is a right old hoot!'

It was obvious that everything was being fixed to reassure Ginger. The broken glass was being cleared up. The windows were going to be sorted. Perhaps most importantly, everyone had accepted that Craig's face had been bruised by shrapnel. Plus, of course, Pammie was on hand to give whatever loving care was needed.

Aware of how hard everyone was working to make

things come right after the explosion, Ginger thanked Pammie again. Her humility warmed my skin and slowed my pulse. Gently clasping Ginger's hands, Pammie lowered her head until their hair touched. 'You did beautifully by your family all those years, my dear,' she whispered. 'Quite, quite beautifully.'

Craig had moved close beside me. His left fingers rested between my ears. All the twins knew it was my favourite spot for being tickled. Pammie looked aside at him. I again noted her eyes: they were the same peaty shade as Bill the copper's. He'd married the human who was exactly right for him. I hoped they would go to the kennels and rescue a mangy mutt from the lethal syringe of Psycho-Vet. Their home would be rich with love and that canine's life would be blessed.

The kid was all but mesmerised by Pammie's thoughtfulness in congratulating Ginger on what she'd done for the family. So much of her long struggle since Raymond's death had been taken for granted. That's the nature of young humans. He waited until Pammie gave a slight nod. He and she had become a team whose aim was to prevent Ginger being overwhelmed by stress. 'C'mon, Mum, darling,' he encouraged her, 'they all want you at the party.'

Movements from within the front room startled me just as Ginger and Pammie moved apart. The kid, too, was taken by surprise. Bill the copper had been inside all along. He'd been earwigging on the conversation with his wife to make doubly sure Ginger was okay.

On seeing Craig's bruises, he pulled an exaggerated face and winked at him. Purposefully stepping into the hallway, he asked Ginger and Pammie if they might get some of the younger guests to assist with the down-stairs glass. Ginger took this as her moment to depart for the garden. Jack would be sure to help, she told Bill. Following in her footsteps as far as the porch, the kid called after her that he would do it, no need to trouble his brother. Turning back to Pammie, he thanked her for helping his mum. Pammie gave him a shrewd look and advised that he shouldn't go near dodgy steam-roller whistles in future. Promising her he would be careful on all accounts, he went into the front room to pick up glass with Bill.

Pammie's smiling eyes rested upon me. 'Well now,' she said, 'I dare say you got quite a fright when the whistle blew.' I thought again that she and Bill should visit the kennels. A thoroughly deserving mutt would surely be waiting for them.

Refreshed by a long drink of water, I flew off the high front step and landed midway down the path. My paws barely touched the concrete until I was beyond the wide-open gate and standing where the flash gold van that belonged to the glazier was pulling up.

I'd heard Bill tell the kid that, rather than temporarily

boarding up the windows, the glazier would cut the new panes and install them straight away. I guessed that would keep them busy for hours. To clear space for them to work, Zenon had apparently taken the Canny Lass to the seafront. With her destroyed whistle by-passed by an improvised tube she was, according to Bill, working perfectly again. It was good to know that a bigger problem with the boiler had not lain behind the explosion. Grandfather Kalaknowski's welding had survived a massive excess of pressure with flying colours. The sad old whale could swim off in peace.

I heard Jack calling: 'C'mon, Brucie! C'mon, Brucie!'

He was one of several stragglers among a group that was crossing the seafront road to join the revellers on the promontory.

'C'mon, Brucie!' added an unfamiliar, yet clearly female, voice. My eyes bulged as I saw that the owner, whose hand now rested upon Jack's shoulder, was none other than the pretty young human who, for two summers, had worked with Vanessa at Mr Garrity's Liquor Emporium.

'C'mon, Brucie!' she cheekily repeated, while Jack fell around laughing because I, the ageing family mutt, was now haring down the centre of the steep red road to join them.

'Faster, Brucie!' they jointly urged. 'Faster!'

The salty sea air was drawn deep into my lungs,

which helped sharpen my memory. The girl with Jack was called Lisa-Jane. They looked to be getting on very well indeed. If Jack was now falling in love I certainly wasn't staying in the dark. It had been embarrassing enough that I hadn't grasped what had been going on between Vanessa and Zenon, then Rachael and her young man, Ernest. We mutts are proud of our intuition. Mine seemed to have been on strike.

76

Amazingly, the spook who'd led the big scrap with Hitler was leaning against the plinth upon which his statue faced the sea. Peace had broken out between Sir Winston Churchill and the two Raymonds, with whom he was amiably chatting. I hoped my earlier message of reconciliation had brought this about. In my excitement I splashed upon my usual corner and was chased by Jack. He was laughing and I barked loudly in response.

'Oh, do be quiet, our Brucie!' cried Vanessa. She, too, was amused and I caught a look between her and Lisa-Jane. Jack getting together with her friend was a big bonus to the wedding day. She'd always been worried about her twin brother and now it was clear that he was going to be fine. So much was suddenly turning out right for my beloved humans.

A folk group, known to Zenon and Vanessa, arrived. Milos Lampredi played along to their music on the flugelhorn. Soon people were dancing.

As if all that wasn't enough for me to take in, from the corner of my eye I spotted more activity where the gently steaming Canny Lass was parked at the bottom of the curvy road that came from the town centre.

Dr Pimento, Nigel the therapist, who'd died some years before, and two or three spooks that I didn't know from Adam were cheering Grandfather Kalaknowski as he sat at the controls of the steamroller. It seemed the perfect place for him to be. Happiness was everywhere I looked.

Within the blink of an eye, or so it seemed, the stretch of promenade that took the direction of the Gay Hussar had become the parking site for the red and yellow van of Tony the Italian Number Two. More than a year had passed since Zenon had bought an ice cream from that vehicle and covered it with tomato sauce because he was falling headlong in love with Vanessa. Tony had not forgotten. As a queue formed for the burgers – the smell was making me drool like a Great Dane – he declared that his Italian sauces could bring on *amore*. Jack made a rude quip about the human-sized plastic hot dog that was set at an angle upon the roof of Tony's van.

Mr Garrity, who had joined the party earlier, laughed hard at that. After his deliveryman, Artie, had parked the white van with 'Mr Garrity's Liquor Emporium' emblazoned on the side, he'd thrown his arms wide and announced a wedding gift of twenty bottles of champagne. He'd even brought boxes of glasses.

Much to Rachael's surprise, her normally reserved Ernest clambered onto Sir Winston's plinth and made a speech: he was proud to be joining a much-loved family led by a very special mother. That was when the other three twins really began to take to him. Afterwards I made sure to brush my flank against his leg.

The dancing became livelier and the light changed from day to evening. Word came that the glaziers had finished the repairs and were even scooping up the broken glass from the garden. In need of a scamper, I padded down the concrete steps from the promontory to the sands.

That was where I happened across Jack proposing to Lisa-Jane that they might one day view Turner's seascapes together. My tail drooped. At this rate he'd drive her into the arms of a young human who wasn't afraid to make an advance.

I'd reckoned without Lisa-Jane's determination. She kissed him with such passion that, when she finally took a breather, he remarked, 'Sod Turner,' and buried his face in her breasts.

Smiling down upon them from the sea rail forty feet above were Dr Pimento, Nigel and Sir Winston. My loud barks were a friendly warning to the spooks to let the young humans have their privacy.

Yapping with joy for Jack and Lisa-Jane, I returned to the promontory just as the music for the latest dance was coming to an end. In the seconds of quiet before an astonished Rachael cried, 'Well, look who's coming now!' I spotted a long-absent human approaching from Sea View Road. Here was a big surprise indeed.

77

After Raymond's suicide in 1975, Big Eddie from across the lane had become the kid's replacement father, teaching him to weld at fourteen, and otherwise boosting his confidence in every way he could.

Things had soured after Big Eddie's beloved missus Vivienne died on the same day as Elvis Presley in 1977. Unknown to Ginger and the family, when Big Eddie was in his thirties and Vivienne had first got cancer, he'd briefly become a boozer. In grief at losing her ten years later, he'd hit the bottle harder than he had the first time round.

I, Brucie-Dog, could do nothing to make the kid smell the profound loneliness in Big Eddie's scent. He was too young to understand. All he could smell was booze, which had brought back his father's worst excesses.

Wounded by Craig's rejection, Big Eddie drank until he was struck down by a heart attack in the town centre. His close encounter with death was what he'd needed to kick the bottle for good, though his rift with

Craig was seemingly unbridgeable.

At forty-nine he'd employed a caretaker to look after the Heartbreak Hotel, which he'd run with Vivienne, and returned to Texas, where they'd previously lived for fifteen years. His job as a welder on oil pipelines had always been open for him. In the half-decade since his departure the kid had barely mentioned his name. Perhaps it was his silence that had given Ginger the idea that he was secretly pining for big-hearted Eddie.

Vanessa's impending wedding had been the ideal excuse for her to ring him. I'd lain under the table as she got the operator to make the connection with America. If I was a human, Ginger would have said I was earwigging. Of course I was. Her confusion at reaching Big Eddie in the middle of the night was funny but it was obvious that he was pleased to hear from her.

They spoke for thirty minutes. Ginger enthused about Zenon, the Canny Lass and the coming wedding, to which he, of course, was invited. That was when the tone changed. The fun went out of it. I didn't need to hear the words to know that he was unwilling. My skin itched. I'd always hoped that Big Eddie would return one day. Probably he'd remarried and would spend the rest of his days in Texas. Nobody could have blamed him for that.

Ginger had already said goodbye when she added a final thought. If Big Eddie was by any chance able to attend Vanessa's wedding, her younger son Craig would surely be delighted. However scattered her marbles were, I thought that was a touch of genius.

Big Eddie had solemnly promised Raymond that he would always look out for his younger son. His real betrayal of Craig had not been his drinking but his escape abroad. Only hours after Big Eddie had pledged to look after the kid, Raymond had thrown himself from the promontory. He, too, had trusted Big Eddie, and with a few simple words, Ginger had reminded him of all this.

She was pensive afterwards. To me, she commented that at least Big Eddie was now as dry as the Texas desert where he was working. That was what she'd always wanted Raymond to do: get sober and stay that way. Sadly, it had been beyond him. After a day or two, it seemed she'd forgotten her call to Big Eddie. He was part of the family's history, not its future.

78

U pon reaching the promontory Big Eddie came straight to Ginger and lifted her in the air. I realised then that when he'd left for America he'd been falling in love with her. So much became clear so quickly. It was too soon after he'd lost Vivienne for him to admit his feelings and therein lay an added reason for his boozy spell. Tall, broad and tanned, he wasn't anything like a troubled old alkie now.

'Aren't you looking wonderfully well?' cried Ginger, when he finally set her down. I had to agree. The whites of his deep blue eyes were clear of the yellow that had tainted them before his heart attack. Where his once big tum used to drag his upper half down, he was now upright. Though his black hair had turned silver, it was thick and shiny. He radiated good health and a happy redness showed around him.

Playfully lifting Ginger's face with his right hand, he boomed that she looked younger and even more beautiful than he remembered from six years earlier. Ginger pooh-poohed that, but the surrounding humans were amused. She enjoyed Big Eddie's flattery.

If anything Old Raymond was even more pleased by Big Eddie's arrival than Ginger. He whooped on the spot, then cartwheeled across the wide promenade. The kid's number-one protector had returned and that was what counted. Young Raymond looked on. His happiness was for Old Raymond.

Life had come right for three of Ginger and Raymond's kids. They each had love. If only Craig could discover it, then Old Raymond would be able to rest in peace.

Big Eddie shook Ernest's hand and hugged Rachael, then gave Vanessa and Zenon tickets for a ten-day trip on the Orient Express and an envelope containing a thousand pounds' spending money.

Reds, golds, greens and many other shades glittered all around Ginger, Vanessa, Zenon, Rachael and Ernest. Grandfather Kalaknowski and Old Raymond were so moved that they linked arms. They were like long-lost comrades who'd been reunited.

While the commotion generated by Big Eddie's unexpected arrival took place, Craig had slipped to the far side of the promontory. Way beyond his shoulder, the neon lighting that traced the mock-Tudor beams of the Gay Hussar came on. The green haze it cast blended with the red that was now drifting around him. From this, I knew that he was thrilled by Big Eddie's return but didn't know how to deal with it. All the family now faced his way. Even the many guests who didn't know Big Eddie tuned into the anticipation. A straight line opened across the promontory that was in front of the statue. It was like a parting of the sea. Nothing and nobody now stood between the kid and Big Eddie. Whatever his feelings Craig was not going to speak first. I wished that wasn't the case. His heart was loving. Bearing a grudge suited him about as well as boils on his smiley face. Still, it was only right that the older human should break the ice between them.

The silence dragged on. Padding closer to Big Eddie for the best possible view of Craig, I wagged my tail but held back from giving blue moons. It was a long time since I'd learned that, of Ginger's kids, he was best left to discover things in his own way. Cajoling would not have helped. Big Eddie had travelled thousands of miles knowing there was a rift between them. Whatever occurred now would only be worthwhile if it was authentic. I waited. The humans waited. Waves that were withdrawing from the shore made the shingle sing. It was a lonesome melody. My heart ached. So much needed to be put right.

Big Eddie had loved the older Elvis Presley. After Vivienne died, Ginger had explained to the kid that his infatuation with the unhappy singer's most heart-wrenching ballads had been grief in advance of his wife's death. Vivienne had battled cancer for a decade.

During that time, Big Eddie had even come to dress like Elvis. He was, claimed Ginger, the original imperson-ator.

Now, however, he was done up as Enrico Caruso, the famed Italian tenor, because Ginger had told him about the wedding-party dress code being Victorian. If he was at all self-conscious about facing Craig in a burgundy velvet suit, frilly white shirt, gold bow tie and gleaming black shoes, he didn't show it. The kid, who was done up as a nineteenth-century sailor, tried to suppress a smile that leaked at the corners of his mouth. That was Big Eddie's cue to speak.

'Doin' all right there, young 'un?' he boomed.

His voice had always been exceptionally loud. Some humans considered him OTT. The cleverer ones saw that, for all his noisiness, he was as sensitive as a sniffer dog. Regarding the kid, his instincts were sharp as ever.

No sooner had Big Eddie asked his question than Craig's hand shot to the bruising Ginger had inflicted. In the same instant his green peepers rebelliously flitted her way. Big Eddie didn't need to see or hear more to grasp what had been going on between the kid and his mother. My own instinct became laser sharp. His mind was now set. He would never return to the States. Not only did he love Ginger, he was big enough to absorb the hurt that Raymond had caused. The kid needed to be free. That was why Ginger had phoned him in

America. He had heard her call for help loud and clear. This time he wasn't letting anybody down. His spook-missus Vivienne understood. She was standing beside Vanessa and Zenon. When she was alive she'd loved the family as much as her husband did. Big Eddie still had a mountain of love to offer, and she wanted him to lavish it on Ginger and the kids. Especially Craig, to whom she'd been a second mother of sorts.

Raymond, too, had been reading the workings of Big Eddie's heart. His gaze now settled upon the kid. If he could have shaken him into answering Big Eddie, I'm sure he would have done so. As it happened, it was the kid's twin sister who broke the awkwardly long silence.

'Stop gawping like that, our Craig,' she snapped. 'You're being bloody rude, you are.'

Big Eddie laughed and winked at her. He wanted to make it clear that the kid could take all the time he wanted. Still, her intervention chivvied things on, though not quite as the kid intended. Goaded into giving Big Eddie some kind of response, he was not in full control of his faculties. I know this for sure because I was looking directly at him.

Upon attempting to control a second smile, he broke into a huge, welcoming grin. There was no pretending otherwise. He truly was thrilled that Big Eddie was back. Striding forward, he offered his right hand. 'Hello, Big Man!' he cried. Eschewing the proffered handshake,

Big Eddie hugged him as he had the others. The rift was healed. Barking, I ran new circles around the stone plinth where the statue was. The humans and spooks were suddenly gone. It was like being on a roundabout powered by my own fast-moving legs. Sir Winston's black Labrador pounded at my flank. We were the happiest dogs in the world. I could have run like that for ever.

79

A hand closed around my collar and I was yanked to a halt. 'Whoa there, Brucie-Wucie-Lucie!' ordered the kid. As I twisted to look at him, I saw that he'd been laughing at my antics. Other nearby humans were likewise amused. Remembering my earlier escape when Zenon had brought the Canny Lass to number twenty in the middle of the night, I thought I'd further entertain them by twisting free of Craig and running circles in the other direction around Sir Winston. Before I could make a move, Vanessa cried, 'Oh, my God, they're coming again!' Nobody knew what that meant but she was pointing at the horizon. The kid let go of my collar and stepped to her side. I followed.

The flat sea was silver-blue. It was always like that on late summer evenings. That was when I thought it was most beautiful. Because I couldn't discern what Vanessa was on about, I went onto my hind legs and set my front paws to the top slat of the seaward-facing bench. Now I saw what she meant.

A thudding red cloud was approaching at great

speed. 'Oh, heck!' exclaimed the astonished kid. 'It's our Vanessa's bloody ladybirds back!' His elder sister had just enough time to retort that the invading insects were not hers. As millions of them swept over the promontory, the wedding guests screamed, hollered and scattered in all directions. I was most concerned for Vanessa. The last time this had happened, she'd got a ladybird stuck in her sinuses. That had freaked her for a long time afterwards. Upon half opening my right eye, I saw that her mouth was shut tight and her nostrils were clamped between her thumb and first finger. If anybody else got an unwelcome visitor behind their face, we'd know how to get it out.

Already the swarm had cleared the promontory. Pointing to the slightly distant Canny Lass, Rachael called for everybody to look at what was happening there. Once more Craig exclaimed in astonishment. Others did likewise. As ladybird upon ladybird hit the gleaming blue boiler of the steamroller, they instantly became little yellow flames that fell to the red tarmac. The colourful cascade was both grim and beautiful. Soon all the humans were watching. What they couldn't see while this continued was that Young Raymond, Old Raymond, Vivienne, Dr Pimento, Grandfather Kala-knowski and Nigel the therapist were, one by one, ab-sorbed into the swarm. Gone.

When I was a young dog my brains had been fried

by distemper. Psycho-Vet's argument for offing me at the time was that I might later become unstable. Perhaps the excess of spooks I'd been seeing was a symptom of that. I was a mad old dog. My front legs became weak and I expected my chin to whack the grey paving stones. Vanessa took hold of me. She was crouching and I was reflected in the huge green and black pools that were her eyes. 'It's all right, ya big soft mutt,' she cooed, as the ladybird stragglers flew by.

Already, though, my attention had shifted to where Big Eddie, Rachael, Ernest and Zenon were standing in a clump around Ginger. She was amusingly indignant. Why did younger people, who'd 'never lived through a damned world war', as she had, think she wouldn't be able to cope with a 'few insects'? That made everybody laugh. Big Eddie took her hand and kissed it. I doubt there was a human on the promontory who didn't see the depth of feeling that existed between them.

My heart felt warmer than ever before. Craig wryly opined that Vanessa needn't have sent a wedding invitation to the flying creepy-crawlies. A lone ladybird hit the Canny Lass and turned to flame. I had a sense that, whatever their purpose had been, Vanessa's ladybirds would never visit again.

Milos Lampredi picked up a gentle waltz on the flugelhorn. The other musicians joined in. Watched by the family and their guests, Big Eddie and Ginger danced. Holding Vanessa's eye, Craig smiled. Maybe they'd always known about their mum's feelings for the Elvis impersonator who'd become Enrico Caruso. That was another thing I'd been lax in perceiving.

80

The curtains were drawn across the new glass and Ginger slept in the comfy old armchair that had always been hers. The wedding day had been long. Noting that her French accent was returning, the family had insisted she must rest. I, too, was tired. It was lovely to be stretched out on my back before the small coal fire Rachael had lit for her mum. Craig stole into the room and sat by me on the rug. His Victorian fancy dress had been discarded in favour of blue denims and a black T-shirt. As he stared into the flames, his hand rested upon my belly. 'Well, Brucie-Wucie-Lucie,' he mused, 'I wonder what Daddio would've made of it.' I let out a contented groan. That was as near as I could get to reassuring him that Old Raymond had been thrilled by the wedding and the return of Big Eddie. He looked to where I'd got my head tilted backwards upon the floor. I crinkled my brow. 'C'mon, Big Dog,' he whispered, 'let's go late walkies.'

We left Ginger in the flickery room with the guard in place against the burning coals. It seemed that fire had become a theme. Unable to give a departing toot on the Canny Lass's destroyed whistle, Zenon had earlier performed some technical wizardry that had resulted in whooshes of yellow and red from the steamroller's chimney, which delighted the many humans who, in giving the newlyweds a special send-off, had formed a line along each side of the seafront road. Craig had called that Zenon better not blow the Canny Lass up after all or Vanessa would be getting the wrong wedding-night bang.

Two or three more risqué jokes followed but none too graphic. As the Canny Lass drove slowly away, the humans converged into a crescent-shaped group that straddled the road. Big Eddie stepped forward from the centre. 'Hip, hip, hooray!' he boomed.

'Hip, hip, hooray!' chorused the gathering.

'Hip, hip, hooray!' they roared, as a final whoosh of flame came from the Canny Lass's chimney.

By the time Craig had led me out of the house and onto the pavement that sloped to the seafront, the Canny Lass had long since rumbled past the small hotel where a Cortina 1600E had stolen the kid's heart way back in 1970. She had passed the Gay Hussar, where Raymond had boozed to excess, and reached the white 1920s house where Zenon had grown up.

'Thank you, Grandfather Kalaknowski!' I barked, in celebration of the wondrous day that was coming to a close.

'Thank you Grandfather Kalaknowski!' I barked again, before the kid had gathered his wits enough to tell me to shut up before the whole street woke.

Yet in truth he wasn't so much concerned with me as with the big human leaning against the sea rail that fronted the promontory. Following the exchange of letters in the *Gazette* of a year before, the council spotlights no longer made Sir Winston Churchill resemble a drag artist. Ordinary white beams had replaced the controversial magenta. I remembered how that colour had entertained the four twins and distressed Ginger.

'C'mon, Brucie-Wucie-Lucie-Darling,' said Craig, as I felt my walkies-chain tighten in his hand. 'Let's go and see our old friend.'

81

Big Eddie had turned away from the sea when I'd barked. He was still wearing his Caruso outfit. Beyond his back the nearly full moon was hanging low in a particularly dark sky. The same silver that bled into the inky black sea made the tips of his hair glow. Craig chuckled as we got nearer. 'Your hair's shining like well-polished chrome,' he remarked. Big Eddie smiled. Last time they were properly together his now silver-white mane had been black. For a moment or two his gaze rested on me. 'Brucie-Bruce,' he murmured. That set my tail wagging. Craig pulled on my chain. I'd been tugging him towards his old friend. Relaxing my muscles, I made the last steps at the gentler pace the kid wanted. When he stopped close to Big Eddie, I parked my bum and set my ears at points. Craig wasted no time in coming to a point of his own.

'You going to marry her, then, Big E?' he enquired.

Big Eddie grinned. It had been a mistake not to marry Ginger five years earlier, he replied. The kid's fingers found their familiar spot between my ears. He was glad that Big Eddie and Ginger would be tying the knot, he said. His mum needed someone to love her and Big Eddie was the only man he could imagine as being right. You could tell he'd rehearsed this speech over and over in his mind. There was no doubting that he meant every word of it. I was so happy that I couldn't prevent a yap. Its embarrassing squeakiness made them burst into laughter. Then, looking fixedly at Craig, Big Eddie apologised for having become a boozer and admitted he should not have gone to Texas. This, too, had the ring of a speech that had been practised many times. As I anticipated what the kid might say in reply, I felt another tug upon my lead. It was confusing. I'd thought I was still sitting on the ground, but evidently I'd licked Big Eddie's chin. Maybe I really was becoming a deranged old mutt. I'd never been unaware of my actions before. Quite possibly my marbles were beginning to scatter. Still, it had been an exceptional day for highs and lows of emotion. It was only natural that in my sheer dog-tiredness, I was liable to confusion. Now I succumbed to the day's finale as the kid himself was experiencing it. My second sight ensured that my looking back became his looking back.

82

I intended to reassure Big Eddie that he had nothing to apologise for. It was a long time since I'd blamed him for anything. When Vivienne died, I'd been too young to understand his grief. All I knew at the time was that, in becoming a boozer, he was bringing Dad's drinking and suicide back. I couldn't cope with that. Before I could say any of this, though, he was off talking again.

'Want to know the real reason why I drank, son?' he asked. The answer to that seemed obvious and I promptly said it: grief. He looked at me for a long time, weighing up the pros and cons of saying more. I became irritated. In my family you said what was on your mind and dealt with the consequences. There were times when Zenon had a cautious way of speaking that drove me nuts. I knew that was unreasonable, but it was how I was.

Suddenly he sighed and amiably shook his head. We hadn't been in contact for years but he still understood me better than anybody else. I was reminded that I loved him. My impatience at his delay in piping up made me laugh. 'Well, go on, then, Big E, out with it!' I insisted.

'I was relieved by Vivienne's death,' he responded. 'Relieved, Craig, laddie,' he stressed, keeping his eyes firmly upon me.

The hairs on my neck prickled. I'd never heard anyone admit to being glad at the death of a loved one before. Nonetheless, while the idea seemed wrong, the way in which he was looking at me seemed right. He was treating me as the adult I'd become and there was something unfathomable in his honesty. Whatever it was I needed to connect with it. 'Explain for me, please,' I requested.

There was a pause. Then Big Eddie began to speak. When he was a teenager a nail had gone into his eye as he was going up a ladder. His dad had accidentally dropped it from above. They were building a treehouse. It was the last thing they'd done together. Soon afterwards, his dad was killed, fighting the Germans. The eye had healed but its centre would always resemble a broken egg yolk.

It was years since I'd thought about that. I winced. It had never occurred to me that Big Eddie's childhood had been difficult, too. I made a mental note that, when the time was right, I would ask if he'd found a replacement father, such as he'd become to me.

He saw me looking at his imperfect eye. Given that

half my face was purple, that was pretty ironic. I shrugged. 'You were going to tell me about being relieved,' I reminded him. There was no more delay.

'After ten years of fearing I would lose Vivienne,' he explained, 'I no longer had to live in fear. Wondering when the cancer would return. Wondering if this time she'd be a goner. Seeing her get weaker and weaker.'

I'd watched to see if his eyes filled. They didn't. I knew he'd loved the ground that Vivienne walked upon. Relief at her death must have been the hardest feeling he'd ever had to reconcile. Now I understood why he'd hit the bottle. Falling in love with Mum at the same time could hardly have made it easier. He'd survived, though. And I understood that, in permitting himself to tell the awful-seeming truth about his own feelings, he'd become well again. That was the thing I'd needed to connect with. Before I knew it, words were spilling from my lips. 'When my dad died,' I confessed, 'I was glad not sad.'

I paused. Nothing I needed to be wary of had entered his expression. I knew he would never push me to continue until I was ready to do so. I sped on. Had I not, I might have chickened out of equalling his honesty. 'Let's face it, Big E. He was violent to Mum and cruel to me.' I'd astonished myself. Throughout my teenage years I'd played down how deeply Dad's cruelty had cut into my soul. Now, if Big Eddie could tell the truth, so could I. I looked him harder in the eye. 'If I had kids, I'd build 'em up, not smash 'em down to feel for ever bad.'

Those last three words bounced off my tongue. I'd been compelled to acknowledge something. Dad's bullying had done more harm than I'd cared to admit. He'd smashed my confidence and left me ashamed of who I was. It had been convenient to jog along with the self-deception that this had been sorted out years before. The truth was quite different. Having it drilled into you that you're a retard and a loathsome little queer goes deeper than any inch-long nail to the eye.

Dad had screwed me over and I'd been struggling ever since. I told Big Eddie the truth. Dad was a bastard for what he'd done to me and a bastard for what he'd done to Mum. My grieving fifteen-year-old brother Jack had kissed the coffin and said goodbye to our father. My guilty secret at the funeral had been that I was glad he was dead.

That was an outpouring I hadn't expected to make. I was appalled to have used the word 'glad' as I had. Dad was long dead but I was ruthlessly adding the killing touch where his memory was concerned. 'Glad' was a bullet I'd fired into his temple. I could almost smell cordite. At the same time I was enraged that he'd made my early life into a dark and difficult place. There was a particular time when he'd hurled a socket wrench down and a spark had come off the concrete floor. That single spark had said it all. It had terrified me. I was twelve years old. I was now twenty-one, but it still terrified me. Dad had done that again and again. He was a bully. Never had I acknowledged it with such clarity before. I spat out the truth once more for Big Eddie. I was glad when my father had died.

83

In the silence that followed, I feared I'd appalled him. Eventually he drew a breath and said, 'What I should have told you long before now, Craig, is that on the day your father died, he said the only thing that counted was love.'

That bamboozled me. I'd never heard Dad wax lyrical about love. At the same time, though, I knew Big Eddie had barely started. Sensing he feared sticking one of his size twelves in it, I kept my eyes on his. 'Well, that tells me just about nothing, Big E,' I retorted. My intention was to press him into continuing. If there was something more to be said between us, now was the time to say it.

He smiled and became pensive. I didn't want to make him sad but it was important that our talk was carried to its limit. Taking several steps to his left, he spread his arms across the back of the bench that looked out to sea. I knew he'd been sitting there with Dad on the day he'd topped himself. Big Eddie had scolded him for blaming me when he couldn't fix the suspension on an old brown Vauxhall Victor. It was a piece of junk, that car. After Dad had jumped from the sea rail directly in front of the bench, it'd gone to a breaker's yard owned by a bloke called Bernie. According to Bill the copper, who'd told Mum, Bernie had sobbed when he was told about Dad. Many people came to the funeral. One of the mourners who spoke was called Mr Gregson. He was a business contact of Dad's and sold life insurance. Although his old friend Raymond had 'more flaws than a multi-storey car park', he'd said, there was a 'fundamental humanity' in him that only a fool would have denied. I saw Dad's fist flattening Mum's nose and an icy shiver ran down my spine. It was years now since my father's suicide. I realised that I'd carried it with me every single day since. I needed it to become yesterday.

The glare that shone onto Sir Winston from the pavement-level spotlights was reflected off the shiny white marble. It gave Big Eddie's burgundy Caruso coat a metallic sheen. I had a crazy notion. He was an angel at the threshold to the rest of my life. Our Brucie whimpered and I saw that he was giving me one of his most quizzical looks. I wondered if he was reading my mind. That was my second crazy thought in fifteen seconds. I had to laugh at myself. In all probability, I'd got delayed concussion from when Mum had clobbered me with the mop handle.

Big Eddie gave me a sideways look. With the moon upon the sea to his left, and the brightly illuminated statue to his right, his chrome hair was even shinier. I almost told him about his similarity to an angel. But then it crossed my mind that I'd never seen an angel, and Big Eddie would have thought I was crackers. Or maybe not. When I was younger I'd been able to say anything to him. Whatever he'd meant about Dad and love, his own heart was enormous. 'Go on, Big E,' I urged. 'Tell me what Dad meant.'

He knew how important this was to me. When he smiled next, it was like the first time I'd met him. I'd been eight. He'd opened the Heartbreak Hotel across the lane and found me crawling under his bright red 1960s Ford Mustang. At first he'd been annoyed. But when I'd drawn myself to my full height of four feet two inches and explained that I was checking the chassis for rust, he'd laughed and gone to fetch a huge bacon sandwich from Vivienne. We were friends from that moment.

When Dad died six years later he'd asked me to re-store the car. By then it really was rusty. Much later I understood that he'd protected me from terrible grief. The parallel with Zenon and the Canny Lass restoration suddenly glared. Coming back from the bench, he stood near me and Brucie at the side of the promontory.

'Raymond was talking about you, laddie,' he explained. 'He knew what he'd done was wrong.' That made me shudder. I'd long accepted that Dad hadn't intended to be cruel, even though he was, so there wasn't anything new in what Big Eddie was saying. My disappointment must have shown big-style. Then he said, 'Look, lad, whatever your father may have said about homosexuality, on the day he died he told me that he wanted you to be happy with being who you are.'

I don't know what astonished me most. The idea of my queer-loathing dad giving his blessing for me to be queer or Big Eddie actually using a word like 'homosexuality'. After all, everybody knew I wasn't one of those.

Big Eddie had the look of one who believed he'd stuck a size-twelve boot in it, after all. Seeing that I was totally nonplussed, he quickly rallied. I'd later think that his next words were impressively clever.

'Did he ever come back for you, son?' he asked.

I knew exactly who he meant. At any other time I would have been crucified with embarrassment. But since we were candidly talking queer and my initial shock had gone, I wasn't thrown. 'No, Big Eddie,' I replied, looking him in the eye. 'Marcus Wright the kennel lad never came back.' I was mindful not to add 'for me'. That would have been a step too far.

Sensitive to the last, Big Eddie looked back to where the silver light of the moon was upon the sea. 'Pity is that, Craig, lad,' he concluded. 'Have to go a long way to find a laddie nice as young Marcus.'

Had I been braver, I might have told him that, ever since Marcus had pedalled out of my life on his gleaming yellow Raleigh Chopper, there had not been a day when I hadn't thought about him. Big Eddie was right, of course. You would have had to walk a million miles to find somebody as open, funny and loving as Marcus. Pity he was queer. Otherwise we could have been great mates. How Big Eddie would have responded if I'd said that, I'm not sure. There was one thing I was absolutely confident in talking about, though. I reached for it without delay.

'It's bloody brilliant that you're marrying Mum!'

That made him throw his head back and laugh. 'I'd best tell her first, laddie!' he boomed.

We both knew what Mum's answer to his proposal would be.

Dad had been right to value love. It was going to make Mum and Big Eddie happy. They each deserved that. My own heart warmed. I thought of Dad. Now that I'd at last confessed it, I understood that I hadn't been glad when he'd died. I'd been relieved that all the trouble was over. Except, of course, that it wasn't over, and only now were the decks beginning to clear. Still, I'd arrived at a new beginning of sorts and it felt good.

'You okay, lad?' Big Eddie enquired.

'I am, Big E,' I confirmed. 'I really am.'

84

When I got home Mum was in bed. Some-body had damped the fire before also turning in. No sooner had my own head hit the pillow than our Brucie-Dog jumped up and lay nearby. He often did that. I rested my hand on his head.

Upon falling asleep I had a dream in which I became him. It was sunny and Sir Winston's big black Labrador joined in the fun as I ran circles around the promon-tory. Then at some point I was Craig again and the black Labrador became Marcus Wright. Now also in his early twenties, his lovely mop of blond hair was as thick as ever and his light blue eyes shone with love. 'Hope and joy can do a tango in the sky!' he cried. That was crazy dream-speak. His face was clean-shaven and tanned. When we were at school, the girls had said he was the handsomest boy in our year. Now he was even better-looking. Some of those girls who'd admired him now appeared on the promontory. They laughed and asked why on earth I wasn't kissing Marcus when he was obviously in love with me. When I did so it was beautiful. I'd never known happiness like it. I told Marcus I would always love him with all my heart.

He decided we should go for a ride on his yellow and chrome Raleigh Chopper. As I clung to his waist from behind, I felt his muscles working. We sped along the promenade towards the lighthouse. It was like we'd become one. Brucie ran at our right flank; the big black Labrador kept pace at the left. The dogs barked while laughter poured out of me and Marcus. It was the best ride of my life so far. I relished it.

When I woke, laughter was carrying up to me from downstairs. I realised that Big Eddie and Mum had told the family they were getting married. I looked to the clock. It was midday. Still, Big Eddie had worked fast. That was a good thing. Mum had been getting vaguer recently, and I hoped that, with Big Eddie's love, she would fare better.

I was readying to throw the covers back when I became aware of our Brucie. He was sitting to the side of the bed, watching me. Sometimes his eyes were so big and blue that I thought of them as blue moons. That's what they were now. Huge blue moons. I no longer knew if I was awake or not. It seemed he was entrancing me. No doubt I was still mildly concussed from the blow of the day before. Whatever the explanation, what happened next was real enough.

Dad sat on the side of the bed and faced me. He looked well and he was sober. I wasn't scared or surprised. It was just a fact that he was there. I reached to touch him, but somehow I couldn't. Brucie kept his big blue eyes on us. Finally Dad smiled and spoke.

'Vanessa and Zenon.

'Rachael and Ernest.

'Jack and Lisa-Jane.'

He drew a breath.

'Barbara …' that was Mum, only nobody had ever called her by her name except him '. . . and Edwin.'

He went on looking at me. I knew what he was saying. It was my turn next. But for all that it'd been wonderful to kiss Marcus in my dream, I was still adamant about one very important thing.

'Dad,' I said, eyeballing him as I never would have dared when I was younger, 'I'm not queer.'

The sparkle in his blue eyes became stronger as he looked at me more keenly. He stroked his bushy grey beard. 'The only thing that counts,' he persisted, 'is love.' I knew what that meant: he was telling me it was perfectly fine to be queer. Big Eddie thought the same. I was irked that they were agreeing I could be something they weren't. Dad's eyes had often terrified me when he'd been angry. Now they were kind. 'You'll get there when you're ready,' he concluded.

Brucie yapped. Dad was going. As he did so, he remarked that he would always be with me until I accepted who I was.

More laughter carried from downstairs. Number twenty Sea View Road was teeming with people in love. Suddenly Brucie was licking my face and I became properly awake. I'd had the oddest dreams. It had been good to see Dad. I'd always loved him and I still missed him . . .

ACKNOWLEDGEMENTS

Winston and the Canny Lass is the second volume in *The Winston Tails* quartet. It would have been harder for me to find the time to write either book without the support of my life partner, Paul Simpson. Thank you Paul. As I said last time, you're one in a million.

Documentary maker and publisher Mike Wallington has kept faith in my work for twenty years. His offer to publish *Winston and the Canny Lass* under the Berry Press imprint came as a wonderful opportunity. Big thanks, Mike. You're a gentlemen and a friend.

Times cartoonist David Haldane – another good friend – kindly gifted the cover illustration and I offer a million thanks to him. My editor Hazel Orme is a stalwart who has pushed me into being a better writer. I cannot thank her enough and I'm delighted that she too has become a friend.

Big thanks to my old pal Mike Davis who has done a fine job with the typesetting and also to our proof reader, Tony Russell.

Andreas Campomar at Constable & Robinson Ltd has been a most encouraging friend to the publication of *Winston and the Canny Lass*.

It would be remiss of me not to mention that the following friends read *Winston and the Canny Lass* as a work in progress: Wendy Young, Lisa Harris, Rodney

Wood, Margaret Lewis and Jill Clark. Thank you all, your comments were invaluable (and so too was your input, Tim Dickinson).

Writer Richard W. Hardwick took time out of his demanding schedule to read the manuscript. Richard, you too are a gentleman and I'm proud that you have endorsed my book.

Barbara Hadaway was one of the first people to believe in *The Winston Tails* and her encouragement gave me added confidence. Barbara passed away at the beginning of 2013. Rest in peace, Barbara, you were a dear friend to myself and Paul.

Lastly, many thanks to the thousands of people who bought the first volume of *The Winston Tails, Barking at Winston,* as published by Zircon Press and Constable & Robinson Ltd. Without your support there would have been no further books.

Barking at Winston – ISBN 9781780332420 – remains in print with Constable & Robinson Ltd.

Coming next

BOOK THREE

THE WINSTON TAILS

WINSTON LOSES HIS HEAD

Barry Stone was born in 1958 and likes to think it was 1988. He has been a writer for over twenty years. *Winston and the Canny Lass* is the second book in his quartet *The Winston Tails*. A lifelong dog lover, Barry partly attributes his good physical health to the thousands of miles which he has clocked up whilst exercising the adored – and none too well behaved – canines that have been a major part of his life. Barry has a delightful young black Labrador called Bonzo. Or Asbo when misbehaving.

Contact Barry: barry@barrystone.co.uk
www.barrystone.co.uk